ENTWINED

ALSO BY NED LIPS

The Reset Series:
First Steps, the prequel
Reset
Entwined

Other Books:
Freed (coming soon)

ENTWINED

NED LIPS

Elliptic, LLC

St. Louis

Published in the United States by Elliptic, LLC, St. Louis, Missouri

First Edition

This is a work of fiction. Names, characters, places and events either are the product of the author's imagination or are used fictitiously. Any similarity to real persons, living or dead, is coincidental and not intended by the author.

Cover images from Shutterstock and Unsplash

Library of Congress Control Number: application pending

ISBN 978-0-9980325-9-7

Cover design by Jamie Wyatt, imnotskippy.com

Edited by Karen L. Tucker, CommaQueenEditing.com

Dedicated to my patient wife, Barbara, and my two wonderful daughters, Jessica and Christine. I am grateful for their loving support.

ONE

Sitting in this beautiful place, Sarah felt freedom. A huge weight, the darkness that was Tony, had been lifted. She moved her hands over her golden caramel skin, feeling its warm, sweaty smoothness and the powerful muscles beneath. As the positive spirits of nature returned to their compound, soaking into her, the blood that had coated her from the battle flowed off, as if with the moisture of the early morning dew, into the ground below her. She slid her fingers to where the wounds inflicted by Tony and his gang had been healed by her Elephant spirit without a trace. She was happy but physically exhausted, and her muscles were sore. It was a minor price to pay for her girls, for Tom and for the Family. Tony was vanquished.

The Family gathered around her, staring with concerned eyes. She relished the love that emanated from them, and she poured out her love, extending her soul to all and feeling theirs within hers. Positive, empathetic, loving, singing. They were a true Family of people, sharing a single universal spirit. She could see it as their eyes changed, reflecting the beauty and love blossoming within their souls.

Joy. Pure joy.

The Family surrounding Sarah applauded their leader then began to pat each other on their backs, hugging and kissing. The children began a song and the entire Family joined in.

Her four spirits—the Horse, who gave her speed; the Bear, who gave her strength; the Elephant, who brought her the power of healing and protection of her body; and the Tiger, who brought her grace and a determined ferocity that gave her courage and confidence—settled inside her. Asha's spirit strengthened and bound the other spirits completely within Sarah's soul. From within Sarah, from among this universe of spirits to which she was so connected, her guru spoke, "I am with you always." The voice of Asha, like her spirit, was both loving and strong. The Tiger was the soul of Asha, the final spirit that had saved her, that gave her the strength to defeat her own personal demons, to escape the Storm and to save her girls and this Family. A tear came to her eye, and she let it slide, unimpeded, down her cheek.

Then Sarah felt the spirit of the Storm, the more positive side, the part of the Storm that had brought nature back, but she could also feel its fierce unpredictability. It was not part of her nor was it from Asha. It merely lived within her where she'd trapped it with her Bear spirit in her battle with the Storm. She was not sure she controlled it, even though she'd used it to defeat Tony. She'd have to deal with that later as her thoughts turned to Jazz and Janie and, of course, Tom. Fear welled up within her.

TWO

Jazz and Janie came running from the back of the compound. Janie leaped into her arms, and Sarah wrapped her in an embrace then pulled Jazz to her. Mark had tagged along behind Jazz, and Sarah gathered him in. Tears flowed down Sarah's cheeks. Tears of joy, relief and love. Tears of overwhelming emotion. After several minutes, she pulled back from her girls.

She was barely able to croak out, "How's Tom?"

Jazz and Janie exchanged a worried glance. Both looked at Ms. Watson, who nodded, and then Jazz returned her gaze to her mother. "Not good. He's in a lot of pain back in the infirmary."

Janie continued, "Doc thinks he may be bleeding inside."

"OK, down. Let's see what we can do. He can't die." As Janie landed on the ground, Sarah raced with grace and amazing speed through the crowd the more than 40 yards to the back of the compound.

Tom's groans were deep and struck her soul even before she reached him. He lay in a clearing near the infirmary on soft grass. His body was streaked in blues, browns and reds. He bled from deep and gruesome cuts. A trickle of crimson fell from his mouth as he turned toward her. Blood stained the dirt and grass around him. She recoiled at the site of him, focusing instead on Olivia.

Olivia said nothing, but her eyes belied her fear for him as she desperately tended to his wounds and those of several others with their limited resources. Helpers ran back and forth from the river bringing water, while others hurried into the woods to gather herbs, leaves and barks for various medicines. The pharmacists, Bethany and her father Franklin, were frantically mixing ointments, most of which Sarah had taught them.

"Oh my god, Tom. Tom!" She fell on her knees at his side and took his hand in hers, holding it to her wet cheek. Tom's eyes, barely slits, bloodshot and weak, brightened at the sight of her. "Honey, what did they do to you? I'm so sorry. I was too slow. Too late. If anything happens to you . . ." Doc arrived. "Doc, what do we know, or think?"

"He took a beating, but that's obvious. We've got compresses of juniper and peppermint on the open wounds. Your concoction. We have some medicinal teas brewing, and Bethany's making a compress from alder and elm barks and leaves, but those injuries are deep. I'm afraid of how deep. He may have damage to organs and internal bleeding. No way for us to stop it if he does. He has several deep knife punctures. Luckily, I guess, they were designed as torture and not to kill, but they did plenty of damage, most of which we have no way to resolve. All we can do is work as hard as we can and hope."

There's that word again—hope. "Well, that's not enough. Not for Tom," Sarah cried, so close to sobbing, but she forced herself to think about Tom rather than her own fears. She accessed her spiritual connections, reaching out to Asha for help. Sarah sat back and wailed into the sky. "Spirits of the universe, as you have come to my aid so many times, please, please be with me now!"

Sarah bent over Tom, tears pouring down her cheeks and onto his burning hot skin, her hands hovering over him so as not to cause any pain or harm. She wanted to gather him to herself and hold him close.

THREE

A familiar and powerful presence caused her to look up. Daffodil appeared out of nowhere and lighted beside her. The depth of their spiritual relationship always startled her. It was different from any other—fuller, richer, purely ethereal. It was as if Daffodil had only a fleeting physical existence. Sarah could never truly grasp it. Daffodil seemed to understand it, living peacefully within it, within everything. Nothing phased her.

Even though she, like everyone else, was naked, Daffodil appeared to be wearing a most delicate lace gown that shimmered around her—not a glow like Sarah but more like incredibly tiny, floating gemstones. The sun seemed to always be shining from behind her long golden curls. Other than Erika, Jazz, Janie and Ms. Watson, no one else saw the sparkle or, sometimes, even saw Daffodil. Tom hadn't seen her in the field as she'd guided the lost souls of the poor addicted teens into the spiritual universe. She was a special being in this very special place.

"You can save him, if you want," Daffodil said with a melodic tone of complete indifference.

Sarah sat bolt upright. "Of course, I want. I want it more than anything in the world."

"It will hurt. It will hurt you a great deal and for a very long time."

"I don't care. I can handle it."

Daffodil looked her in the eyes, put her delicate hands on Sarah's shoulders and spoke in her soft, sweet voice as though they were talking about butterflies, not the life or death of her eternal love. "This will take some of your powers of healing. You will never get them back. You will be weaker, more vulnerable. It shouldn't take them all, but the sort of injuries you just healed yourself from, you may not be able to recover from next time. They may kill you." The more serious change in her demeanor was barely perceptible. "Do you understand?"

Sarah turned to Jazz and then Janie. They both nodded, and Sarah looked Daffodil directly in her eyes. "I do."

"This will be the last time you can heal a human near death. To do it again, under any circumstances, will kill you." Daffodil paused as Sarah nodded. Daffodil continued, her voice still soft and dispassionate, "That includes your girls. If either becomes deeply injured or sick, you will not likely be able to heal them without killing yourself in the process." She paused to make sure Sarah perceived the gravity of what she was about to do. Then, with the same indifference, almost like a kindergarten teacher addressing a five-year-old, she asked, "Do you understand?"

Sarah thought about this for several seconds. Nothing had ever been as important to her as her girls. Her love for Tom was now in the balance. Sarah looked at Jazz, who nodded, and then at Janie, who did the same.

Jazz pulled Janie to her, and Janie put her arm around her sister. Then Jazz spoke with more confidence than Sarah had ever heard from her oldest, "Mom, save Tom!"

Sarah smiled as a tear slipped down her cheek. She wiped it from her face, turned and rose as upright and sturdy as possible on her knees, now looking the standing sprite in the eyes. She knew at that moment she was speaking to the spirits of the universe through this woman. Sarah spoke to Daffodil with clarity and sincerity, "Daffodil, Asha, Mom, I do understand."

The crowd murmured, having no idea who Asha was or why Sarah mentioned her mother, but neither Daffodil nor Sarah heard them. Their spirits were now entwined in this one mission. Daffodil nodded, maintaining eye contact with Sarah, searching her soul.

When she found the depth of love Sarah had for Tom, she continued, still matter-of-factly, "This will hurt more than anything you have ever endured, and you will not be able to escape it. You cannot let the intense pain interfere with your concentration."

Sarah nodded. "I've endured great pain to protect those I love. I can do it again. I will do it for Tom."

Daffodil now faced Tom, and Sarah regarded the man she loved, dying before her eyes. "Sarah, we are going to move through Tom's body, slowly from head to toe. You will take on his pain—all of it. It will be excruciating, and it will last. You will not be able to ignore it or leave your physical body to get away from it. It will be debilitating, but you will not take on his injuries. They will be healed. Do you understand?"

"Yes, I understand."

"Sarah, if you lose your focus while we are doing this, it will kill all three of us." Daffodil paused, still not the slightest urgency in her voice. She gazed into Sarah's eyes. "Do you understand?"

Sarah carefully considered this new information for several seconds then stared into Tom's eyes. Tom moved his mouth, but she couldn't hear him. She lowered herself down to listen to him closely.

"I love you," his whisper was barely audible. "You can't save me, sweetheart. It's too risky. Too many others need you, rely on you. Your strength is their protection. Let me die and save them."

Sarah raised up, took his hand in hers, then told Daffodil, "I understand. I can handle it. I know the risks. I need to do this. I'm ready."

Daffodil smiled ever so slightly then guided Sarah, still on her knees, up to Tom's right side. Daffodil slid in behind her, Sarah's back touching Daffodil's front. Daffodil slid her arms above Sarah's, her hands resting lightly on Sarah's wrists.

"We begin."

Sarah nodded.

"Close your eyes and bond completely with me." Sarah did as requested. She felt the warm, soothing soul of Daffodil fully enter hers. Sarah released her soul and all her spirits to her guide, providing her with all the powers she might require. As her healing Elephant spirit rose within them, Sarah could feel Daffodil's soul entwining with hers at a level deeper than anything she'd ever felt.

Daffodil's guidance was spoken nonverbally through their connection as she moved Sarah's hands onto Tom's forehead. "Feel his body, all the way through. Feel the pain, the injuries, and absorb them. Release your healing spirits into Tom. They will heal his wounds."

Sarah did as instructed. She could feel and envision the injuries Tom had sustained to his head and brain. She felt the healing powers from her Elephant grow and envelop Tom. As it healed him, she felt a deep, searing pain in her head, worse than she'd imagined. She instinctively recoiled but did not lose touch with Tom.

"You must maintain your concentration," Daffodil reminded her as she held Sarah's hands on Tom. Sarah recovered, her head still racked in agony. It was hard to think, and this was just the beginning.

Daffodil guided Sarah's hands, moving them down, her Elephant spirit healing his facial bruises and a cracked eye socket as the pain from Tom's wounds slashed into her face. Sarah responded to the attack, closing her eyes and feeling the pain, trying to ignore it. This time she maintained complete concentration on Tom and returned with determination. *If Tom survived this for me, I can do this for him. For us!*

A fractured cheekbone healed as sharp daggers drove into her own. She jolted back but withstood them, feeling the love inside her helping her. A moment, Robert punching her, flashed through her mind. *It's like that. You handled that. You can take this. He beat you worse than this. You can do this.* Her soul was in warrior mode as it had been so many times in her life. *Strength against time, and time doesn't matter.* The lesson she'd learned during meditation amid the ancient spirit of a majestic oak tree in a park in D.C. on the worst day of her life, now many years ago, repeated in her mind. *You can do this, Sarah; time doesn't matter.* This was the most important challenge she'd ever faced. Her spirits and soul were united. She could do this. *Focus, ignore the pain. Strength against time, and time doesn't matter.*

A contusion in his neck, fractured vertebrae, severe bruises, healed. Pain seared through her neck. She struggled to hold her head up. She felt deep love from Tom's soul, which allowed her to persevere. *It's only his body. He loves with his soul, and that's still strong. This is only pain. It's not real. I can do this!* She was convincing herself as her brain railed against continuing.

She heard Daffodil inside her: "Good. It is all the pain the injury has and would inflict. Bear it. Feel it. Take it in, and you will save your beloved. Use that love to absorb it for him."

The deep, jagged stab wound in his shoulder ripped into her as though she were being stabbed over and over. This was not the sort of pain she was used to dismissing. Not the natural nerve pain that was simply a warning signal to her brain. This pain penetrated her core, to her inner being. Burning like hot coals, she pushed on. She could feel his love, his soul hanging on for her, barely, within a body on the edge of survival.

Punctured lung, damaged liver, broken ribs, torn muscles, gashes through the chest, bleeding within, all healed but piercing her like red hot swords and skewers. Her powerful Elephant spirit healed Tom's injuries as her Bear spirit gave him strength to survive. Feeling Tom grow stronger emboldened her soul, but her brain rebelled, trying to protect its body. *Can I handle any more?*

Daffodil, in a voice sweet but firm, answered the unspoken question, "You must, Sarah. This is pain. No more injury. But you must continue. It is too late now to stop."

She had no choice. Her mind swirled as her brain and body revolted against her will, demanding over and over that she relent, release Tom to his death, join him in the universe. Dying seemed a better option than the searing torture she was enduring.

She heard Jazz's soothing voice. "You can do it, Mom. Stay with it. Love him. Love him so deeply."

She drew strength from her oldest. *I can do this! I've never felt a love like this. I need to love. I deserve to be in love. Tom is MY love.* Gashes in his side, torn muscles in his back, organs bleeding, oozing, failing. She reeled left then right as though feeling the infliction of the beating Tom had endured, but many times over.

Pain tore at her from head to midsection. Excruciating, unrelenting pain, and she was only halfway done. Again, Robert's face exploded into her mind's eye. "YOU DO NOT DESERVE TO LOVE!" It was the tiny shard of the Storm, reaching through, throwing doubt into her spiritual consciousness. Her Bear rose from within her, rearing onto his hind legs, muscles rippling, providing her confidence and strength to force the image down. She reached for her Tiger spirt, and with its power coursing through her, Sarah yelled into the universe, "I CAN DO THIS! I DO DESERVE LOVE!"

She refocused, feeling Daffodil guiding her, connecting her. A perforated intestine. Escaped waste. Infection, puss and putrid buildup. Healed in Tom, but pain penetrated her midsection, a driving ache and searing heat beyond her comprehension. She fell forward, her arms on Tom's abdomen, head bowed, her long black hair wet and tangled, spread across his sweaty skin. She was trying to avoid the pain, pain to every part of her upper body. Her healing Elephant spirit was too engaged, irretrievable, unable to heal her, but then she was not injured. It was just pain. Her other spirits were of no use. She writhed back and forth, struggling in a battle between her brain and soul.

Daffodil kept Sarah's hands connected to Tom. "Come back, Sarah, it is too late now. You must continue or we all die." There was still no hint of panic in Daffodil's voice.

"Mommy, you can do it. Save him. Save yourself. Love him. Fight for all of us. Mommy, you can do it." Janie's higher voice was sweet but panicked. She knew inside that she couldn't leave her girls.

I've withstood pain my whole life for love. I can do this!

Sarah redoubled her focus and felt Daffodil's spirits reinforce hers. Stabbing knives tore deep into her gut, as if rupturing organs, crushing bones. Tom's spine was badly damaged, but she felt it and healed it completely as what felt like jagged saw blades ripped at her back and insides. Again, she paused a moment, fighting her own mind, her own body's demands that she stop. Pain, unbearable pain, raged through her from head to abdomen, and she reeled against it.

FOUR

She felt she couldn't bear anymore. Perhaps they should die together right now. As the thought grew, she felt Tom strengthen as she healed his body. He was there with her. She could feel him, his love, their shared love. It swept through her. It didn't diminish the terrorizing pain, but it made it bearable and her mission clear. He was now fighting for their lives alongside her. As his strong hand rested on her shoulder, warmth flowed through her soul. It was love deeper than she'd imagined was possible. It glowed like a beacon for her. Her spirit, although in crushing pain, smiled.

Now it was two against one, and she'd win that battle any day. She felt his love pour into her. His powerful, gentle, wonderful hand resting gently on her shoulder gave her strength.

His testicles were beaten. She focused on healing them, feeling the pain in her groin, a feeling like she'd never felt. It was debilitating, and she bent over, putting her head on Tom's stomach. She felt Tom's right hand brush her hair gently. His strength fueled her resolve, and she refused to release herself from the connection. She absorbed the pain. Cuts on his penis, healed. Searing burns in his anus jerked her forward as the pain transferred to her. She gasped and held her breath.

"Take a moment, but do not lose your connection."

"I won't!" She felt weakened but determined.

A long gash down his thigh along with deep bruises. Torn tendons and cartilage, a crushed kneecap, regenerated as scorching heat and ragged knives lacerated her soul, attacking her courage with each advance. Cartilage, broken tibia, crushed bones in his feet, toes ripped from their sockets, toenails gone—now all repaired and replaced. *How had he endured all this? If he could for me, then I can endure it for him!*

When she cleared Tom's toes, Sarah fell to the earth in a heap. The pain throbbed through her head, face, neck, shoulders, abdomen, arms, hands, crotch, legs, knees, feet, toes—jagged, shredding, blistering, pounding, festering, over and over and over. Sarah was writhing, shivering, pawing at the ground for relief. She screamed out into the universe and the world around her as everything she knew flowed from her mind, leaving nothing but brutal, wrenching, excruciating, tortuous pain.

Focusing on her soul, she tried to meditate, but the agony was too deep. It wasn't physical. Leaving her body made no difference. No spirits appeared to guide her. Nature was not there to soothe her. She couldn't reach her animal spirits. Couldn't feel her girls or Tom any longer. She couldn't hear. Couldn't see. Couldn't sense anything. She was alone in darkness with pain boring into every cell of her body in an unending circle of torment.

FIVE

A hand touched her shoulder. Kisses fluttered across her face. Brisk water. Love from everywhere reached through the pain. Her senses began to return. The burning heat dulled. The jabbing, tearing of her spirits lessened.

As the pain weakened, she felt cold, soft rabbit skins, loving hands and Tom's sweet kisses. Clarity awoke her mind. The pain settled into the background, and then, like a light switching off, it was gone.

When she opened her eyes, they were met with the bright blues of her loving man. Tom teared up, and she reached a hand up to wipe his cheek then around to the back of his head, pulling him to her. He kissed her, and love rippled through her body, eliminating any residual effects from the supernatural treatment that had saved their lives.

She sat up and took in the sights of the compound, the grass and forest trees green with life. The sky a deep azure blue. Flowers blooming in every color imaginable.

"Hi," she said to Tom with a huge smile. "Are you alright?"

"She's back!" came a cry nearby. Everyone in the compound scrambled toward her and gathered around.

He chuckled at her concern for him, though she could see he was not completely healed. His face was still slightly discolored, but his eyes were clear and his smile radiant.

"Right now," he said, "I couldn't be better. Still a little sore, but alive and doing great, especially now. Way more important . . . how are you?"

She took a deep breath. "Well, my sweet dear, that sucked worse than anything I've ever endured, and I've endured *a lot*. But right now, I feel great. You'd better be worth it."

He embraced her tightly. "I'm so sorry, sweetheart. Why'd you do that, you crazy woman? You should have let me die."

"No way. You still owe me an adjustment and back rub. I wasn't going to let you out of that so easily!"

The Family chuckled.

"I promise to fulfill your every need, for the rest of our lives together."

The crowd let out a collective "awwww."

"Of course, if you keep doing the insane things you do, that might not be all that long." He kept her close within his big arms and kissed her.

The Family cheered.

When they finally separated, she said, "OK, sweetheart, let me up. We have things to do around here, I imagine." He released her and stood, then reached down a hand to help Sarah to her feet. Her legs were wobbly and weak. Jazz and Mark ran to help stabilize her. Once she gained her balance, Sarah looked around. "Things have changed. How long was I out?"

"Three days," answered Doc.

"Three days?" Sarah exclaimed. "Holy crap. Three days." She regarded the Family members around her, who nodded. "Well, I'm not doing that again, so all of you better stay safe, alright?" She pointed first at Tom, then Jazz and Janie and then the rest of the Family, who giggled and began to disperse.

"Alright, Doc, so how's Tom? He's not quite healed despite all I went through."

"He's fine. He's left with some minor residual discolorations and a little stiffness, but his body's virtually healed. No broken bones, internal bleeding, infections nor anything else that could kill him." Doc bent over and whispered, a bit too loudly, "And his really important parts are all healed and fully functional."

Sarah blushed and those still nearby snickered. Tom smiled and wrapped his arm around her.

She whispered with a big smile, "And I can't wait for you to prove that to me." They kissed deeply for several seconds until the Family began to ooh and aah. She gently pulled back from him and addressed Ms. Watson. "Where's Daffodil?"

A hush fell over those remaining. Ms. Watson took a step forward. "Sarah, I hate to be the bearer of this news, but Daffodil did not survive the healing. We could see her fading physically during the healing process."

"She sorta dissolved, Mommy," Janie piped up, as usual.

Ms. Watson continued, "When you reached the end and fell into convulsions, Daffodil looked more like a ghost than a physical person. She floated off and, well, dissipated."

Jazz added, "A little like Tony, Mom, but Daffodil faded into a golden mist of diamond dust."

"She sparkled into the air," Janie said but stopped short as she saw tears pour down Sarah's cheeks. No one else knew or appreciated Daffodil, but perhaps that was Daffodil's way.

"That's the second person to sacrifice her life for me," Sarah said. "Asha and now Daffodil." No one knew who Asha was and yet Sarah had mentioned her twice in front of them. She hadn't told the story of her life before the Storm, or her battle with it, to anyone but Tom, but all sensed now was not the time to ask. As her tears turned into sobs, she hugged Jazz and Janie, and Tom engulfed them.

Sarah spoke haltingly, "I'm so . . . sorry. I should 'ave . . . taken care of . . . Tony a long . . . long time ago." Guilt flooded over her. She took a deep breath and looked through foggy, tear-filled eyes at her Family. "I should never have left here with Tony and his mob in this place. I'm so sorry. This is all my fault. I'll do everything in my power to make it up to you. To everyone. To make Daffodil's and every other life lost in that battle honored and valued."

Tom held her tightly, and she buried her head in his shoulder. The Family stood, hushed.

Ms. Watson broke the silence. "Sarah, this was not your fault! Tony was an evil, evil man! It was bound to happen. He was going to try to take over one way or another. You couldn't be here every minute of every day to protect us."

The Family streamed toward her, patting her on the back, reaffirming their faith in her, assuring her that this was not her fault and that they loved her. She tried to smile, but the tears continued. Something deep was lost. Something special to this earth—beyond words—was gone because of her. Daffodil, the spritely healer of all things and guide to the lost spirits of the dead, was gone. The strange woman to whom she felt a connection so complete that even she couldn't understand it had died so that Sarah could save her lover.

SIX

Breaking the mournful silence, Sarah croaked between sobs, "Everyone . . . I need . . . a few minutes."

"Alright, she's back. Let's give her some time." Ms. Watson, as always, took command. "Back away, and let's get to work. Amy, do we have some food for Sarah? Can we get something together?" Ms. Watson's orders were, as always, followed by the Family without question.

Sarah leaned into Tom, her arms hugging herself, crossed between them, her head tucked into his shoulder. Visions filled her head with missed opportunities to take Tony out: when he attacked Latifah, after he goaded that simple man to molest Holly, any number of moments. She'd been incapable of acting. Something inside her—the Storm, the destructive side—had prevented her. She mumbled, "I knew he was evil. I should've taken him out."

She found refuge in Tom's embrace. Warmth. Love. Tom said nothing while he held her. After she'd composed herself, she pulled back and whispered, "Tom, I need some time alone. Just me. I won't be long, I promise." Tom nodded and released her. She turned to Jazz and Janie and put a hand on each of her daughters' outside shoulders, squatted and gazed deep into their eyes. There was a "knowing" in Jazz's eyes she hadn't seen before—a maturity, maybe even a hint of grace. Sarah smiled and hugged them, whispering, "I love you so much, but I need a few minutes."

"Come on, girls, let's give your mom some space." The two nodded as Sarah kissed and released them. Tom led them off into the rejuvenated compound.

Sarah watched them with love then took a lotus position, settled into her meditation and was soon floating with the spirits of the universe. She'd missed this world.

"Sarah, welcome." Daffodil's voice was every bit as melodic and sweet, while her words were straightforward and dispassionate. "The pain is gone. Tom is healed because you loved him enough to endure. You know now how deeply you love him. Show him. Be there for him, always and in every moment of every day. Do what it takes to make him happy, and he will do the same for you. Love heals all. He loves you deeply. Love him as deeply, for you now know that you have it in you to do so."

Sarah thought about this. Had she really released herself to totally and completely love Tom, or did she only accept his unquestioning love for her? She looked at Daffodil, as ethereal here as she was in real life. "I'll try." Daffodil shook her head. Sarah paused, gazing into the soft sky-blue eyes of the sprite, and said instead, "I *will* love him with all of my being." Daffodil nodded. "Thank you, Daffodil, but I'm so sorry you lost your life for Tom and me. Thank you so much, but that was too great a sacrifice. The new world needs you. *I* need you."

"My dear Sarah, you are more special than you yet know. This is where I belong. I was but a visitor. A bit player. I did my part. Asha has done her part. Others have done their parts." Daffodil paused and engaged Sarah with her eyes. "Sarah, my dear, now comes the hard part. We are all gone, and it is now upon you to do your part, and your part is to play the leading role. We were ensemble players. You, Ms. Sarah, must carry the show. Love and lead but collaborate with all around you. It is not over. There is another. A threat. There will be challenges, great and small. Thank you for being willing to do what has to be done."

Sarah reached out a hand for her, but Daffodil faded into sparkling dust and floated off into the bright depths of the void, surrounded by the full assembly of spirits and souls. Instead of loss, Sarah felt the pure joy that emanated from that world. She could hear Daffodil's voice, distant but melodic: "Sarah, come back when you need us, and those who love you will always be here." Here, in the holy universe of spirits, Sarah was but a visitor. She smiled as she settled back into her physical body.

When she opened her eyes, Amy and Herb were there with a basket of food. Tom and the girls sprinted back to her side. Janie jumped into her lap, and Jazz sat beside her. Tom slid in behind her, serving as a backrest so she could eat and chat. She felt the warmth from all of them, each different, each pure and very real.

Amy handed her the basket. "Girlfriend, you had us scared out of our wits. We were sure you wouldn't make it. It was certainly touch and go there for a while. Take this slow. I'm sure you're famished, but eat a little at a time."

She savored the strong venison, bitter greens, soft mushrooms, delicate fish and sweet berries, enjoying the unique flavors as they settled on her tongue. It was the best meal she'd ever tasted, as though she'd never really appreciated the full range of joy food could bring.

SEVEN

After the meal, Sarah stood on her own, tested her legs, felt her Horse flow within them and strode out into the compound. The hawthorn branches in the barrier were budding. They'd rooted. Given how nature exploded in this new world, she shouldn't have been surprised. Living roses and other vines had been planted at the base of the barrier and woven into its fabric. The grass was thick, lush and bright green. The air smelled of nectar from the many flowers that were blooming. Birds sang in the trees. The breeze rustled the bright green leaves. The sky was blue from horizon to horizon, not a cloud in the sky. She could feel the spirits within it all, connected, in harmony, breathing and living as one. So it was with nature—a single, integrated ecosystem, now largely uninterrupted by humans. They'd need to keep it that way.

The bustle of Family members gathering around her broke her from her trance. Smiling people encircled her, wanting to interact with her, to touch her as though she were a rock star from the old world. She was swept up in it all. Tom and the girls guided her out into the Family. She glided through the crowd, touching hands, reconnecting, feeling their love and returning it with as much power as she could muster.

She moved slowly, quietly, almost in a daze. The spirits of the universe, the plants and the animals swirled with the warming emotions and deep gratitude of the Family. The spiritual experience was mesmerizing, and she knew she was glowing. No one bowed to her. They felt the love she had for them, and they allowed her spirit to mix with theirs.

She had no sense of how long the process took. *Time doesn't matter.* She was a river, flowing within the Family, her spirit flooding over and through them.

When she reached the end, standing before her was Erika, bruised and proud, a spear in her left hand. Beside her was tiny Randi, a bruise on her left cheekbone, her left arm in a sling and a spear in her right. Warriors. These two women were every bit as important to saving the Family from Tony as she was. The most fearsome and fearless warriors she'd ever known. Sarah stopped, the bulk of the Family now behind her, and gazed into their eyes. Then, to the two women's surprise, Sarah genuflected before them, bowing her head to honor them. The rest of the Family followed.

When Sarah stood, the Family remained on one knee, unsure what would happen. A grin spread across her face from ear to ear, and she bolted into the arms of her friend Erika, whom she loved like a sister. Sarah reached down and scooped Randi into their embrace, her feet dangling off the ground. Erika and Sarah shared a long powerful kiss. Then they both turned and kissed Randi on her forehead.

They broke the embrace, and Randi slipped down. Sarah and Erika stared into each other's eyes before Erika spoke the first words, "Great to have you back, sister." The sound of the slap of Erika's strong hand on Sarah's back resonated through the camp. "I wasn't sure that was going to happen." She exhaled a long breath and added, "I'm glad you're back."

They hugged again as the Family stood and cheered.

EIGHT

Very little was accomplished the rest of the afternoon. Ms. Watson realized the Family needed time with their leader. Sarah was regaled with stories about what had happened while she was writhing in pain. Several people merely recounted the battle with Tony, what they saw, marveling at some aspect of Sarah's heroics, and how they were thankful to Sarah for saving them. A few others updated her on the plantings around the barrier. Marsha provided information on various structures they'd been working on.

Ms. Watson stood a few feet to Sarah's right, quietly listening. Sarah could sense concern in her demeaner but was so engrossed in the storytelling that the feeling faded. Jazz and Janie joined her, sitting at her feet, and Tom appeared and stood near Ms. Watson. Sarah winked at him, and he winked back; they dopily stared at each other like teenagers in love as the stories continued.

Finally, it was Erika's turn, who called Randi and a couple of others to join her.

Erika leaned over and kissed Sarah, short but sweet, and stood. Many in the Family were new to their way of greeting each other, which caused murmurs, but Erika launched right in.

"Wanna know what happened to Tony's gang?" she asked Sarah.

"Sure. I hope they're gone."

"Forever," Erika stated. "I'm not a storyteller, so Randi's going to tell it." Erika sat down next to her friend and put a hand on her knee. "Listen up. This is good." She turned to the tiny woman who was brave and tough beyond her size. "Randi."

"Well, Erika, me and a team of armed guards drove what was left of Tony's revolutionaries, injured and all, far west of here, across all the fields." As Randi continued, Sarah received her first report as to what the world looked like in that direction. They'd explored so little, and bad things seemed to happen when she strayed from the compound.

"Our grasslands continue, like, for miles that way," Randi explained as she pointed west. "They get very wide as you get out there. We were guessing they went from the woods and bluffs along the Meramec on the left, or, I guess, the south side, to the Missouri River, which is north. We stayed along the south edge of the grasslands, so we don't know what happens as you get closer to the Missouri River. There are lots of pretty big hills and ridges on the left as you head out that way along the Meramec. Pretty quickly, you can't see the northern side of the grasslands.

"There are big herds of all kinds of herbivores. Many I've never seen, except maybe in the Zoo, but I preferred the carnivores and penguins when we went there. So anyway, they were all roaming around and eating grass. Lots of babies. Each herd was separated from those that weren't like them, and they seemed to ignore one another."

Sarah called Samantha and Marshall out of the crowd. They trotted over with a few others from their team.

"Sarah, what can we help you with?" Samantha asked.

Sarah said to Randi, "Randi, would you repeat what you know about the herds out west for our hunters?"

"Oh, Sarah. No need," Marshall interrupted. "We've been hunting out there for a couple of days now. Ever since Erika, Randi and the team got back. Wait 'til you see what's for dinner."

Erika smiled at her friend. "Girlfriend, a lot's happened in the three days you were loafing on the ground." Sarah smiled, and the two bumped shoulders.

Randi continued, "Sarah, most important, there's a small herd of cattle really far out there, and about ten horses a little farther than them."

Sarah was impressed. "Awesome. It'd be great to bring in both the cows to breed for milk and beef, and the horses to use for all sorts of things."

A portly man with very pale skin, whom Sarah felt she should know but didn't, chimed in, "Before the transportation systems in the old world existed, horses were invaluable."

Sarah nodded and wondered how heavy he must have been to still be rather rotund, then shook herself out of that negative thought and said, "Thank you so much. I agree. Those horses will be a big benefit. Erika and I saw three other horses not far to the north of us, and with those ten or so, we'll have a nice herd of our own. Let's figure that out as soon as we can."

Ms. Watson piped in, "On it, Sarah. I'll talk to Gus. He's the only cowboy we have in the Family, that I know of."

Sarah welcomed her trusted partner and dear friend. "Thank you so much, Shirley. If he's the only one you know of, then he's the only one." Sarah winked, and Ms. Watson smiled. "Thank you again, Shirley." Remembering the concern she'd felt from Ms. Watson earlier, Sarah grinned with deep affection and said, "Shirley, I hope you know how much I love you and am honored to be part of your team."

Ms. Watson blushed. "I'll talk to Gus . . . and thanks." She started to leave but looked back. "I love you too, Sarah." Then off she moved through the crowd.

Joe interjected, "Just so you know, Sarah, we had this place covered. I stayed back to protect the Family against any new problems." The Family stared at him. "Well, nothing happened. Thank heavens." A gentle giggle rolled through the crowd. His face turned red, and Sarah stepped forward.

"You did great. Thank you for protecting us. Not only then, but always. You're a great man around here, Joe." The big man blushed then, to Joe's surprise, Sarah began to clap for him. Everyone joined in. It lasted a few seconds, but it was clear Joe was deeply touched. Erika stood, put her arm around him and kissed him gently on his cheek, then backed a foot or so away. Joe was red-faced and smiling as he retreated into the safety of the masses.

Sarah returned her attention to Erika as more Family members gathered around them. "So, Cap'n, what does it look like out there? The terrain and all that?"

"It's awesome for us." Erika jumped into her role as military logistics expert. "As Randi mentioned, the grasslands stretch wide, and the northern forest, which is very dense and dark, fades north out of sight, presumably to the bluffs along the Missouri. At the far western edge of the grasslands, the forests on the north and the wooded southern hills come together. Passing through that forest would be pretty difficult, with the dense underbrush among the trees. So, it should provide some protection from anything coming from the north. Of course, somewhere up there is the Missouri River and its bluffs, which would also be tough to get across."

Randi added, "And all along the edges were nasty sticker bushes."

"Getting through there will take some doing." Erika seemed proud of this fact. "To the south are some pretty steep hills and ridges. There were a bunch of parks out there before the Storm and areas where man had cut down hills and ridges for roads and subdivisions. Well, whatever man removed is back. The Missouri and Meramec come rather close together out there, and between them are some pretty daunting, heavily wooded hills and ridges."

"There's a narrow passage, maybe 10 feet, between two pretty tall ridges: one runs north and the other south," Randi continued. "They're climbable on our side, but they go down pretty steep on the west side into a valley. I think that narrow gap is, like, the only way in or out of our grasslands without thrashing through that forest or climbing those steep, rocky hills. After we told the rebels never to come back, we made them scramble down through that gap. After a while, it becomes a pretty steep slope."

"We've had guards out there ever since to make them stay down there," Joe added.

"So, after leaving them to fend for themselves, we started back home. Without the prisoners to guard, we started to explore. There are several small creeks that run across the grasslands, from north to south, and pool beneath willows and birch trees like ours does. They all flow from the hills to the north and then across the grasslands into ravines between the hills on the south side."

"Olive Boulevard, well, the original Plank Road, is the high point. The creeks south of that ridge run our direction, and the creeks north of that run into the Missouri," the portly man spoke up from within the crowd. "It's way more hilly north of that ridge, which is probably even higher if everything's returned to what it was like before humans tore things down."

"Great to know. Thank you." Sarah acknowledged him, and the man smiled. A few Family members patted him on the back.

"We should be able to explore that forest by heading up those streams to avoid fighting through the underbrush," Erika interjected then nodded to Randi to continue.

"On our way back, we explored the southern edges of the grasslands and walked a few of the ravines the creeks travel in through the hills. The bluffs overlooking the Meramec are pretty steep. A few slope gradually then fall off at the end pretty hard.

"The water rushes down them, mostly in rapids, and then some in falls over little cliffs. As we got closer to here, the southern hills get higher and steeper. We couldn't get close enough to see past the edge, but the water pours over and makes its way into the Meramec, just like our river does."

Sarah asked questions about the terrain and was formulating a pretty good vision of that area in her mind. That they seemed to be encircled by formations that would be difficult to penetrate by outsiders was comforting.

Sarah stood and announced to the Family, "It's good to be protected like that, right?" The crowd nodded in agreement. "All the same, let's make more spears, arrows and long knives than we need for everyday activities in case we have any other unwanted visitors."

"OK, OK, that's enough storytelling," Ms. Watson announced upon her return, noticing that Sarah was exhausted.

NINE

$\maltese$om explained that Joe had taken charge of the arsenal. He and Erika also began to train the Family in the tactics for defending the compound. The strategy was developed by Erika with consultation from an older gentleman who sat with the Seamstresses and told stories all day long. The children were drawn to him, enwrapped in his tales. Everyone called him the General. Even still, Sarah had yet to formally meet the elderly man and saw no reason to do so.

Carmen and Candy showed up and stood before her silently, waiting to be acknowledged.

"Hello, ladies," Tom finally said.

"Ms. Sarah, we'd like to help you clean up . . . if you'd like us to," Carmen responded.

"Well, I'm sure I look terrible. I guess I've been thrashing around in the dirt for three days. Sure. I'd like that. It'd be nice to look halfway decent." She smiled at the two women. "OK, Tom, Jazz and Janie, I'm going to the beauty parlor. You can head out and do whatever you're supposed to be doing."

Sarah stood, and the beauticians led her down to the river. "We're going to fix that hair, Sarah. You simply have to let us." Carmen and Candy were the Family gossips, and now was Sarah's time to catch up on what was really going on in camp.

Apparently, relationships were blooming. She heard about who was having sex with whom and who was mad about that and what they said they were going to do about it and on and on. Many people spent time with more than one partner, and, according to Candy, "some even have threesomes."

"You and Jake have threesomes, Candy. No one else does," Carmen teased.

"Their loss." The two giggled and continued to spill the details on Family interactions that Sarah had largely ignored.

A few spats had occurred over who was entitled to the exclusive intimacies of a desired partner and Sarah tuned in. "How does that get resolved?"

Carmen explained, "Ms. Watson handles the issues. She asks the target of the suitors' affections what they want. Whatever he or she says goes, even if he or she decides to enjoy the pleasures of both or several other folks. It doesn't matter what the suitors want, but of course, they can decide to back out of the relationship entirely."

The two continued to prattle on about the comings and goings in camp. Sarah's exhausted mind struggled to keep up and finally gave up trying. She laid back and let the ladies take care of her. As she relaxed, her mind wandered to the affairs of the Family. She was contemplating the new home and realized from the beauticians' stories that there should be plenty of babies born in the middle of winter. Sarah decided to discuss this adjustment to their planned quarters with Marsha. Soon, her eyes grew heavy and she dozed off.

After the ladies were finished with her, they woke her and had her look into a still pool.

"Doesn't she look perfect?" Candy drawled with her borderline Southern accent.

"You look simply stunning, Sarah. Tom will not be able to keep his hands off you." Carmen added a lilt that seemed to imitate her colleague.

"Not that he could before." Candy gave a delicate wave of her hand, and the two snickered.

Sarah gazed at her reflection in the pool and had to admit she looked as good or better than she had in a long time. "Amazing. Who is that?" The confused looks on the ladies' faces confirmed stand-up was not in her future. "Thank you so much. I feel great. I'll be back, if that's OK."

"Oh, of course," the two said at the same time. Giggling, Candy added, "Sarah, you come by any ol' time. Can't have our leader looking disheveled." A couple of other women showed up at the edge of the river, and the two artists turned to their new customers.

As Sarah made her way up the bank, the two bowed to her and Carmen said, "You look awesome, sweetie. You really do."

"Thank you." Sarah blushed but felt good. "And please, no one needs to bow to me. We're all equals around here." The women nodded and held their heads low in deference. Sarah sighed. *I suppose like everyone calls Shirley Ms. Watson no matter what she requests, some people will bow to me no matter what I say.* She shook her head as she emerged from the river.

"Sarah," came a pleasant cry from her left. Sarah was needed, as always.

She toured the barrier, marveling at the flowers and how the vines were working on both sides. She checked out the garden the children had made before the Storm, which was growing nicely. The fruit trees were in bloom. She individually thanked all the gardeners for their hard work.

She visited Claire and Samantha and the dogs, visited the Seamstresses and Ol' Mac, and was generally guided around all afternoon by someone who wanted to catch her up on things they'd accomplished in the three days she was out. She had a moment, a simple shared glance, with the man they called the General, which touched her spirit and made her smile. He smiled back and nodded. She was pulled away before she could introduce herself.

With Tony's malcontent rebels gone, the Family was getting along nicely, settling into the rhythms of nature and camp routine, and thrilled to have their leader back and in charge.

TEN

After dinner with Tom, Sarah was back at work, going over the improvements to the trap design John had made and discussing fixes for other issues they'd run into when she heard Marsha call, "Sarah, have you got a minute?"

John told her, "Sarah, this is great. I get what you mean. I can take it from here." He smiled.

Sarah patted him on the back and stood to address her friend. "Marsha, wow, the whole crew. How can I help?"

"Well, we need bamboo. For the new big house you want us to build."

Another member of her team, a tall slender man with red hair, spoke, holding out several pieces of bark with charcoal markings on them. "We've designed nearly every aspect of the building, including the ventilation issues you pointed out. We've practiced making thatch. We've figured out the walls, where the fire will go, how to set up the cooking area and even where to put the families with infants." He pointed at the bark as he spoke.

"Glad you thought of that. I was planning to mention it," Sarah said.

A slightly built woman spoke next, also holding out some bark, this one filled with numbers. "And we've got all of the stresses and structural issues worked out, even if we get a couple of feet of snow or a tornado."

"Thank you, Patricia," Sarah replied, proud of herself for remembering her name from somewhere. The woman beamed.

Marsha took back the floor, "So, Sarah, this is a weird world, and we were wondering if you could help us get some bamboo. We understand that leaving is kinda scary, since the first time you left the zombie teens attacked, and the second time Tony and his gang revolted. But they're gone, and we need you to find us some bamboo so we can begin to harvest it and bring it back."

"It's urgent we start building our winter home," the tall redhead added.

"Marsha, you're right. Well, Erika and I found it right before the revolution. I'm sure she told you. But I'll have to get back out there to locate that bamboo stand and figure out how to get it back to camp." She took a deep breath and turned to the man with the red hair. "You're right, um . . ."

"I'm Leonard, ma'am."

"Sarah, please, and Leonard, nice to meet you. You're right about needing to start the winter house, but leaving here concerns me. Who knows whether there are any crazies out there, or something worse."

"Like an organized army that won't die mostly of its own mistakes, like those teens did," Leonard suggested.

"Precisely."

"The guards out west are keeping watch over Tony's remnants. We've even begun bringing supplies and food to them. With Tony gone, they've kinda changed. Not so much that anyone's willing to let them come back, but some. They've established their own rudimentary camp along another tributary stream that leads to the Meramec. So that threat is done," Marsha summarized.

"Good to know. It's been too long since the Storm for many other people to still be alive, but we have to be careful." Sarah remembered what Daffodil had said. "There could still be a threat out there. Alright. I'll start figuring out how to get back out there, collect some bamboo and then get it back here. Meanwhile, we'll all keep our eyes open."

ELEVEN

Sarah called for Erika. Erika was near the barrier helping plant some climbing plants Janie had found. There were many gardeners in the Family, and the task of turning the barrier into a living thing was something many had taken to. That the hawthorns were rooting was unexpected but certainly welcomed. As those trees grew, the barrier would become much stronger, and it'd already proved its worth against the attack of the zombie teens, as the Family had taken to calling the incident.

Erika perked up, excused herself and sprinted toward Sarah. Of course, Ms. Watson began to waddle toward Sarah, and others followed.

As Erika arrived and the small crowd gathered, Sarah asked Marsha, "Want to tell those gathered why we called this meeting?"

There was a chuckle among the Family leaders as Marsha answered Sarah, "Sure. So, as you all know, we're going to build a large building for us in the woods. We've done all the designs and calculations and are ready to get going. What we need is bamboo, which is what I was asking Sarah about."

Erika jumped forward. "We found some! I completely forgot in all the chaos. We were coming back from that trip when Tony ambushed us. But before that, we found a nice stand of bamboo trees!" Sarah knew that bamboo wasn't a tree but a grass but decided no one cared.

Erika was still talking, "The bamboo is a long way out there, but it's reachable. There are also three other horses. One is a draft horse, which would make hauling that bamboo a heck of a lot easier."

Sarah agreed, "Erika's right. We need to get those horses first. I'll have a plan by morning, and we'll get a team to head out to get them."

"Sarah talked to the horses. I could feel it. I sorta communicated with one of the horses myself." Erika puffed out her chest and then launched into the story about tracking the horses, how Sarah connected to them and how that felt. "Then, whoosh, out of nowhere, a huge Bengal tiger—that tiger that helped save us from Tony—flew out of the trees and took down the colt. The other three horses bolted, and the tiger killed the colt in one bite.

"Then Sarah and the tiger locked eyes. They stared at each other for several seconds. Sarah was talking with the tiger and the tiger was talking back, though not out loud, through their spirits. Then the tiger bowed to her, and she nodded back. Then he came to our aid in the battle. How cool is that?"

"Did you really talk to a tiger?" one of the women in the crowd asked.

"Communicated. You can't talk to a tiger," Sarah explained. "His soul and mine are connected, like I am with Latifah and the big male bear and the female elephant who came to our aid in the battle. We have an accord with them all. I'll explain tonight. Claire has this relationship with the dogs. I'm sure many of you will develop these relationships over time. They do all begin with me; so as long as we are in range of one another, you'll have your connection with whatever you relate with. We have many allies right now, and they've helped to save us. We now have to do our part for them."

"You got all of that from a tiger?" someone said skeptically.

"And from the bears?" someone else asked.

"Sure, and Latifah, of course. And my elephant friend out there as well. I connect with animals the way Ms. Watson connects with people and Janie connects with plants."

There was a pause as the leaders contemplated this. Sarah winked at them. "Alright, we need to get those horses."

Ms. Watson chimed in, "I spoke to Gus. He's in. We'll find other volunteers, I'm sure."

"I'm in, if I can ride Latifah again," Erika volunteered.

Sarah nodded with a sisterly smile. Ms. Watson and Erika strode off to the east. The others dispersed. Marsha and her team wandered off to their other projects.

TWELVE

For the first time since she'd come to, she stood in the middle of the compound without anyone demanding her time. She had one person on her mind. It was time to start living up to the promise she'd made to Daffodil. She walked south toward Tom's clinic. When he spotted her, Tom smiled and immediately headed her way. Sarah ran to him and jumped into his strong arms. She whispered into his ear, "I want your body, and I want it now!"

He embraced her tightly and kissed her long and deep.

Sarah begged, "Where can we go? I want you so badly, I could do you right here and now in front of everyone."

They scanned the compound and saw that everyone was busy or listening to Erika, who glanced up at Sarah and nodded. Tom put her down. "This way. There's a clearing on the other side of the river that can't be seen from our side."

"How do you know that?" she asked as they bounded off in that direction.

"The evening of the first day I needed to get away to grieve. I wandered across the river and found it by accident. I've gone there to think a few times since. It's my safe place. You're lucky I'm gonna share it with you, but I, for one, am looking forward to it." On the west side of the river, her hand in his, he guided her up a steep bank, down a thin space in the woods and up a short slope to a small grassy opening at the top of the rise.

Sarah gasped as she gazed down at the broad valley that spread out before them. The Meramec River ran from the west and pooled into a large lake that began at the foot of the hills they were standing atop. "The Meramec River. The folks who headed west talked about it," she said. "Now covered with water, that valley was a busy town and industrial area not long ago. Somehow it's been dammed up to create that huge lake."

A dark green forest spread over numerous hills as far as she could see to the south. Sarah scanned the horizon. No smoke. No indication that anyone had survived in that direction.

The ridge they were standing on fell sharply down to the lake's edge. To their west, the ridge rose in random peaks and gullies up from the river. Small waterfalls, the ones she'd heard about from Erika and Randi, raced down steep slopes, some parts green and tree covered, while other areas were rockier and more scattered with determined plants growing from cracks and crevices.

To her left, the ridge they were on curled south around the lake. It seemed less steep, covered by trees and brush. Somewhere well south, the river exited the lake and continued onward, presumably in a similar path to that of the old river. *Is that lake what would've happened if man had never been here to take control of this land?*

She stood there for several minutes taking in the view, contemplating the land's history and wondering if more humans existed somewhere out there. The sun shone down on them with radiant splendor as a gentle breeze blew from the west, bringing with it the subtle sweet scents of wildflowers. The world spread out at her feet. "Magnificent," she said out into the vastness.

Tom slid in behind her, wrapping his arms around her shoulders. She stared up into his big blue eyes and said, "Wow." She turned in his embrace, all her spirits raging. She was sure she was glowing. She wanted to tell him she loved him, to comply with her promise, but something caught in her throat. Her mind objected as a brief image of Robert flashed through it. She grimaced. Her only experience with a serious relationship had started too fast and ended too terribly. *It's OK, Sarah. It's early in the relationship. You'll get there.* She heard the familiar voice from within her and from somewhere in the universe and smiled. *Thanks, Mom.*

"You OK?" Her focus returned exclusively to Tom, and he sensed it. Perhaps a radiance in her face told him it was time. He lifted her up to him and kissed her then lowered her to the ground. He followed, hovering above her, kissing her on her lips but ever so gently.

"Close your eyes and enjoy," he said, and she obeyed. It was nice not to be in charge for once, and she took a deep breath to relax into his love.

He moved his body above hers, their auras overlapping. She could feel his soul dancing with hers. He kissed her left eye and then her right. She settled into a shallow meditation that allowed her to feel everything. His kisses flitted across her forehead, down her nose and cheeks, along her jawline. Slow, soft, tantalizing.

He moved down the side of her neck. His chest hairs brushed her nipples. She let out a short gasp. His lips hovering, breath soft and warm, his tongue flicking her skin gently along her neck, up the side of her jaw, breathing slowly in her ear. Electrifying energy rippled through her. His tongue behind her ear, under and around, tender and sensuous. Shivers raced down her spine, and she giggled. His body radiated heat to hers. She deeply breathed in his luscious aroma, powerful and masculine.

His lips and tongue moved leisurely down her neck, along her collarbone, down her chest, between her breasts. She exhaled as her body tingled. The gentle breeze enhanced the sensation as it folded between them, lighting up the moisture.

His tongue traced the underside of her breasts, then up from below and around her nipples. She could feel his love pouring into her, loving her like she'd never been loved before. Her spirits were in a state of frenzy. Her Tiger spirit wanted to grab him and make love to him right then, but she settled back and drank in the dreamlike moment. He continued around her breasts until his tongue flicked her left nipple lightly then circled it. He applied a kiss before gently sucking her erect nipple. She let go as the pleasure raced through her. He crossed over to her other breast and repeated the sequence.

Tom's right hand skimmed over her skin. Holding himself up with his left arm, beginning at her shoulder, he slid his fingers down her left side past her hip and thigh then crept over to her inner thigh. Her heart rate and breathing increased, energy rising, swirling, extending to every part of her body.

Tom's mouth moved under her right breast and down the center of her stomach as he grazed her pelvis and legs with his chest. He slid his tongue down the soft sides of her belly and licked and kissed her. It tickled, and she giggled like a little schoolgirl but didn't try to stop him. Her hands now rested on his upper back. His right hand caressed her butt, moving under her left cheek then down the back of her leg, across her thigh and again up her silky inner thigh, his fingers exploring her body as his tongue played with her left nipple.

As his hand slipped down the inside of her right thigh, he moved his soft lips with it, down her stomach, past her pelvis, her hands now on his head. His tongue glided down the inside of her right leg, moving his head out of her reach. Supported by his knees, Tom used both hands to grip her waist, stroke her hips and down her legs to her feet, his hands encircling her legs. He kissed her feet then caressed them, taking his time. Passion flowed throughout her body as he masterfully stimulated and opened spiritual blockages from the chakras in her feet. She felt so much negative energy she'd pent up inside leave her, flowing out freely and smoothly, and she relaxed into his love with more depth, perception and willingness.

She could feel all of nature around her, coursing through this moment: the cool breeze, the heat from the sun, the flowers perfuming the air and the birds singing their songs for them.

He started the return trip up her leg, guiding his tongue along her inner ankles, back and forth. Then the insides of her calves, the backs of her knees, the insides of her thighs. The anticipation was intense, building, growing. She put her hands on his head and guided him to her, and when his tongue touched her where she'd never been kissed before, a bolt of energy leaped up her spine, bursting into her brain then flowing back down through her body in waves. Her back arched, and she moaned as his tongue flicked and licked her in all the right places. No one had ever done this for her. Sex had never been about her.

The Tiger was now insatiable. She couldn't stand it anymore, so she grabbed his shoulders and pulled him up to her. She guided him inside her, kissing him fervently with each thrust. Her mind was flooded. She lost all sense of everything but Tom and the feelings boiling within her. Faster, faster, then just right. Building, building, energies rising, entwined in love, intensifying the experience. Their souls were dancing in the pleasure of their physical bodies and the joy of their spirits.

Together, the energy released within their souls, exploding at once into expansive orgasmic bliss—electricity, passion, warmth and love fusing as one. Sarah's ecstasy guided them into a deep meditative state to extend the feeling for both of them. Pure orgasmic penetrating joy radiated into the universe around them.

THIRTEEN

Joyful and wondrous as it always was, the universe of spirits engulfed Tom and Sarah. Tom was present with her. Asha was there. Her parents were there. Daffodil was there. All smiling.

Another woman was there with three children. Tom smiled at them. The woman smiled back and whispered, "We're wonderfully fine, my sweet. Enjoy your new life, Tom; enjoy your life with Sarah."

"Dad, we love you and want you to be happy," his son said.

"Daddy, we're fine. Thank you for being such a great dad! We're always with you," his oldest daughter added in a sweet, melodious voice. His youngest smiled and waved.

"Honey," Tom's wife continued as he reached for her, "it's time we move on. Our spirits will always be there for you. We will always love you. Love Sarah with every ounce of your being because that is what I, what we, want for you."

The universe was then empty, dark, but warm and embracing. The two of them remained, immersed in joy, then a bit of sadness and, for Tom, confusion and maybe guilt. Tom lost his bearings. This was too new for him.

Sarah was also shocked to have met his wife and children, especially while making love to her husband and their father. She felt the incredible love that flowed between them. It unnerved her. A twinge of jealously, maybe more than that, attacked her conscious. Suddenly, the connections were lost. The universe became cold. She'd never experienced that before, and it frightened her.

They seemed to fall, tumble out of her control, down into their bodies, spent and exhausted. She focused to gather herself and felt Tom roll away from her onto his back. Her heart was beating quickly. She lay on her back in the warm sun, feeling the breeze and nature glide over them as she regained control, slowing her breath, plugging back into the spirits of nature around her.

After several minutes, Sarah lifted herself up so her face was above his. "That was your family, wasn't it?"

His eyes were damp, and he could barely speak. "Yes." She reached around and held him close, but he kept his arms at his side. She wanted him to return the embrace with a bear hug. Finally, he whispered from somewhere far away, "Thank you."

After a while, Tom took a deep breath and asked, "Sweetheart, where was that?"

Sarah thought for a moment. She'd never even considered that question. *Where was that?* "I'm not really sure, honey. Um, it's the place where all spirits exist, whether their physical bodies are alive or dead."

"Do you go there often?"

"I do. I've been going there for most of my life. I learned to go deeper into the spiritual universe with my guru, Asha, but my Mom and grandmother took me out there when I was a child. That's where I fought the Storm that changed the world and where I got my unique strengths."

There was a long silence as he thought about that. "Has anyone else been there with you?"

"No other man. Of course, Jazz and Janie. I took Erika there when Tony and his crew were kicking the crap out of her. I couldn't find you then. I tried. I don't connect as well with men as I do with women."

"What?" He was overwhelmed and confused.

Sarah sat up. "Well, my love, I can feel you," she poked his chest, "deep inside me." He smiled mischievously. "Not there, silly, though that *is* wonderful. Inside my soul." She put her hands to her heart. "You're the only man I've ever let in there."

An old, worrisome sensation crept through her. Fear. She knew it well. "Tom, I'm going to tell you, that scares me. It scares me a lot. My experiences with men have been disastrous, to say the least. To let a man into my soul is a big deal for me. This is all new to me too."

The fear grew inside her, the Storm igniting it. "You can't trust him! You can't trust men!" came a voice from the Storm, a strange voice combining men from her past: a part Robert, her pink-faced boss, the much older boy she dated at 14 who'd forced her to have sex with him in the back of an old musty car, a college boyfriend who'd pawed her top off at a party before she slapped him, Herb, who'd she'd considered almost a father but had betrayed her, the partner at the firm who'd leered at her in his office before she'd threatened him. Others flowed through her mind—torn blouses, beatings, unwanted advances, being trapped in a corner, boys touching her. So many men who'd mistreated her in her past all mixed together but still separate. "You can't trust him. No one loves you!" It shocked her.

She closed her eyes and reached for Asha or her mother. Her Bear grabbed the memories and the Storm and forced them down. Warmth flowed through her, but the effect on her psyche had been unleashed. She tried to ignore it by deciding to change the subject. "It was nice to meet your family. Tell me about them if you want." A pang of jealousy struck her, but she remained outwardly calm.

She listened as he spoke for what seemed to her like hours about his life before the Storm. A simple story full of love. Unlike her life, his had been special—nothing anyone would want to leave. She struggled throughout with jealousy as she compared lives, holding her attention to his words, but it all hurt. Hearing about how much he loved his wife bore deep into her spirit. *Could he love her that much? Was there enough love in him left for her?* He began to cry, and Sarah took him in her strong arms and held him. He needed this. He'd helped her cry out her horrid past. Now she needed to help him cry out the loss of his idyllic one.

As she listened, she thought, *Strength against time, and time doesn't matter.* Time for sure doesn't matter, not now.

All cried out, his stories over, they lay in the grass, Sarah on her back, Tom tucked under her right arm, his head on her shoulder. Through all of this, something had happened between them. It was as though being the conduit to his former wonderful life and the recipient of his tales and tears, combined with her fears, had somehow come between them instead of tightening their bond. She could feel it—small at first. Doubt, sadness and need lurked within him.

As the evening wore on, he rolled onto his back. *What's bothering me? Love? Being in love?* She considered this for a bit but couldn't shake the feelings. As they lay there staring at the stars, lost in their respective thoughts, her ability to feel his soul disappeared. *Has he closed me off? Have I closed him off?*

"Relax, Sarah. The wounds, yours and his, are out there to deal with. They are in your pasts, which cannot be changed, but they do not rule your futures. They'll heal like all the others," her mother whispered.

The sun went down, but still, they didn't move. They simply breathed, matching breath for breath in a strange place on top of the world.

FOURTEEN

Stars filled the sky from horizon to horizon. Billions blinked down at them. They'd been there, in full display like this, since the end of the old world's light pollution, but Sarah hadn't noticed until this moment, lying on her back with Tom beside her.

"Amazing, isn't it?" Tom had been thinking the same thing. "The universe extends for infinity. *Infinity*. I don't think we can comprehend that term."

Sarah didn't say anything. For her, infinity had always been a reality. She still couldn't feel him like she had just an hour or so ago. She was romantically invested in him now. No matter what the demons of her past told her, she did deserve love. Yet another woman had seemed to come between them, his beloved wife. Sarah considered this complication, but she couldn't lose him. Not to a spirit. She curled in closer and felt better as he wrapped her in his arms.

There was still something there, something she couldn't put her finger on. It was inside her, for sure, but the relationship was different. She had so little experience with being in love, and what little she had was not healthy. She used the burdens of the Family that had crept into her mind as an excuse for them to get up. She sighed deeply. "We should probably be getting back."

"You're probably right."

She waited for him to move, not sure why she wanted him to take that first step. He didn't. He didn't have the same burdens of leadership that she had, so he could lay there as long as he wanted. Several minutes later, she repeated the suggestion that she needed to get back, laughed a little but still lay there a while longer. Wasn't he going to get up and then help her up? Then Sarah mentioned the Family one more time, but this time she stood, and then he reluctantly followed. He kissed her on the forehead. She wanted so much more and was feeling a little panicked at the same time.

As he led her back into camp, a strange thought crept into her conscious. *Is this the same way I started with Robert?* The images stuck with her, and even though she tried not to, she began to compare the early days with Robert to the last several days since she'd met Tom. Should she allow herself to trust him?

The Family was meeting around the central fire as usual. Sarah's spot to Ms. Watson's left was occupied by Jazz, Mark and Janie. As Sarah and Tom emerged from the shadows, Janie leaped to her feet and ran to their mother.

"Where were you guys?" Janie demanded.

Jazz giggled and nudged Mark. She may not have known where they'd been, but her look let Sarah know that Jazz knew what they'd been doing. *Girl, you have no idea.* Sarah's insides were still churning with the emotional confusion of the last couple of hours. As Sarah and Tom approached, Jazz's eyes grew worried as she felt her mother's troubled aura. Mark, however, was as clueless as Janie.

"Spending some alone time together, honey," Sarah answered as she picked up her youngest and kissed her. "Just some alone time." Satisfied by the answer, Janie wriggled down to the ground, and they all returned to their seats at the fire.

The Family politely applauded her arrival. Sarah blushed and sat down. Tom sat behind her, but she hesitated before she leaned back into him. Janie climbed into her lap. Jazz moved next to her, placing a sympathetic hand on her thigh as their eyes met. Mark moved closer while Sarah hugged her girls close.

Erika was in the middle of a grand story of the trip before the rebellion, a story that had been forgotten with everything else going on. Of course, it centered around the miraculous events that occurred through Sarah, but it also helped the others to appreciate the intervention of the animals in their fight. There had been a great many rumors. Erika continued her tale describing how Sarah, with no reins or bridle, guided Latifah solely with her mind through the connection between them.

Sarah noticed the crowd staring at her. "We should've stayed on that hill," she whispered to Tom.

"Wannna go back?" He blew in her ear.

She shuddered and pushed into him with her shoulder. "Shush now," she admonished him, although her eyes crinkled into a smile. She needed that moment of reassurance from Tom, but for the first time, she wasn't completely sure she wanted to return with him.

Erika talked about how Sarah knew what the newfound horses were thinking and how to relate to them. She told them Sarah knew the tiger was coming before her or even the poor horses. She went on to tell in graphic detail how the tiger erupted in a flash from the dark woods, tackled the colt and what came after, characterizing Sarah's interaction as master over the beast.

"Really?" Tom asked.

"Yeah, that's how it happened. That's my tiger. It's not the first time we connected, but that's a story for later."

She said it so matter-of-factly. Although she'd told Tom about battling the Storm, absorbing its power and the four spirits that often raged inside her, she wasn't sure if he completely believed or even understood that part, even after she'd taken him out into the universe of spirits. She'd yet to share that with anyone else, but people were getting the picture.

Erika continued on with how Sarah had found the bamboo even though it was in the middle of a forest and even attributed to Sarah the idea to find a path along the tree line without going through the woods.

"Hey, that was all Erika," she whispered. "I was going to go straight through."

"Don't spoil it. Erika's on a roll," Tom insisted.

"Fine, but I'm not some kind of witch or something."

"They know, they know." He paused. "More like their god." She elbowed him hard in his side and gave him a mock look of grave threat if he continued. He smiled, but there was a look in his eyes. A twinge of something she couldn't recognize, but it definitely wasn't the 100 percent, all-in look of love she was used to. He was struggling inside, as she was, and she still couldn't feel his soul.

"Watch out, boy, or I'll smite your sorry ass," she said to break the uncomfortable moment.

"Whoa! I'm sorry, your heinie-ness." He grabbed her tight before he caught another elbow. Janie and Jazz, who'd heard their entire conversation, muffled snickers.

"Shhh, all three of you. Erika's speaking, and then I guess I have to say something, for crying out loud. Now, hush." Janie put her hand over her mouth and fell to the ground laughing.

Sarah rolled her eyes, shushed her and helped Janie back into her lap.

Erika finished with a rousing description of the mad dash back to the camp. Thankfully, Erika left out the ambush by Tony when they'd returned. No one wanted to relive that.

FIFTEEN

When she finished, a hush fell upon the Family, then a smattering of applause as everyone stared at Sarah.

"OK, let me up. I guess I need to say something." She scooched Janie off her lap. Jazz moved over to Mark, and Janie settled comfortably into Tom's lap rather than sit on the cold ground. He hugged her to him. Janie giggled. Sarah grinned and stood up. For some reason, it felt good to stand, to break contact with Tom. That startled her.

"Thank you," she managed to utter to the Family while holding up her hands to signal an end to the applause, thankful for the moment to collect her thoughts. "First, thank you, Erika, for that electrifying story. I want to point out a couple of things. Erika connected to the lead horse, the male quarter horse."

"Through *you*," Erika emphasized.

"Yeah, but it's your connection, not mine." Here, she lied a little. She knew that she was critical to the connection, even going forward.

"Like me and the dogs." That was Claire. "I connected to them through you. Now I can communicate with them even when you're not around. Thank you, Sarah."

"Thank goodness, too. You and the dogs were so critical in quelling the revolt. Thank you so much, Claire!" Sarah clapped, and the Family joined in.

"I'm sure that we all have the ability to connect with things in this world. Janie is connected to the plants, so perhaps not all will be with animals. We'll work on that. Now, back to the story, it was Erika who knew to go around the woods rather than through them, and she found the ideal path to the bamboo stand. So, kudos to Erika. Who knows what might have been in those woods?" She applauded Erika, and a few others followed her lead.

"Alright. Several good things came from our little adventure. First, we need those horses. The draft horse I recognize and maybe some of you will as well. It's the horse owned by that microbrewery in the city. It used to pull their wagon in the parades and stuff like that."

"City Brewery," someone shouted.

"Right. Very creative name. Anyway, since there are no longer any cities or breweries, I think that horse and his compatriots are now free agents. We need to sign them up." She got a few chuckles.

Tom said, "Don't quit your day job." There was more laughter.

"Just a minute, folks, I need to conk my boyfriend here on the head. I'll be right back." As she swung around to him, he leaned back and lifted a cackling Janie up in front of him. The whole crowd laughed.

"I guess I'll take care of him later." She tossed a mock glare at him before turning back to her audience. The playful interaction felt good, and it made the Family happy to see their leader so in love.

"OK, so that's good news number one. The issue is going to be getting them back here. Erika will be part of that."

Gus chimed in, "I can rope 'em."

"And Gus will be on the team, of course."

"Used to be a cowboy back in my youth. From Oklahoma. I was up here doin' some horse tradin' when that dern Storm came through. I can rope anythin', and those horses, if they's anythin' like your horse, will be easy as pie. Prob'ly prefer it to bein' out on their own."

"OK, good. Make a plan, and tomorrow we'll go rope us some horses. Gus, can you put that together? Do we have enough rope?"

"Sure," called a voice from a different area. "Gus, let us know what you need, and we'll have it by midday or earlier." It was one of the Seamstresses.

"Great. Talk atcha in a few. Thanks." Gus looked, walked and spoke like a cowboy.

"Good. That was easy," Sarah said.

Erika jumped in. "The bamboo's pretty far away. It took us most of a day to get there, though we had no idea where we were going and we did go through the whole tiger thing, so I'm sure we can get there faster."

Marsha was thinking like an engineer. "Sarah, the horses will be critical for us to get those stalks of bamboo, which are big, dense and heavy, back to camp."

"I have another friend, the elephant you all met the other night," Sarah reminded the Family, "who might help as well. So, Marsha, we'll need bridles and some sort of contraption that will allow the animals to pull the big stalks. Can you and Gus and the Seamstresses figure something out? I know you're working on a lot right now, but all that other stuff depends on getting these building materials back to camp."

"I'll talk to them and the team. The contraptions you're talking about are called travois," Marsha answered.

"OK, great. Let's talk in the morning."

Randi stood up. "When we were out there, we saw some straight pine trees."

The informative portly man interjected, "Lodge pole pines are pretty common around here since we're back in the precivilization days. They were, of course, what log cabins were made of."

"Good." Sarah thought for a second. "We'll see what our tools are more effective on."

Erika broke in, "The stands are about the same distance, though in opposite directions."

Jake spoke up. "Sarah, as you know, the wood near here, at least for now, is all deciduous forest. Fine for carving into bows and for firewood, but not much is straight enough for decent building materials. There may be some."

"Thanks, Jake," Marsha responded. "We need straight stuff for the travois. If you find anything useful, let us know."

Jake nodded.

Sarah spoke to the larger gathering, "So, either way, it seems we have to travel a bit to get good wood for the house we're going to build."

A general murmur trickled throughout the crowd.

SIXTEEN

"OK, two more things," Sarah continued. "First, there will be no rain tonight." Everyone cheered. They didn't know how she knew, but they had confidence in their leader.

"Second, and this is important, the whole tiger interaction—that happened. We reached an accord. I have connections to the bear and the elephant as well. And, of course, to Latifah. They're a part of me." She paused. "I realize this is hard for you to understand, but my soul and each of their spirits are entwined. I also have a part of the spirit of that crazy Storm in me, but only the good side, the side that brought out this wondrous, bountiful nature. I'm going to be straight with you: I'm still learning to control it, but I'm getting there, and that's what allowed me to defeat Tony."

"How do you know all this stuff, Sarah?" asked Joe, while little Joe sat in his lap. Erika sat nearby but not close enough to touch.

"Joe, good question. I can *feel* this world. I can sense everything living within it, from the animals to the bugs. I can feel the spirits in this world, and some of them can connect with me. That power became stronger when I learned to trust in all of you, to love all of you and came to know, in my heart, that I am loved in return. Your love is what allowed me to defeat the evil within Tony. His power also came from that Storm, but his was from the side that destroys. I believe there may be more of that out there. Near the bamboo is a strange dead zone where nothing grows."

Erika confirmed, "It's brown and barren and goes on for miles to the east."

"It seems that only scavengers who feed on the dead live there. We'll deal with that when we have to, but we must be aware that it's there, and we don't know what's in there or on the other side, if there is another side. So, bottom line, the evil of that Storm is probably not gone with Tony."

There was a murmur through the Family, and Sarah let this message sink in.

A male voice spoke from the back, "Where'd you get your powers?"

"That's a long story. Short version: While you all lived through the Storm, I had a terrible battle with it out in the universe of spirits, or close. OK, that may be way over your heads. I got my powers from my guru Asha, who you've heard me mention, and from the Storm itself. I defeated the Storm with them, and now I am who I am. I'll tell the whole crazy story some time, and I know it's weird, but let's for now deal with the reality that I have these powers and that's good for us."

Following this revelation, mumbling spread and grew louder throughout the crowd.

Sarah raised her voice and her hands, trying to get back on message. "OK, as to the accords with the animals, this is very simple." The Family quieted. "Animals are all fairly straightforward in their approach to life. We leave them alone, and they'll leave us alone. We do whatever we can to protect their families, and, like they did the other day, they'll help to protect ours." She paused to make sure this would sink in. Even though they'd witnessed this firsthand, many couldn't comprehend exactly what they'd seen.

"So, you're friends with those animals that came to our aid?" a man asked. It was hard to see anyone through the fire in the darkness, and she still knew too few of her Family members.

"I don't know what to call it. Animals don't name things like we do. Our spirits are connected, almost as though we are one, but not really. The connections have no labels. I don't know how else to put it. They are as new and strange to me as they are to you, but I'm learning, getting stronger."

Again, the murmurs spread through the Family. She knew this was way beyond them, so she tried to bring it back to something they could understand. "The tiger lives in the eastern woods." She pointed. "He prowls those woods and the nearby grasslands for food for his family."

"Male tigers are loners. They don't stay with their families," the portly man pointed out.

"Yes. In the old world, that was true. I've discovered a lot of things are not the same in this new world. How about you guys?" The Family chuckled. "I don't know why, but we have bamboo, we have tigers and hyenas in what was once Missouri. I'm not going to analyze how these tigers behave. I'm going to be aware of it, accept it and be connected to him and his family. For whatever reason, they've stayed together." Speculation raced through the Family.

Sarah said loudly and firmly, "Stop trying to explain everything." She took a deep breath. "We live in a new world. Let's simply experience it, live in it, learn about it, but not judge or evaluate it, and certainly not based on the old world. Perhaps it was destroyed for a good reason! We're in a new world. It is. That's enough." She paused, allowing the Family to talk this out among themselves. She needed the break. As they settled, she continued.

"OK, so luckily, we hunt in the opposite direction from the tigers, but we do forage in their direction for food and firewood.

"This is the same deal that we have with the bears, who, as you know, live in the woods across the river to our west between the ridges and the grasslands."

Carmen spoke up, "There's a male, Sarah's friend, and his mate, who we just love to pieces, and they have a cub and another on the way. Come down and be with them at the river sometime. They're amazing. And no, we don't talk to them, but we can feel her, the mama bear, and sorta know what she's feeling. I agree with Sarah; you can't explain it in human ways."

Sarah continued, "And I have this with the female elephant many of you met. She tends to roam the northern edge of the grasslands with her herd. Everyone understand?"

"A group of elephants is sometimes called a parade. I love parades. Can we have one sometime, Mommy?" It was Janie sharing a bit of her random knowledge.

"Hush up, Janie, you little pest," Jazz interjected while tickling her little sister. The Family laughed, relieved that the mood had been lightened up.

Ms. Watson stepped forward from behind Sarah and raised her right hand to silence the Family. Sarah looked down at Tom, who winked, then addressed the Family. "Simple accord with all. We protect them; they protect us. We don't harm or mess with them or their lives and families in any way. Is that clearly understood?"

The conversation among the Family members increased.

"This is critically important! Please listen!" The chatter stopped. "If you're out there and you encounter any tiger, big or small, do *not* approach them! Now this sounds like a 'no-duh' sort of instruction, but I want to be clear: no spears, no arrows, no knives. Nothing that could threaten them. Same with the bears and elephants, unless I allow it.

"Here is what you do—no joke. This is what you *must* do. Stop what you're doing, stand up straight, look them in the eyes, convey love and respect to them, bow to the tigers or bears, and back away slowly. They won't hurt you. The animals will do the same. That's the accord. Everyone understand? I'm serious."

Everyone answered in the affirmative. "This, at least for now, does not apply to any other dangerous animals out there, like hyenas or lions or wolves, for example. The tiger, elephant and bear families are valuable allies."

"And the dogs!" Claire wanted to make sure her team was included.

"Absolutely, and the dogs. The horses out there that I mentioned, at least one has a connection to us through Erika. And then there's my dear friend Latifah. There will be others as each of you determines what you connect to. They are and will all be valuable allies; however, it is important to understand that they are not part of our Family, except maybe Latifah. He's special somehow. We'll all coexist. We don't want to disrupt that by being stupid or frightened. This is a weird new world. Allies and relationships are different. Erika will reiterate this to every team that leaves this compound. Please do as you're instructed."

SEVENTEEN

"We have to eat. If everyone is connected to an animal that we can't kill, how will we eat?" asked Taneesha, who'd become quite the spearfisher.

Sarah didn't hesitate. "This world will provide. The universe will provide for all of us. The tigers have to kill to eat; so do the bears, though mostly fish." Sarah paused, searching for answers. "You will know. You will know it in your heart, in your soul. You always know deep in your soul what is the right thing to do. Always. This is how the universe of spirits, or god, or whatever you believe in, communicates with us.

"Many of you pray for things, asking a higher power for things. I don't do that. I listen. I listen and feel. I don't even need to ask. God, or the universe of spirits, or whatever your higher power is, already knows what you need. Maybe it's not precisely what you want or think you want, but it is what you need in your life. When I do this, and when you do this, listen and pay attention to the world around you, to the pull in your heart, to the knowing deep inside you. When you do, you're connecting to this higher power. When you connect, it will tell you what path you should follow, the right next step. You may not learn the long-term strategy, but you'll discover the next right step.

"Each step will keep you in harmony with all other souls, with the world around us." She raised her hands to the sky and in every direction. "A friend of mine in the old world, a woman who helped me through the worst day of my life, called it the spiritual internet. We are connected spiritually to all other souls, alive and dead. Well, souls never die. When we connect into that spiritual internet, that connection of souls, we understand how to proceed, what path to follow, where to go next, how to dig ourselves out of whatever hole we've dug for ourselves."

Sarah paused, but this time there was nothing but silence. Reverent silence.

"By far, the hardest part is having the faith to believe what your higher power is telling you, allowing you to know, in your heart of hearts, that it's the absolute right thing for you to do now. You must do what you know to be right, and you must do it right then—not later, because the moment, the opportunity, the flash in time, may pass.

"Do it no matter what others will think. Don't worry about what you think you *should* do because your pastor in the old world, or mother or even I, for crying out loud, told you it's what you should do. There are no *shoulds* outside of doing what you know—not want or desire or covet or wish for—but what you *know*, right here in your spirit, your soul, is right for you." She put both hands on her chest.

A hush from the crowd was followed by murmurs then gradually chatter. Sarah caught a blur of motion from her left. Erika leaped in front of her, grabbed Sarah in her arms, and they shared a long kiss. Sarah wrapped her arms around her dear friend. Although passionate, the kiss was not even remotely sexual; instead, it indicated two people who deeply loved one another on a spiritual level. That feeling of intense love poured across the Family.

Erika leaned back and looked Sarah in the eyes. "My heart of hearts told me that you needed a big hug and a loving kiss, so I had faith and jumped up to deliver it."

Sarah hugged Erika close. Then she said over Erika's shoulder to the crowd, "I did need a big hug and that great kiss. I feel so loved." Erika broke from the embrace, and the two stood side by side, strong and powerful. Erika had a faint glow about her. *Is this what I do?*

Sarah addressed the Family again, "Feel. Listen. Stop asking. You will know. Alright, so back to your question, when you're hunting, connect to this world. I need to start teaching you all this."

Jazz stood up and stepped forward, catching her mother by surprise. The family hushed. Jazz was glowing, even more than Erika. The 14-year-old spoke with strength and authority. "I've done this. When you do, you'll know where the right animal is before you see it. You'll find it without hearing it. You'll kill it because it's right for the universe of souls for us to be fed. It's the circle of life." She paused to glance at Sarah, who was beaming with pride, and Jazz continued. "It's the way animals hunt. Predators kill the weakest in the herd, and so the herd becomes stronger. They know and do."

Jazz stopped. A blush fell over her and the glow went away. She sat down and scooted back from the limelight.

Sarah smiled at her. *OK, we'll need to build that confidence, but she's off to a good start.* Sarah took back the reigns. "We'll have plenty to eat, but we must learn to connect, to be a part of this world and take only what we need from it. To take only what it gives to us. It'll be enough. Precisely enough.

"OK, that's all I have. Should be a good night for a change. We could certainly use one. I, for one, am exhausted. Amy, do we happen to have any dinner left? I guess we missed it."

"And what were you doing that you missed dinner?" Amy asked.

"None of your goddam business," Sarah responded with a huge grin, which broke the tension. "I can tell you we may miss some other dinners, and it was worth it." A few hoots and catcalls erupted from the audience. Everyone laughed. Despite her special powers, Sarah hoped she'd made them realize that she was also a woman looking for love and relationships to support her in this crazy world, like everyone else.

Herb brought Tom and Sarah some food in a couple small baskets. Sarah held up a basket. "Hey, these are awesome. Major congrats to whoever made them! OK, Shirley, I'll shut up and eat. They're all yours."

She hadn't realized how hungry she was. Tom was hungry as well. She ate what she needed and shared the rest with Tom. Her small immediate family cuddled up together that evening on the now dry, soft green grass inside the safety of the compound and listened as Roger regaled them with a song.

"Mommy," Janie said as they lay down to sleep, "I feel safer knowing there's a big ol' tiger family on one side and a big ol' bear family on the other."

"Me too, honey, me too." Allies were good. Life was good. She was pretty sure something would screw that up again, and soon, but for this night, life was awesome. She struggled to fall asleep in Tom's arms as images comparing those early days when Robert swept her off her feet to these first days with Tom flipped through her mind. An undercurrent of fear, vulnerability and self-doubt emerged as her mind sorted through them. *How can I tell if Tom is doing the same things to me, manipulating me the same way Robert did?*

EIGHTEEN

She awoke suddenly. A brief and irreconcilable nightmare. Tom and Robert, both part of it, led to confusion and pain, but nothing concrete she could put together.

As her eyes cleared, she felt the comfortable weight of Tom's arm around her, his soft breaths on the back of her neck and the warmth of his chest on her back. It felt good to be in his arms. She watched as the first rainbow of sunlight streaked across the sky, pushing back the indigo night, which was stubbornly clinging to the western horizon. As she followed the wispy clouds, scanning the sky east to west, a few stars were still visible above the treetops. The breeze was cool but inviting. She inhaled the pure air, smelling the aroma of the myriad flowers blooming all around them and the musky scent of her beloved. *He was different from Robert. He had to be.*

The songs of thousands of early birds out in search of breakfast or a mate rained down from the branches. Life abounded. She could feel it all: squirrels racing through their interconnected paths, rabbits scurrying about sniffing and nibbling, the dogs resting or milling about, chipmunks, woodchucks, mice of all sorts, a family of mink, all flowing with new life. She focused her attention to the fields beyond their barrier. Thousands of herbivores grazed peacefully, including her elephant, whom she could feel attend to her spirit as it connected with hers. Peaceful. Blissful.

No matter how crazy this is to everyone else, this is heaven on earth.

Enwrapped in Tom's arms, she felt rested and tried to stop her mind from comparing Tom and Robert. *Listen to Daffodil. Love him with all your heart.* After another deliberate breath, she snuggled closer to him. Tom stirred.

"You're happy this morning," Tom muttered as he awoke to find her peering at him.

"Of course. It's a beautiful day. Tony's gone. You can feel the positivity in this place. And, most of all, for the first time in my life, I'm in love." She'd said it this time. It came out naturally. They stared into each other's eyes, foreheads touching and smiling like idiots. His warm kiss was so much better than anything she'd ever felt, and she lingered in it for several seconds.

"I love you too," he whispered.

Thud. "Owww!"

Just as she had back in the old world on Sarah's bed in the mornings, Janie had plopped right on top of them. "We got eight rabbits and four squirrels!" She dangled a dead squirrel in between them, and the two recoiled. Before Sarah could reach her, Janie was bounding off into the compound, behind and past a chuckling John, the trapper, who was holding the other squirrels and rabbits as he sauntered toward the cooking stone. Sarah watched as Janie proudly laid her catch before Gus and Bobbi, who'd skin them. Gus would prepare them to be cooked for breakfast, and Bobbi would tan the hides for the Seamstresses to turn into something wonderful and sorely needed.

Tom was laughing.

"Shhh." Sarah gave Tom a sly look, pointed at Jazz who was still asleep, and then stole a look around the compound. She curled into him and gave him a kiss.

He pulled her on top of him and kissed her with passion and a love that sent shivers of positive energy down her spine. His well-trained hands were firm and warm as he caressed her. She wrapped herself around him, running her hands up his sides, over his shoulders and into his wonderfully soft and curly hair. She wanted so badly to release herself completely to him. To enjoy that vulnerability rather than fear it. She tried. She tried hard. Her mind rebelled, refusing to let her.

"I so missed your touch, girlfriend," Tom cooed. "I was so worried about you. Thank you so much for saving my life. I'm not sure I properly thanked you."

"Oh, yes you did. Our time on your little hill over there was thanks enough."

Sarah and Tom settled into each other, comfortable for Sarah. Jazz moved and snorted a little as Tom caressed Sarah's butt cheek. Sarah gave Tom a face that made it clear she didn't want to be caught but enjoyed the attention. She snuggled into him, and he hugged her tightly. They said nothing. Feeling his love pulsing through her, she craved it, drank it in, tried again to fall completely into it.

As she lay in peace and love, she closed her eyes and felt everything around her: the Family was content; the tigers were content; the bears content, the horses content, her elephant, out in the fields, was content; Erika was happy; and she felt Daffodil, somewhere floating above, probably in a cloud. All was good. *Why can't I let myself love him completely?* She knew the answer—Robert and fear.

Just then, Janie bounced on top of them again, reaching down to hug her mother and adopted father. "Wake up, sleepyheads. We got stuff to do if we're going to keep this Family alive."

Sarah smiled. "It's a good thing I've got the strength of a bear or you would've broken me, you crazy nut."

Jazz yelled at her sister, "Shut up, Janie!" Janie sprinted back off into the bustling Family as Jazz emitted a grumpy "Hrrumph." Mark was standing several feet away, so Jazz struggled to her feet and padded off toward him, then the two adolescents slunk down to the river.

Tom and Sarah sat up, and Tom said, "Welcome back to reality, sweetheart. I'll get breakfast."

She slipped back to sleep and woke as her family returned.

"Good morning, lazy butt. I already gathered greens and stuff for breakfast," Janie bragged.

"And Mark and me already caught fish. We saw the bears. They're nice," Jazz informed her.

"Good, good. Well done, you little overachievers," she snorted in a half-awake state. "I'm very proud of you two." She hugged them, the most important beings in her life, as Tom approached behind them.

Tom handed her a basket of breakfast. "Everyone else has already eaten."

"Off to start preparing for lunch," Janie said with a chortle.

Jazz pecked her mother on the forehead and headed off toward the flints. "You OK, honey?" Sarah asked.

"I'm getting kinda tired of making points all day, every day. I know you told everyone to make their own, and really, all of them are trying and getting better, but they're a long way from making anything very useful. I have to finish everything. Plus, we still need all the other tools. A few of the woodsmen are doing pretty nice work on sharpening and even creating their own axes, and a few others are getting better. But, again, I have to oversee everything and finish the blades. They're all getting better at sharpening tools we've already made, so that's good. Don't get me wrong, Mom, the team is good for a bunch of rookies, but they've only been doing it for, like, a few days now, and it took me years to get it right.

"The problem is that no one can make points for arrows and spears but me. It takes too much skill. So, making all of Rhonda's arrow points falls on me every day. Rhonda's trying, but she's a long way from making a point small enough for an arrow. Ol' Mac always needs a fresh knife, and he'll never be able to make his own. Johnnie and Maggie, his helpers, are starting to work on that for him. Gus needs a new knife almost every day, and while he's getting better, he still makes me do the final sharpening because he says I'm the best.

"It's rewarding but a lot, and I spend all day sitting down there in the shade, whacking rocks together. Half the time, it's just Mark and me down there, and he stays 'cause he likes me." Her cheeks blushed over a smile. Sarah's look conveyed a mother's understanding.

"Janie gets to romp all over the fields and explore the woods. You get to ride out on adventures. I know what I do is important, but it's a lot, and it's tough work. My hands are so calloused. We have some tougher leather gloves, and that helps, but still." Although Jazz was trying not to complain, Sarah could see a sadness in her eyes.

"Wow, sweetie. I'm so sorry. Even though you like to make points, everything is good only in moderation. Let's you and I work together today, make lots of points and knives and stuff, and then tomorrow we'll take the day and go riding out there somewhere cool. Sound OK?"

"OK, Mom. That does sound good. I'll get started."

"Great, sweetheart. I'll be right down." She watched Jazz run off down into the creek area.

"Who knew? There's so much going on, for crying out loud. It's a lot for everyone, even the strongest, to deal with," she said to Tom.

NINETEEN

Sarah shoveled down some food, tossed the basket to Tom, who ate the rest, and was off to find Ms. Watson. On her way, she stopped by Gus. "Counting on you to bring those horses in. I'm not joining you, so it's all on Erika and you, cowboy."

"Doncha worry yer pretty li'l head 'bout a thing. They'll be in by sunset. Just needs m'rope." He could still have been talking about it, but Sarah was on the move to search for Ms. Watson.

Damn! Where is she? There! Ms. Watson was coming out of the infirmary. Sarah sprinted toward her.

"Bad news," Ms. Watson said. "We lost two last night. Jeanne was injured in the rebellion and just couldn't recover. And Sal was a serious addict and didn't make it through the withdrawals. Of course, the stress of this world didn't help."

Sarah took a breath. "More deaths I should've prevented. If I'd only moved earlier against Tony." As she said it, Ms. Watson's eyes scolded her. "OK, it wasn't my fault." Ms. Watson nodded. "OK, tell me what I can do or say and where to be when and I'm there." Still, the deaths gnawed at her. *That will not happen again!*

Ms. Watson broke into her thoughts, "So, you had no idea anyone had died, so why did you want to see me?"

"I promised Jazz that I'd help her down at the river with all the stonework she's been doing so that we can go on an adventure tomorrow. She's stuck down there smashing rocks together all day long. So, to the extent people can get things done without me today, that would be great."

Ms. Watson paused. It was clear she also hadn't considered how trapped the girl was down there. "That'll be good for Jazz. She's so dedicated. Never complains. I should've been aware of this." Deep in thought, Ms. Watson considered who else might need a break from the monotony. "I'll see if I can keep the teams off your back. Heck, they got along fine for three days while you were recovering from the healing. They should be able to give you a few hours with your daughter."

"Thank you, Shirley, I appreciate it."

Gus and Erika were getting ready to go bring in the horses. Sarah stopped by on the way to the river and wished them great luck.

"Don' need no luck, ma'am," Gus said matter-of-factly.

He was condescending, and it unnerved her. She grasped her good friend Erika's hands. "Take Latifah. You're connected to him. Gus can ride anything. I've let Latifah know. When you get out there, connect to the quarter horse. Feel his spirit in yours. He'll come to you. He's your horse; you know that, right?"

"Really? Sure. Alright. I can do this." Erika seemed unsure.

Sarah hugged her close, wrapped Erika's spirit with hers, giving it strength and confidence. "Just do what I do. Stand erect out of mutual respect. Gaze into its eyes. Exude positive feelings, love and courage, and feel the spirit of the animal. You can do this." Sarah and Erika exchanged a look of love. "Girlfriend, you got this. Ride that big horse back here, OK?" Sarah kissed Erika on the lips, and Erika kissed her back. "Now go."

"Alright. Thank you." Erika turned to Gus. "We're taking Latifah."

"You sure?" Gus asked.

"Easy to ride, and I'm sure you can handle him," Sarah added.

"Ain't a horse alive I cain't handle, ma'am."

"Be gentle. He's expecting you. And Gus, call me Sarah, please."

"Yes, ma'am." And with that, they headed to the area where Latifah was being cared for. Gus used a log to mount Latifah and then helped Erika on behind him.

TWENTY

Jazz was showing Mark some of the finer points of stone tip making. Mark was a cute boy. *But, kid, this is MY time, so step aside.*

She hopped down the bank and skidded to a stop on the sand and gravel by the river, ending up with her feet in the water's edge. She almost fell but caught herself.

"Nice entrance, Mom."

"Thank you, daughter. Heelllooo, Mark," she said, imitating as best she could Jerry's snide greeting to Newman on *Seinfeld*. It went right over their heads. *Perhaps I should stick with my day job.* "OK, boss lady, what are we making today?" Sarah picked through some pieces of flint.

"Well, what are we going to cut that bamboo with?" Jazz asked.

Sarah stopped for a second and thought. "Good question."

"Actually, Mark brought it up. He's read some Asian action/adventure stories, and they always cut bamboo with huge super-sharp steel knives. According to him, the stuff might be brutal to cut down."

Mark chimed in, "I think they sorta saw it. The stalks are really tough."

"Well, I don't suppose we have a huge super-sharp steel knife, huh?" Sarah asked with a grin.

Mark's voice quivered with uncertainty, "No, Ms. Sarah, we don't."

Jazz giggled and nudged him before answering her mother, "And we looked *everywhere* for one." Her voice mocked Mark, and as he righted himself, he shoved her back, smiling, finally getting in on the joke.

Sarah stood straight and said, "OK, you two, let's solve this problem, shall we? Jazz, can we make a stone tool like that? Mark, since bamboo is so fibrous, will it splay when you cut it?"

He looked at Jazz for help. Jazz got it right away. "Dude, bamboo's grass, right?"

"Yeah, sorta."

"It's like tons of fibers and stuff. It's not all hard and chunky like wood, right?"

"Yeah, I guess."

"Soooo." She rolled her eyes at him. "Duuuude. So, it's like the strands on a thick rope. When you cut one, it peels back from the stress of the rest sort of pushing it out 'cause they're all so packed together."

"Oh . . . yeah, right. I get it. I don't know. My experience with bamboo is from movies and books, and they didn't get into that much detail."

Jazz pushed him playfully and exclaimed, "All that for nothing. What kind of expert are you, anyway?" They chuckled. Sarah enjoyed watching them.

"I'll bet there's someone in this camp who does know," Sarah suggested. "Shall we see if Ms. Watson, the walking encyclopedia of this place, would know?"

"Know what, Sarah?" Ms. Watson said, appearing behind Sarah as she shuffled her feet down the slippery mud riverbank. The two adolescents laughed but tried to hide it. Jazz mouthed the word, "Busted."

Ms. Watson smiled. There was so much misery in this camp, when she saw this oddly unaffected family laughing and joking, knowing that it was rubbing off on everyone else, she encouraged it.

Sarah recovered. "Shirley, I was just commenting on how you know everything there is to know about everyone in this camp."

"Well, I don't know about that," she said humbly.

Sarah replied, "Come on, Shirley, if there's anything worth knowing in this camp, you know it, and you know you know it, and you know that I know that you know it." Sarah crossed her eyes at Jazz, who devolved into giggles again. Mark's expression was one of confusion. *That boy's bright, but he needs to get a clue.*

"Alright, back on task," Sarah continued. "We have a problem. Mark, would you care to explain?"

He was caught completely unprepared. He stammered through a few words before finally giving up. "This is way above my pay grade."

Jazz lost it. She laughed out loud and pushed him again, and the two fell back into the sandy edge of the river behind them, giggling as they struggled to get back up. "You doofus!"

Sarah tilted her head and shot a motherly glare in Jazz's direction. Then she smiled at Mark and encouraged him to continue.

As Mark and Jazz righted themselves on their rock again, Mark mumbled, "That's something my mom said about work all the time when someone asked her something she didn't know."

Ms. Watson stepped in as always. "You're right, Mark. It was unfair of us to put that on you without warning. Sarah and I are important adults around here, and it's tough to talk to adults in any case, but young man, you can handle this. Sarah wouldn't have asked you to present it to me if you could not."

Mark looked inquiringly at Sarah. Sarah nodded while marveling at how Ms. Watson handled people issues so smoothly.

"Mark, take a deep breath and calm yourself like we used to in class," Ms. Watson instructed. He did so. "Good. Think about what we need, give me a little foundation, a little background, and then ask me what you need to ask."

Mark paused to look at Jazz, who reassured him with a gentle shoulder bump.

Mark began, his voice still unsure, "Ummm, we were talking about bamboo, and I was saying that I've seen these shows where Asian guys cut the bamboo with really super-sharp knives. We were talking about what we could make to cut the bamboo, but none of us has ever actually cut big bamboo like that. Do you know if there's anyone in the Family who knows anything about bamboo, like has actually cut it themselves?"

"Well done, Mark," Ms. Watson remarked. "Well done. Great foundation. I understood what you were talking about. Excellent job of getting to our problem and to what you need from me. Excellent. If we were still in school, you'd have earned an A." Sarah could see his young hairless chest rise and his confidence with it. Jazz patted him on the back with a slap, a little too hard on purpose. Mark grinned from ear to ear.

"Now, as it turns out, I know just the man."

"Of course you do, Shirley," Sarah said with a wink to Jazz.

"His name is General Armstrong. He's one of the few in the Family who demanded a more proper title early on, but most everyone refers to him as the General these days."

"Sure, I've heard of him. Joe and Erika consult with him, right?" Sarah remembered.

"That's correct, Sarah. He was a general in the Marines, but when he was a lower-level officer, he was a POW in Vietnam. He was forced to cut bamboo and do other backbreaking jobs for endless hours every day in the viciously hot sun. He'll know how bamboo works. Of course, we'll have to go to him. Shall we?"

TWENTY-ONE

As they walked through the compound, Ms. Watson provided them with some background. "The General is the oldest person in the Family. He used to be a tall and powerfully built leader. He's been reduced to a gaunt man who can't move very well. A makeshift backrest has been made for him, and he's pretty much confined to it. He's quite frail now but sharp as ever and still has a strong handshake." Ms. Watson stopped for a moment and taught Mark how to properly shake hands so he'd be prepared to meet the General.

Mark spoke next, "The General tells stories all day long. He has some great stories. Jazz and I sometimes take breaks to listen."

The Seamstresses were seated around the General making gloves, arrows, rope, animal-gut thread and other items the Family required. Bobbi, young by comparison to the Seamstresses, was working several hides. Ol' Mac sat on the ground next to the General carving. He joked that he was an honorary Seamstress. His two young apprentices working next to him not only learned how to carve, but also helped the overall group by fetching materials, delivering finished products, cutting plants, bringing water and meals, and helping the less mobile get around and go to the latrine. Jazz greeted them as they were also the two learning how to make the tools this group used.

This place was the manufacturing hub of the Family. The General was, as usual, regaling them with some story as they approached, flailing his skin-and-bones arms about to accentuate the tale. His tattoos, which Sarah guessed were once stretched over large muscular shoulders and biceps, were wrinkled and faded. However, she didn't sense sadness. This man's spirit was strong and vibrant, even as his body was failing him.

As they arrived at the outside of the circle, they stopped and waited for him to finish. The General's story was about a leave in Korea and involved a couple of women. Ms. Watson leaned over to Sarah and whispered, "The General considers the Seamstresses to be 'his girls,' and they're more than fine with that. His stories to them are more graphic and often quite racy." She cleared her throat. When he saw the children, he adjusted the story to their ears. "Molly brings the youngest children around to listen to the General every day after lunch. The Seamstresses love the kids. He tones down his stories for the children, of course, and everybody loves him. We all realize that telling stories is about all he can do, other than consult on military defense issues."

As the old gentleman finished, he and the Seamstresses turned their attention to their visitors. Sarah could see the surprise and pleasure in his eyes when they met hers.

Other than a walk-by, Sarah had never met him. She'd been busy driving the things required to keep the camp alive. The General was part of Ms. Watson's team—the glue that kept the camp together. She'd met a few of the Seamstresses while walking the gauntlet from the stream to the infirmary and hoped she could remember their names.

"Hello, General Armstrong." Ms. Watson smiled and extended her hand. He returned the warm smile and extended both of his hands to hers, though Sarah could see him glancing in her direction.

"How are you, Mrs. Watson?" He was the only person who used the older personal title for a married woman, which Ms. Watson disdained as discriminatory. Of course, she was now, through no fault of her own, the only person besides the General with any official title of respect.

"I'm fine, General. May I introduce you to a few friends? They have a question to ask you." Ms. Watson had learned to be formal with the General.

Sarah whispered to Jazz, "Curtsey when introduced. You remember how, right?"

"Yep, OK. He's weird."

"A little old, but not weird. Let's do it his way."

As they spoke, the General made a few cursory inquiries of Ms. Watson, as though these may be ruffians and not worthy of his time, but he soon gave her permission to proceed with a wave of his hand. She smiled, bowed with her head and shoulders, and turned to the three of them. Ms. Watson introduced them in proper order: oldest woman, Sarah, next oldest woman, Jazz, and then Mark. The General was the only person for whom Ms. Watson made such formal accommodations.

She introduced Sarah. "Hello, sir. It's nice to make your acquaintance." She bowed her head to him and held out her hand in a daintier manner than her normal powerful handshake. He took it with respect and held it with both of his shaking hands.

"Miss Sarah. Very good to meet you. I've heard so much about you and all the fine things you've done around here. We must spend some time together."

"I'm sorry I haven't come by sooner, General, but there's been a great deal to do, and I didn't want to trouble you with such things." She was being quite formal and hoped it was appropriately deferential. This man had no authority here, but he had once been very powerful and had sacrificed a great deal for the old country, and she felt, for the first time, that he deserved both her respect and momentary deference.

Ms. Watson turned next to Jazz, who stepped forward. "This is Jazz. She's Sarah's oldest. She leads our stone tool–making and fishing teams." Jazz curtseyed as though she had a party dress on. He nodded his approval.

"Impressive work, young lady. I've seen some of the tools you make. Extremely impressive. And the fishing has been excellent as well. Nicely done." Then he dismissed her with a nod and a smile.

"Master Mark," Ms. Watson announced.

Mark stepped forward. He stood erect and with confidence, walked right up to the General and held out his hand. The General took it and looked him square in the eye, clearly impressed.

"Young man, I'm told you have an issue that is most urgent and that I'm the only person in this compound who can help you resolve it."

"Yessir."

"Fine, with what can I assist you?"

Mark took a breath and began. He explained that they wanted to build a shelter. The General nodded. Mark continued that bamboo would be the best building material. The General again nodded. Mark continued, "Well, Sarah and Erika—"

"Miss Sarah and Miss Erika, young man," the General interrupted. "They're your elders and must be treated with respect and honor. You will address your elders properly."

"Yes, sir. Sorry, sir."

"Carry on."

"Well, Miss Sarah and Miss Erika found some bamboo out there. The problem is, we don't know how to cut it down. We've never dealt with bamboo, and of course, we don't have large super-sharp steel knives like the Japanese have."

"I understand. You're aware that bamboo is a grass." Mark nodded. "When it's green, it's extremely strong and very fibrous. In the old world, of course, we could saw it down. One used a chainsaw for larger culms." Mark's face reflected his confusion. "A culm is the trunk or base of the stalk. We obviously don't have those types of saws. However, it's fairly easy to saw through. Much faster than wood." He paused and appraised the boy. "Master Mark, are you one of the stone cutters?"

"Yes, sir. Jazz is teaching me."

He was speaking so that Sarah and Jazz could hear but continued to focus his attention on the young man. "You'll have to make something that's as sharp as possible with a jagged edge rather than the beautiful sharp ones I've seen. Early on I saw some knives that might work, probably made by lesser artisans than you and Miss Jazz over there."

Mark began to speak, but Ms. Watson put her hand on his shoulder to stop him.

"The blade should be 8 to 10 inches, longer if possible, but that could be tough with stone, I'd imagine. The good thing about bamboo is that, unlike wood, if it's still green, a saw should cut through it fairly easily, and the longer browner pieces are hollow, so it should allow for a thicker blade, but the teeth will have to be about as wide as the widest part of the blade for it to work well. You'll need a good handle because it may take a while with a stone blade to cut through the culm. Are you getting this, young man?"

"Oh, yes sir." Sarah and Jazz also nodded so he could see them over Mark's shoulder.

The General continued with some additional pointers and launched into a story about his days in Vietnam cutting the plant with handsaws, which were often dull to make the work more difficult for the prisoners. They patiently listened. He was a marvelous storyteller, and Sarah could see why everyone was drawn to him. Finally, when he'd finished his reminiscence, he looked directly at Mark. "Master Mark, you run off and make a bamboo saw for me and bring it back here. I'm sure Miss Jazz and Miss Sarah will assist you. I'll let you know when it's ready for use. Does that meet with your approval?"

"Oh, yes sir. Yes, sir." Ms. Watson kept him from running off to get started. The General smiled and put forth his hand. This time it was trembling. Mark took it and shook it.

"Good grip, Master Mark. You're dismissed." He smiled at Ms. Watson and then at Sarah, as the two youngsters ran back down to the river to make their bamboo saw. Jazz was already jabbering on about how to make it work. Mark was listening, still overwhelmed by the interaction with the General.

Ms. Watson and Sarah bowed to the old man and thanked him for his time. Before they could turn away, the General reached out and touched Sarah's hand. Sarah could feel the power of his spirit and the deep physical pain he was enduring. She took his hands in hers. The connection was immediate, if not terribly deep. They gazed into each other's eyes for several seconds. Then the General squeezed her hands, smiled broadly and whispered so only she could hear, "Thank you." Then he bowed his head to her. She squeezed his gaunt hands and nodded back.

TWENTY-TWO

As she and Ms. Watson walked through camp, Sarah asked about the General, and Ms. Watson filled her in. "A few days ago, as Doc and I were talking about many camp issues, the General's name and status came up. The Doc told me that the General has late-stage cancer and probably doesn't have much time left—a few more weeks or maybe even days, especially in these conditions. He's likely in great pain, which he refuses to show."

"I could feel it when we held hands. I'm sorry it took so long to meet him."

"At that time, the fate of the entire Family was in the balance, and I knew you didn't have time. You had the Family to protect, so I've kept the General's condition to myself."

Sarah understood. "You were right to. A few days ago, I wouldn't have had any interest in the General; in fact, I thought he was a burden. Anyway, he has a strong spirit. I could feel it. Things have changed."

The fate of the entire Family was now in balance, and a bright future lay before them. So, from this day forward, making the General's remaining days livable and honorable was a priority for Sarah.

"Shirley," Sarah said as they walked together, "I realize how precious hides are, but have the Seamstresses make that man a proper uniform top and have Marsha's team make him a comfortable chair. He'll die soon, and we can repurpose the wardrobe then, but for now, he's a man of great distinction, and we need to make sure he feels and is treated that way. Plus, it'll be a great chance for them to practice making clothes and for others to see that clothing is in our future. Distant future, but a foreseeable one."

"I agree. I'll get them right on it."

"Thank you so much for that. Great moment for those kids, wasn't it?"

Ms. Watson nodded. They'd reached the middle of camp, and as usual, pretty much everyone was watching them. Sarah stopped to face Ms. Watson. "Shirley, I want you to know how much you mean to me and to the Family. Oh my god, where would we be without you? I realize that people look up to me like someone above reality or something." Ms. Watson nodded. "But you know I'm just a woman who was fortunate enough to be taught a whole host of skills that we need to keep us alive in this strange new world."

"You're so much more than that, Sarah. You know that as well as I do. You're our leader."

"Yeah, I know, and thank you, but I want you to know that this place would've been just as big a mess without you as it would've been without me, and there's not a person here who isn't completely aware of that. I've needed to say that for a long time. So . . . thank you so much. You're the best teammate anyone could ever ask for."

"Thank you." Ms. Watson was moved. As Sarah noticed Ms. Watson trying to hold back tears, she realized how important and necessary that reaffirmation was.

Ms. Watson willingly hugged kids, not adults; however, when she reached out her hand, Sarah remembered that first encounter on the Day of the Wall, when hugging between them wasn't an option. Things had indeed changed. Sarah accepted Ms. Watson's hand and pulled her close and gave her a huge hug in front of everyone. She could feel Ms. Watson's discomfort as she wrapped her arms around Sarah. However, within seconds, Sarah could feel the warmth of their sisterhood. That embrace cemented the clear co-leadership of the Family, just in case there was any doubt. Two unique people with different skills, critical to the past and future of their beloved community.

The two separated. Despite her smile, Ms. Watson's eyes implored Sarah, "Please, don't ever do that again." Then her face returned to business as usual. Ms. Watson said, "I'll get the Seamstresses on that uniform."

Sarah fondly watched her go. Janie came running up, and Sarah gave her a hug as she listened patiently to her youngest jabber on about that night's performance. Sarah glanced back toward Tom's treatment area. He was working on a young woman's back. She felt a sharp pang of jealousy. Before she could react, Janie grabbed her around the neck and kissed her, then bolted off. When she turned back toward Tom, he and the woman were gone. *Where is he? Is he with her?* Sarah took a step in that direction when Tom sauntered out of the woods to the southeast, alone. He didn't look around for her, but there were several patients waiting for him.

She scolded herself for doubting him and started for the river to work with Jazz. When she arrived, Jazz and Mark were hard at work on the saw for the bamboo.

"Look, Mom. I think we have a great piece. It's long, like maybe a foot," she paused to look at Mark, who nodded, "and pretty thin already and has this cool arc to it, like that saw the landscapers used to cut branches with." Jazz handed it to Sarah. "Mark found it."

"Yes, Miss Sarah."

"That name is only to be used around the General. I don't want that spreading around camp. Just Sarah, Mark, if that's OK."

"Yes, ma'am."

"This is a great stone, Mark." Sarah returned the blade to him, and he handed it to Jazz.

"We're going to thin it out here a little where it's thicker," Jazz explained.

"Then Jazz is going to see if she can make this edge like a saw blade," Mark added.

"Mom, I think if I use a sharp flint rock and this antler tool I made, I can chip out a rough edge that should act like a saw. While Mark was finding this perfect stone, I tried out my idea on this piece. It took a few tries to get the angles right, and I broke the piece in two," she said, pointing to the other half of the practice rock on the ground, "but I think I have the method figured out. I'm going to practice a bit more and run it past the General before I work on Mark's rock. I'd hate to screw that one up."

Sarah accepted the practice rock and looked at the cut edge. "Wow. This looks great. This end is the newer attempts, right?" Jazz nodded. "Excellent." She handed the rock back to her daughter. "What can I do?"

"Well, we need to make at least three arrow and two spear points today. More if we can. We need to sharpen Gus's knife before lunch since he's out wranglin' horses." Jazz and Mark smiled at each other. "We need to sharpen Ol' Mac's knife. He has two and is using the other one. He and his two apprentices are busy making something, and they've been going through knives faster than we can make them. I think he needs a new one. I've been working on a long knife for cutting the plants the Seamstresses use to make rope. We have two axe blades to sharpen and a new one to make because one totally broke. So, lots to do. Can you work on those things?" She'd pointed to the various pieces as she went.

Sarah relished the simplicity of focusing on the tasks Jazz had assigned her. They chatted and laughed and enjoyed some mother/daughter time. After a while, Sarah was in her zone, and Jazz and Mark were engrossed in perfecting the techniques for the bamboo saw blade. Sarah was happy to see them collaborating with the General on the practice stones to get the serrations right.

Jazz was about to start on the real stone. "Mom, what do you think? The General approved the last practice stone, and now I have to start on Mark's. What if I break it?"

Sarah took her oldest in her arms then guided her back so she was holding her shoulders with her hands. Sarah gazed directly into her eyes, pouring love and confidence into her soul. "Girl, you got this!" was all she needed to say.

"Yeah, girl, you got this." This phrase coming out of Mark's mouth struck Jazz as funny, which broke the tension. She fell back from her mother's grasp, laughing, and gave Mark a playful slap on his upper arm. Mark looked confused, again.

Sarah smiled. "She's not making fun of you, Mark. Jazz thinks you're cute, and that's how she shows it."

"MMMOOOOOMMMMM!" Jazz looked aghast. This time Mark laughed. He liked her and had thought she liked him. It was nice to get it out in the open and with the clear blessing of Jazz's mother and the leader of the Family.

TWENTY-THREE

Gus arrived with the horses in tow, and Sarah jogged up from the river to greet them. Erika was riding the quarter horse. No one was riding Latifah, who trotted in last and went straight to Sarah, expressing his displeasure. She hugged his big neck and made it clear to him that he was her horse, which settled his spirit. He bent down to the grass.

Gus guided the big draft horse and pregnant mare to the grassy area where Latifah lived, smiling from ear to ear.

Erika slipped off the quarter horse and hugged Sarah. "We connected immediately."

"Excellent." Sarah was happy, but her relationship with Tom was gnawing at her. "Erika, you have a minute?"

"Of course. What's up?"

Sarah searched her thoughts as she guided her friend across to an unoccupied corner of the compound. They sat in the soft grass in the warm sun, cross-legged and facing each other.

Erika reached out and took Sarah's hands. "What's up, sis?"

"I'm kinda freaking out. I'm falling in love or am in love with Tom—"

"Oh, girlfriend, you are so in love with that man. No questions about that."

"Well, it scares the crap outta me. My experiences with men—well, my one serious relationship with a man—started out a lot like this. Same kinda guy. Big and strong and muscular and good-looking. They both wrapped me up and made me feel safe when I felt my world was falling apart. Different situations, but the same kinda thing. And I fell for both fast. I mean, it's only been a few days since I met Tom. That happened with Robert." Sarah launched into an abridged version of her life with Robert, from the trauma of losing her parents, the way he had swooped in to care for her, his big loving family, to the abuse, her final retaliation, being chased down and shot, and then her escape with the girls. Tears poured down her cheeks. Erika had taken her in her arms partway through. Sarah gazed through tears into Erika's eyes. "I would never have believed any of that would've happened when Robert and I got together, but it did. What if it happens again? What if Tom is manipulating me for his own purposes?"

"I'm sure he isn't," Erika said uncertainly.

Erika shared her own history with men, which was heartbreaking as she told of losing her husband in Afghanistan and then finding out he'd been having an affair with another officer there. "And now I'm in some weird-ass relationship with Joe, who's still married in his mind. That's so fucked up."

"I get it." Sarah related the visit to the spiritual universe and meeting Tom's family.

"That had to be just as fucked up. Our guys are in love with fucking ghosts!"

They held each other and cried.

Erika pulled back. "Well, sister, I got your back. No matter what!" Erika's voice broke from crying.

"No man will ever take advantage of either of us ever again!" Sarah promised.

They had resolved nothing. In fact, Sarah's feelings for Tom were even more conflicted, but at least she had a true sister to rely on, no matter what happened.

TWENTY-FOUR

Sarah walked back down to the river and found a quiet spot along the upper falls to be alone. She focused on the stonework Jazz had assigned her. She needed the peace and the distraction. Without any more interruptions, Sarah got her assigned tasks completed before dinner, even crafting several extra spear points, numerous simpler arrow points from chips for defensive purposes, two new knives and an axe blade.

It was nice to get away and focus for a few hours like she used to in the seclusion of her garage. At least she wasn't doing it to get away from a violent alcoholic husband. Now it came from a place of strength and purpose. With each finished stone, the soothing sounds of the gentle breeze, the rustling leaves and the gurgling rapids calmed her.

Her mind drifted to Tom, to Robert and back to Tom. Why did she love him? Sure, he loved a ghost, but was she fearing a ghost? Doing the same thing? Not releasing herself to love him because of her past?

Further downstream, Jazz and Mark had come and gone many times during the afternoon. They were engrossed in finishing Jazz's bamboo saw invention. She watched through the leafy branches as the two courted one another. It wouldn't be long before they'd be involved in a full-fledged, physical relationship. Another deep breath.

"Come and get it or we'll throw it out," came Gus's call to dinner and the signal that the workday was over.

The two 14-year-olds scurried up the bank. Sarah heard her daughter say, "I want to show this to Mom."

"Yeah," good ol' Mark said, "she'll be so impressed with us."

They have no idea how hard it is to love someone. Well, maybe Jazz does, but it's not the same.

After they were gone, Sarah slid from the stone beside the rapids, gathered the results of her work in her hands and set them on the big flat rock Jazz and Mark sat on when they were working. She stretched her arms high above her, leaned back so she faced the sky, then bent down to the ground before she wandered up the bank into the melee of dinnertime for a Family of over 70. She was always impressed at how Amy, Herb, Gus and their crews got this huge brood fed three times a day, with meals for the watchmen, dried foods for the hunters and sweet fruit snacks for the children. Amazing.

That evening around the campfire, Ms. Watson reviewed the rules that had been developed in camp.

"I want to remind everyone that there are no formal marriages, and any marriages before the Storm will not be formally recognized. Each of us must work hard every day to make happy anyone with whom we'd like to be in a relationship. Each person has the right to determine what he or she wants in their relationships, however many that may be. So, we need to stop fighting over one another.

"Is it mutually agreeable? That is the only question. If so, there is a relationship that can move forward. If not, we move on. Does everyone understand this? Disputes are always resolved by asking this question, so discuss it openly between you in the beginning. Good?"

The Family nodded.

"No, I need a unified, 'Yes, ma'am, we understand.' Now, shall we try that again? Ready? On three: one, two, three." Ms. Watson held out her hands to the Family.

"Yes, ma'am, we understand," came the response in near unison. There were many chuckles from the crowd, but the point was made and hopefully the disputes resolved.

Ms. Watson reemphasized the no-shaving rule and asked Doc to drive home the point. He addressed the risks of cuts and infections and the difficulties they were having in treating them. He urged everyone to stop getting close shaves. It turned out that Sarah's "earn your mate" rule had only increased the desire on the part of Family members to enhance their appearance. For many, that was the only weapon against others of their sex in the battle for the best mates.

Ms. Watson acknowledged this, saying, "So, as you now stop fighting over who gets whom around here, we will also acknowledge that shaving is not attractive. Period. Let's change that beauty standard. Hair is lovely and sexy . . . and safer. You'd rather have a person to be with than someone back in the infirmary being treated for infection."

Carmen and Candy then stood and explained that while they will still cut and style hair and trim beards, they would no longer offer a close shaving service. There were a few moans, but Sarah sensed that most were relieved to end that aspect of the competition, an unintended consequence of the new rules. *Good, at least now that'll stop.*

Sarah noted that Jake was sitting with Candy and hoped that'd become a relationship, reducing the stress, at least, between Candy and the other women in the Family. After a moment, she realized she should care first about the happiness of Candy and Jake as a couple. Smiling, she shook her head at herself; in the old world, Sarah would never have bothered to "ship" anyone.

As she considered relationships, hers with Tom again began to spin in her mind. However, she noticed Ms. Watson was asking her if she wanted to say anything. She had nothing to add and, for the first time, elected not to speak. Ms. Watson seemed to sense the unsettled feelings in Sarah and moved on. She introduced Roger, who brought Janie and others up to perform. Sarah didn't pay a great deal of attention. *How is Tom like Robert? How is he different? Well, this time, I'm physically stronger, so that's good. Does that mean anything in love?* She considered how vulnerable she was. Tony knew Tom was her kryptonite and had used him against her. Her girls were as well, of course, but they would always be priority one, and her desire to protect them made Sarah stronger rather than weaker.

Just then, Janie bounded back into her lap, "What did you think? Wasn't it great?"

TWENTY-FIVE

The subtle rays of the morning sun were starting to crease the sky, highlighting the numerous fluffy clouds with reds and oranges. Sarah wanted to get an early start with Jazz, but this was too early, so she cuddled back into Tom. This time, as Janie came skipping up from behind, Sarah was ready. Janie bounced in the air to land on top of them, and Sarah reached up and put her open hand on her daughter's stomach, guiding her horizontally down into her grasp. Janie giggled, hugged her mother and said her usual, "Wake up, sleepyheads."

Jazz shifted and rolled onto her back. "Shut up, Janie, you lunatic. It's too early." She and Mark had spent a lot of time together the previous evening. Jazz hadn't arrived at their sleeping area until pretty late. She claimed they just "talked," but Sarah sensed that Jazz wanted to take the relationship a bit further. No sex yet, thank heavens, but she suspected lots of kissing, at least, but possibly some explorational touching. Jazz had been in a very good mood when she'd returned.

Sarah decided she should have the sex talk with Jazz on their ride this morning. She had no idea how much knowledge or awareness Jazz had on the subject, but she'd gone through puberty well before the Storm and needed to understand the consequences of her actions . . . not that Sarah bothered to worry about that with Tom.

Sarah lifted a squealing Janie from atop them as she and Tom sat up. Jazz dragged herself to a sitting position.

"Today is the day for our adventure, Jazz," Sarah reminded her.

Janie jumped in, "Can I come, can I come?"

"No. This is my time with Mom out of this old camp." Jazz was still waking up and tended to be just as crabby in the morning now as she was before the Storm.

"But Moo-oommm," Janie complained.

"Janie, honey, Jazz has a very hard job that keeps her down in the river area all day while you get to romp all over the grasslands, exploring the woods with your team to find plants. I'm proud of both of you, but Jazz needs some time outside the barrier. She and I have a few mother-daughter things to talk about as well. So, this trip will just be the two of us."

Janie pouted but relented. Tom faked a pout as well, and Sarah slapped him on the upper arm then moved in and let him hug her. They all laughed, and when Tom released Sarah, he grabbed Janie and held her high above his head before dropping her in his lap. "We'll have to have our own playdate then. What d'ya say?" Sarah smiled, noting in her mental ledger that his attention to her and the girls was certainly a dramatic improvement from Robert.

"Yeah, we're going to do something WAAAAYYY more fun," Janie said as she grabbed Tom's hand and yanked him to his feet. Tom's smile said, "What the heck have I gotten myself into?" Sarah shrugged, signaling "you dug your own grave."

"What are we going to do today, Mom?" Jazz asked.

"We're going riding. You remember how to ride a horse, right?"

"Sure, but we had saddles."

"I'll show you. It's easy. I'll also help you connect with the horse so that the two of you act as one. Nothing will hurt once you get used to it, and you won't have to direct him. He'll know what you want and do it. It's pretty cool. I'm sure you can do it. Let's get some breakfast; I'm famished."

Breakfast was as expected: smoked meat and sausage, greens and berries. Everything was well prepared with fresh herbs. Herb brought Sarah and Jazz the standard lunch provided to the hunters: jerky and berries in a leather pouch and a bladder of water. The sun had finally taken charge of the sky as they wandered over toward the horses. Latifah headed for Sarah, and Sarah put a hand on his neck and kissed him on his cheek. The quarter horse, named Sergio by the children—or more precisely, Janie—grazed nearby.

Gus followed them over. "Ah'd heared you was goin' riding, young lady, so ah made you a sorta saddle for that big quarter horse. It'll make ridin' him easier." Gus had tried to ride Latifah bareback the day before, and without pants or a saddle, it'd become quite uncomfortable. So, despite Sarah's and Erika's ability to ride bareback, he'd taken it upon himself to make life easier for Jazz. The saddle was a simple but supple older dog hide. He laid it soft leather up, fur down, across the horse's broad back. A slender rope was tied tightly to each side around Sergio's chest. Gus had crafted leather loop stirrups on each side. He helped Jazz up, measured and tied them for her.

"Thank you, Gus," Sarah responded. "Nice work for only a couple of hours."

"Thanks, Gus," Jazz offered after being prodded by her mother.

"Been workin' on it since I rode yesterday." Gus put Jazz's feet into the stirrups. Jazz looked tiny on the big reddish-brown beast but sat confidently, very excited. Sergio was at least two hands taller than Latifah and much broader. He was a work horse. Latifah was built and bred for speed and show.

Suzette, one of the Seamstresses, who spoke with an East European accent, appeared with two thin belts adorned with ties holding knives. She handed one each to Sarah and Jazz. "You might need knives. I'm right, yes?" Sarah put her belt on and thanked Suzette, as did Jazz.

Sarah mounted Latifah and settled onto his strong back. Tom brought her a spear, "just in case. The world out there's proven to be anything but safe for travelers." As she accepted the spear, she thought, *Would Robert have been that thoughtful?* Her answer was, of course, no. Sarah watched as Jazz leaned down to peck Mark on the lips as he stood on his tiptoes to reach her. *OK, game on. Cute but another reason for our talk.*

Sarah scanned the compound. "Hey, Joe and Erika, got a minute?"

"Sure," and the two jogged over.

Erika walked over to Sergio. "Now, you'll take good care of my buddy Jazz back there, won't you?" She looked up at Jazz. "He says you're in good hooves." Jazz smiled.

"I'm going to be out of range, so let's be extra careful today. I don't want to be away and have our compound attacked again. Got it? Be diligent."

"Sarah, sweetie, we'll be superdiligent. Go, ride with your daughter. We'll protect the family," Erika reassured her and patted Sarah on the thigh. "Now git."

Randi arrived beside Erika. "Sarah, we'll be OK. Don't worry." She said it with such calm certainty. Sarah didn't know why Randi was so confident, but it helped.

"Thanks, Randi. If you three are on it, I'm sure the camp will be fine." Sarah smiled in relief and asked Jazz, "You ready?"

TWENTY-SIX

Sarah and Jazz exited through the front gate and spent some time in the maze of hills and valleys in front of the compound. Gus gave Jazz some pointers to make sure Jazz was comfortable on the horse. They tried trotting and then galloping. Jazz hung on for dear life and then, at Gus's urging, started to relax and settle into the rhythm of the horse.

Sarah added, "Listen to Gus. The more you fight it and tense up, the more difficult it is and the more it hurts." Sarah watched as Jazz began to get the hang of it. Gus smiled as Jazz walked Sergio over to Latifah, who was nibbling on the grasses, paying no attention to the training session.

Sarah placed a hand on Jazz's arm. "Now, sweetie, I want you to connect to the horse. Feel his spirit. Connect to his soul. To do that, close your eyes, take a deep breath and sense him below you." She paused. "Exhale slowly." They went through this a few times until Sarah could feel that Jazz had made a small connection with Sergio. That was enough for now.

After the lesson, Sarah thanked Gus, and she and Jazz headed north to the edge of the woods. They stopped there for a moment. *Which way should we head? We've been east.* Sarah felt as though she was talking to Latifah then smiled as she realized he didn't care. *OK, if they moved east, while not completely safe, they'd be moving along the tiger's territory. Then again, she'd never been west but only heard about it. Maybe that way?*

"Where's the bamboo, Mom?" Jazz interrupted her thoughts. "Let's go see that. I brought the saw. Mark brought it to me as we left."

"Really? Excellent. I saw you kiss him and figured that he was just wishing you luck, but he brought you the bamboo saw. Smart kid. Good choice, girlfriend."

Jazz beamed. "Thanks, Mom."

"Alright, the bamboo it is. That's this way."

They walked the horses and talked about boys and sex. The little kiss she witnessed was the perfect segue. Sarah was surprised to learn that beyond the basic physical processes, which she'd learned in school, Jazz knew very little about having sex, how to do it, foreplay or anything else. Sarah decided in a world without clothing, walls and little privacy, she may as well go into some detail. Jazz soaked it up and asked lots of questions as they delved into the subject. Jazz admitted to touching herself, experimenting a little. Sarah was shocked at how forthright Jazz was and felt obligated to share some of her exploits with Tom, though not in much detail.

"Mom, I'm a little scared, especially after what happened with Dad. I mean, Mark's sweet and, like, totally harmless. He'd never do anything like that to me. I like that about him. But still, what if when I want to do it with someone, that whole thing, like, comes back?"

Sarah thought about this for a moment. "I don't really know, honey. Your father was brutal to me, as you know. But when I was with Tom, it all felt right. It was real and sweet and wonderful. The images of your father doing things to me never came up. Sex should be lovemaking, special and tender, but raucous and fun and crazy sometimes too. It's that way with Tom. It was never that way with your father. So, I guess you need to let yourself feel and do what you know in your heart is right. Trust the universe of spirits in this like anything else."

Jazz donned a bright smile and guided Sergio toward Sarah. She reached out and put a hand on her thigh, gazing lovingly into Sarah's eyes. "Thanks, Mom."

Sarah had dreaded the discussion, but it turned out to be a wonderful interchange that brought the two closer, perhaps than ever before.

Then Jazz, to whom she'd always been connected, said, "Mom, I hope you listen to your own advice." Jazz winked. Sarah stared at her daughter. *Does she feel my conflict and confusion with Tom? Either way, she's right.*

As Jazz lifted her hand off her mother's leg, they reached the point in the ridge above the stand of bamboo. Sarah fought the urge to compare Robert and Tom, which would only bring her down, crafted a smile and said, "We're here."

"Where?"

"Right down there is the stand of bamboo."

"Cool. What're we waiting for?"

"Jazz, we just had a great talk and I loved it, but you paid no attention whatsoever to your surroundings. It's dangerous out here. There's only the two of us for miles, and all around us are animals looking for dinner. So far, I've neither seen nor sensed any danger, and I've been watching out, of course. We needed to have that talk, but from now on, we're adventurers out in the wilds of this new world. So, before we plunge headlong toward those woods and the bamboo stand, tell me what you see."

Jazz surveyed the area and described the high grass, the higher grass to the east and the dead zone to their right, south. "Wow. What caused that?"

"I don't know, but it's kinda scary, right?" She could feel the negative spirits in the area, the hyenas to the southeast, millions of rats, mice, vultures and insects. Unlike their last visit, she also sensed some other life much farther out. "We are *not* going that way."

"I agree. Yuck."

"Alright, so look around you. What could be lurking in this shorter grass or out there in that taller grass?"

"Snakes?"

Sarah nodded.

Jazz stared east. "Ummm, out there, like, big cats. Maybe cheetahs like at the Zoo?"

"Where is the Zoo these days?" quizzed Sarah.

"Gone."

"Right, so where are those animals, in particular, the big cats?"

"Out here. Out here where we are."

"And lots of other creatures. The hyenas that threatened Janie and her group are out here somewhere." Sarah pointed. "So, bottom line, when we come outside the barrier, we have to be vigilant and on guard. What is the most dangerous predator of them all?"

"Lions?"

"Nope."

"Tarantulas?"

"They're not really that dangerous unless you seriously interrupt them, but still, we do have to be wary of big spiders. But none of the spiders out here, and they're everywhere, are the most dangerous predator."

"Wolves?"

"Animals, including lions, wolves and spiders, defend their territory or young, hunt for food and avoid unnecessary conflict. The predator we have to be most worried about running into are other humans. Do you know why?"

"I know this." Jazz thought, remembering a prior lecture from her mother on safety in nature. "Unlike animals, humans are unpredictable. We kill for no reason. Humans care about stuff animals don't care about. They're crafty and sneaky and difficult to spot."

"They're also harder for me to sense, which worries me the most when I'm out here," Sarah warned.

"Now you're scaring me."

"I mean to. Just a little. We're fine. We have a friend down in the woods there watching out for us as well."

Jazz turned to the woods to their south and saw two green eyes staring out of the darkness. "The tiger?"

"Nice to have friends, eh? OK, let's check out this bamboo. Be careful."

TWENTY-SEVEN

They steered their horses down the hill toward the bamboo, approached to within fifteen feet of the edge of the very dense northern forest and stopped. Sarah listened and gazed into the trees and underbrush.

"Jazz, I want you to try to sense any animal life inside the forest."

Jazz closed her eyes and took a deep breath. Her eyes shot open. "Wow, I could. Lots of little things—bugs, rodents, and lots of reptiles and snakes. They were mostly moving away. Birds too."

Sarah was impressed. "Good, and most important, nothing big or dangerous. OK, around this way."

They followed the same path she and Erika had taken around the peninsula of trees. Upon rounding the point, they looked into the opening. There at the end were huge stalks of bright green bamboo, with some larger culms already turning brown further in. The stalks ranged from 1 to 4 inches in diameter. The pathway to the bamboo was about 12 feet wide at the opening, tapering to about 6 feet at the stalks. She estimated that the entrance was about 20 feet long from the edge of the first trees in the peninsula. The grass was long at the entrance and shorter toward the bamboo. At that point, smaller stalks of green bamboo grew out toward them.

Sarah thought for a moment then decided that dismounting and entering on foot would be the safest option. The tight quarters would make maneuvering two horses difficult. She led both horses a few feet into the opening to the shorter grass. She listened and connected as deeply as possible with the environment. When she felt safe, she dismounted. She helped Jazz down, and they walked a few feet farther to the even shorter grass. The horses began to feed behind them. *That's a good sign.*

Jazz bent down to some of the smaller bamboo culms that were growing near the base of the larger stalks. She pulled out the saw and cut through one. "Wow. That was easier than I thought it'd be." She held the 1-inch-wide, 5-foot-long stalk up for her mother to see.

"Not bad. Can I see the saw?"

"Sure." Jazz rose to her feet and handed her mother the saw.

"This is exquisite. The surface is so smooth that it glistens in the light."

Jazz explained the craftsmanship, pointing to different parts, walking her mother through the process she'd taken to get it to this point. She was so proud of it.

"The blade's width is tight with the width of the teeth, and it's even width from end to end." Sarah paused, putting it in her palm. "It's beautifully balanced." She next raised it to eye level. "The teeth are ridiculous. Perfectly spaced, incredibly sharp and even offset a little one to the next so that every other tooth is lined up, just like the teeth of a steel saw."

"That allows for the bits cut by one blade to be discharged to one side or the other to avoid binding the blade while cutting," Jazz explained. "The General taught us that when I showed him one of the practice blades. It's attached to a hickory handle Ol' Mac made."

"It fits your hand so comfortably," Sarah noted as she settled the handle into her palm.

"The blade's attached with deer gut that's dried and tightened around the handle. The ladies, um, Seamstresses, said it makes it a single powerful tool with leverage."

"Wow, Jazz. All I can say is wow. This is easily the most perfect tool I've ever seen made from stone. Ridiculously good. Amazing." Sarah couldn't stop staring at it from all angles. "And I love the curve in the blade. Mark found you one great rock."

"The whole thing was a team effort. Sure, I shaped the ultimate blade, but a lot of teamwork went into this. The General was so helpful and sweet."

"Alright, let's see what it does to one of those big ol' stalks."

They walked to one of the medium-sized stalks near the edge, eyeing the branches and leaves of the bamboo before choosing the right stalk. It was about 15 feet high, not the tallest, but a good size. A little less than 3 inches in diameter at its base, it was just beginning to brown. Sarah had the rope Gus had used to bring in the horses. They'd use it to drag one stalk home behind Sergio. She looked around and made sure the stalk could fall into the path in a way that it wouldn't hit and spook the horses or hit either of them. Sarah tied the rope around the chosen stalk as high as she could reach.

"OK, cut here straight across, about a fourth of the way. Then cut at an angle back here to the first cut. I'll guide the stalk down this direction."

The saw cut easily through the stalk. It also slipped easily out of the moist cut made on the front side as Sarah pushed the stalk back. Jazz circled around so that she could cut the back side.

"Wait! Stop!" Sarah screamed. Jazz sprung back, following Sarah's finger. "Look."

"What?" Jazz strained to see what her mother was pointing to.

"Oh my god, Jazz, that's a bamboo snake," said Sarah worriedly. "Get back but move slowly." Jazz obeyed. "They're very poisonous."

As she stood beside her mother, several feet away now, Jazz saw the snake. "Mom, you can barely see it among the bamboo. It's the same green. Amazing." Jazz took a step forward, drawn to it as much as Sarah was repelled by it. This was the first animal she couldn't sense.

"I'm shocked they've found their way from the Reptile House at the Zoo all the way to this stand of bamboo," Jazz said calmly, leaning in for a closer look.

Sarah pulled her back as both scanned the culms for any other snakes.

"I don't sense any others, but then, I didn't sense this one." Sarah's voice was trembling.

"There are more, Mom, but they're back there." Jazz pointed.

"It doesn't really want anything to do with us. We're invading its home. We need to get it to leave." Sarah reached out and tried to poke it with the blunt end of the spear. The snake remained still.

"Mom, do that talking to animals thing you do. Maybe it'll listen."

"OK, but you know that snakes and I don't get along." Sarah had been bitten by a rattler when she was Janie's age. She'd gotten to the hospital in time to save her life. Since then, her respect for and downright fear of snakes bordered on the unreasonable. In this case, however, it was more than warranted. This was a dangerous snake that, until recently, had lived behind a thick piece of plate glass at the St. Louis Zoo. Even then, Sarah hadn't liked that exhibit.

"Mom, that's totally in your head. Snakes are like any other animal, and you know it. You're best buds with a tiger, for crying out loud." Latifah whinnied. "And you too," Jazz said sweetly to the horse.

"OK. I'll need quiet." Sarah spent a few minutes trying to connect with the snake. "It's no use. I can't connect with snakes." Sarah stepped back. "I stared into its vacuous, beady eyes like I've done with the tiger, the bear, Latifah, the elephant and the other animals. They, however, were all mammals—higher forms of life with more developed brains that worked more like ours."

"Mom! Now you're just making excuses." Jazz had a big smile on her face.

Sarah stepped farther back without losing sight of the snake. "We need that bamboo, Jazz."

"Maybe I can. I'm your daughter, and I have no problem with snakes. I sensed them in the woods back there. Maybe I have the power too."

"First of all, I know you have the ability. I can feel it. You have it in spades. You always have. But, snakes?" Sarah paused, eyes fixed on the slippery viper in the bamboo. "OK, daughter. Why not? Be careful. Rock on, girlfriend."

"What do you do?"

"I look at them and calm my mind. I feel their spirit and allow mine to reach out to theirs. Once they touch, well, most of the time, we just connect.

I can sense many life forms without connecting to them, but being really interconnected to an animal, or anyone, means that you have to let them in, you have to be open to their way of communicating, you have to free your mind of any disbelief, fears or other negative thoughts. There's both more to it and much less. If you're meant to be connected, you will be.

"You started to connect to the horse a little. Did you feel that?" Jazz nodded. "Animals don't talk. They just feel, so don't wait for him to say anything. Animals sense the spirit of our souls. All souls of all living things are connected at all times; humans don't usually sense it. Unlike humans, animals sense only positive or negative energy. That's it. Be good and exude positive energy; love is strongest of all.

"Also, animals don't name things. We call Latifah a name, but between us, there's only a relationship between two animals, two souls. I'm not Sarah or a human or anything else to him. I'm simply a positive, non-threatening, loving spiritual energy force in a body. I can't be that with that green thing over there. I can't get there, but maybe you can. Do you get what I'm saying? Animals communicate on a different level. Simpler. More ethereal. Purely spiritual."

"I think I understand. I'll try. You have to remove your negative energy from here, so get back there."

Sarah knew Jazz was right. If this had any chance of working, it would have to be without Sarah's fear getting in the way. Sarah walked back to Latifah, who, sensing Sarah's discomfort, shifted closer to her. Sarah could feel the power and love from her horse, and it calmed her. Latifah seemed to tell her, *Jazz has got this. Chill out.* Sarah took a deep breath, settled her mind and spirits, and looked on as her daughter attempted to connect with the creature.

As instructed, Jazz took a centering breath and gazed into the eyes of the snake. The snake changed its position to gaze back at her. They stayed this way for many seconds. Then the snake retreated and slithered away among the branches of the bamboo stalks.

"It worked!" Sarah exclaimed.

"Of course. One problem, though. She doesn't want us to ruin her home. We can have this stalk, but we have to be selective as to what else we take. I promised we would be, and she promised to help me make those decisions. Like you said, it wasn't a conversation. That's the translation of the feelings that we exchanged, but the accord was clear. There are more of them, and they will defend their home."

"OK, good to know. I understand. We'll have to be selective. Honestly, we shouldn't need that many of these longer stalks to build the structures we want to build. And you just got yourself a new job—communicating with the snake population to keep our workers safe and make sure they don't destroy the snakes' home. Sound good?"

"Sure."

"OK, but I want you to be careful. It's an agreement with a huge 'but' attached, a deadly 'but.' Let's finish this off, tie up the stalk and get back home before something crazy happens."

TWENTY-EIGHT

L atifah made it clear to Sarah that he was not pulling the stalk behind him. Sergio didn't mind at all. When they got to the top of the rise, Sarah glanced back at Jazz, who was riding fine, but then saw something on the horizon. It was unmistakable—a thin pillar of smoke, the amount one would expect from a small campfire. That meant one thing. Humans. *Damn. More?*

"What's wrong, Mom?"

"Nothing. Thought I saw something. I don't think it was anything, but let's move this little parade along. We're back in range of our good jungle friend, so I think whatever it was thought better of it."

She pushed Latifah to a trot. The sun was well up in the cloudy sky as they rounded the bend and began to cross the grasslands toward home.

"It's nearly dinner time. My stomach's growling. We forgot to eat, Mom," Jazz said as she began to nibble on some jerky.

Marsha greeted them first, and Sarah tossed her the shorter 5-foot culm. Marsha caught it cleanly. "So, this is a bamboo stalk. Awesome." She turned to Jazz. "How'd the saw work?"

"Great. No problem. Cuts through bamboo culms like buttah," Jazz replied. "Culm is the right word for a stalk of bamboo—the General told us." Marsha nodded. Sarah dismounted and helped Jazz down. Two of Marsha's teammates removed the bamboo from Sergio, and a young boy guided the two horses to the paddock in the northwestern corner of the compound, bordering a small side pool in the rapids above their fishing pond.

Marsha smiled at Jazz before asking Sarah, "Is that saw the nicest piece of craftsmanship you've ever seen, now or in the old world?"

"Definitely. Really, really awesome," Sarah replied, patting Jazz.

"Alright, we'll head out with a party tomorrow and start hacking away."

"Wellll, we have a small problem. That place is infested with highly poisonous green bamboo snakes. We ran into one."

"Fucking marvelous," Marsha replied. "Snakes. Now what?"

"Well, I hate snakes, so I couldn't relate to this one at all. Too much negative energy. It turns out, however, that Jazz here has a bit of her mother's gifts. She can communicate with snakes, and she did."

"I'm with you, Sarah. I hate snakes. Well, Jazzy, what did the slimy little beast have to say?" Marsha inquired.

Jazz relayed the accord. "There are a lot of them there. I could sense that, and they told me they'd strike if we don't follow the accord. She liked me. She didn't like Mom. Not one bit. Without me, there'd be no deal at all. So, it's not perfect, but it's better than nothing. Plus, we have to utilize our resources in a way that doesn't destroy the planet like we were doing before the Storm."

"I agree. Who better to guide us on that than the animals we share this place with," Marsha said. "OK, we have an accord. We follow their rules. Jazz, you running this show, I guess?"

"Yep," Sarah answered. "I'm not goin' anywhere near that place."

"Me neither," Marsha agreed. "I'll find a team that isn't afraid of snakes but respects them and send that team with Jazz. Bunch of crazy-ass snake lovers." Sarah and Marsha wandered off together sharing snake-hating stories. Sarah looked back over her shoulder and saw Mark run up to Jazz. She grabbed him and gave him a big kiss right on the lips. Then she took his hand, and they strolled off to their lair by the river. *Oh well, I hope I haven't created another monster, but she's my daughter. I had sex the first time at her age. At least this boy's her age and nice.*

TWENTY-NINE

After she and Marsha finished their discussion, Sarah went to find Tom. After the talk with Jazz, she was feeling much better about him and their relationship. He'd set up his treatment areas in a flat space near the southern fire where Tony had commanded his crew. *Very positive reuse*, she thought. As she approached, she stopped. Tom was talking to an attractive blond, who was getting way too close to her man. Sarah's insides boiled. She'd never felt this way before. *Who was this hussy?*

Ms. Watson appeared beside her. "You OK, Sarah?"

"Who's that?" was all she could say.

"Who's who?" Ms. Watson answered with a bit of a chuckle in her voice. Sarah snarled at her. "Oh, the little hottie flirting with Tom?"

"You knew darn well who I meant."

"I did. She's been here since the beginning. Very shy young lady. Her name is Tanya. She sits in the back, sleeps alone and keeps to herself. She helps out, usually in the infirmary where she can be alone. Turns out she was a massage therapist and taught yoga in the old world, so Tom's recruited her to his team. He's really helped to bring her out of her shell. I think it's been good for her."

Sarah listened, all the while staring at the interactions between Tom and this Tanya, who was still standing way too close.

"Sarah," Ms. Watson cautioned.

"What?"

"It was you who made the rule that no one belongs to anyone else. Jealousy is not allowed in this camp, remember?" Sarah tilted her head toward her leadership partner and met Ms. Watson's stern but understanding gaze. Ms. Watson put a hand on Sarah's shoulder. "Sarah, you have nothing to worry about. Tom's a nice guy. He's helping her out, getting her to do what she does best while encouraging her to interact with others. That's all. He loves you."

Sarah took a deep breath. She'd never cared about any man like she cared about Tom. She hadn't cared about Robert's philandering. He was a vicious jerk. It kept him away. But this? "Tom is my, well, my everything."

"You guys are fine. Go to him, for crying out loud." Ms. Watson pushed Sarah a little in his direction. Just then, Tanya gave Tom a little kiss on his cheek, turned and strode toward the river.

Ms. Watson patted Sarah. "It's OK, really. But I've got to take care of something. Go to him, Sarah." Ms. Watson left in the same direction as Tanya.

Sarah was frozen in her tracks, staring at Tom then at Tanya's way-too-nice backside heading to the river, then back at Tom, who was about to return to his patient. It wasn't that she thought Tom was cheating. What bothered her was how devastated she was feeling at the mere possibility that he might be cheating or that she might lose him.

She spun and walked away, her heart in turmoil. *What if he finds someone else? I may be the leader of this place, but I'm plain looking.* Just then, Candy practically danced up from the boutique, her long blond hair waving in the wind, her hips swaying back and forth, looking more like a centerfold than a hair stylist. *Am I happy she's with Jake because she's no longer competition for me? Tom's the best-looking guy in the place. He could have anyone.* She quickened her pace, heading for the front gate. *What if he's only with me because he's afraid of me and my . . . powers?*

She knew that wasn't true, but her mind was screaming distrust at her soul, who so wanted to love him . . . *did* love him. She wasn't sure what to do. Memories of her early days with Robert flooded back. How Robert, big, strong and handsome like Tom, had swept her off her feet. *They're the same type. I fell for both so quickly—too quickly. Is that happening again?*

She glanced over her shoulder. Tom's face conveyed his confusion, which morphed into concern as he started toward her. She was petrified and bolted out the front gate. Latifah galloped out after her.

Images of her early days with Robert spun in her mind as she sprinted well out into the tall grass, Latifah keeping up beside her. She didn't even see Tom, followed by other members of the Family gathering outside the gate behind her. She didn't hear his screams for her as she moved away faster than any of them could. She slowed to a run, then a jog and finally she walked, now entering the path north between their river and the woods toward the rise.

Romantic evenings at the Club with Robert, ruined by bourbon and pain, swirled in her mind. The amazing dinner and lovemaking along the first fairway when Jazz was conceived. The wedding and honeymoon were so lovely. His huge family had taken her in as one of their own. So many similarities to Tom, yet so many differences. *Can I trust him?*

She stroked Latifah's nose, emotions she could not understand coursing through her spirit, and tried to explain, though she knew he wouldn't fully understand, "I can't be in love. Not this fast. What if it's not real? What if it's a mirage like last time? What if he leaves me? What if I lose him to . . ." She paused as her eyes blurred with tears. Latifah nuzzled her face. Even if he couldn't understand the story, he knew that she was troubled.

He whinnied and flipped his head. Sarah, knowing what he wanted, smiled at her comrade and hopped on his back. Latifah headed across the river and out into the grasslands to the top of the next undulation in the middle of the vast prairie. Sarah breathed in the scenery, the gentle breeze, the sweet aroma of wildflowers mixed with the deeper smells from the animals, the rustling of leaves, the sweep of grasses swaying back and forth. The spirits of nature existed, in the moment and all around them. She joined with them, feeling as though she were floating with the air among everything else. It was, as unbroken nature always is, peace and tranquility and balance. *Nature is about balance,* she thought. *It is on us to try not to mess that up. Balance. I need to find some sort of balance.*

Without warning, the pillar of smoke rose in her mind. *It's humans who mess up the balance of the world. Were there more?* Latifah walked

104

back across the river, going east along the top of the rise, though not as far as the bamboo. She was at the edge of her connection to home. This was far enough. She stared at the eastern horizon. Although faint, it was there: a tiny pillar of grey smoke wafting across the tops of the trees, barely visible against the approaching evening sky.

"Damn!" she said aloud. "What do we do about that?"

Latifah had no opinion—not that she expected one.

She reflected for several minutes. *They could be a great help. There could be another Tony. They could all be a mess and use up critical resources. They could be angry and greedy and create disharmony, right as we've restored it to our great Family. They could be, well, humans, hell-bent on taking everything they can from this earth for their own purposes regardless of what it does to the environment they live in and share with so many other souls.* She leaned over and rested on Latifah's neck. *Buddy, I don't think I want to find out. You?* She took a deep breath. The plume of smoke tugged at her. *What is the right thing to do? What does my heart of hearts tell me?*

Latifah snorted. "Damn," she said aloud. "DAMN, DAMN, DAMN! You're right, of course. We have to save them. Of course, we have to save those humans. DAMN, DAMN, DAMN!" she cried aloud.

Her mind in turmoil, Sarah sat upon Latifah on top of the rise between the tiger's woods to their right and the dense northern forest to their left for what seemed like hours. *Time doesn't matter.* The stars beat back the sunlight, which retreated behind her. The bugs and frogs sang as the birds settled in for the night.

It was becoming too much. Her mind and her horrid memories, its strong desire to protect herself, battled with her soul, which knew she needed love. *What do I feel toward Tom? Of course, I love him, but does he love me? Of course he does, but so did Robert, right? And see where that ended up? And if I do love him, what if that ends? Most relationships end. What would I do? Physical pain I can handle, but can I handle more emotional pain? What if something happens to him? I almost lost him once, and I can't save him again. He's a liability to me as a leader, my Achilles' heel, someone a jerk like Tony can use to defeat me. Can I have that in my life?*

And Jazz is going to charm poisonous snakes alone, out there beyond my connections. Why did I allow that? If something happens to her, I'll never forgive myself. What if one of our workers screws up and Jazz gets bitten? She'll be dead before I can even get to her. Even if I could, I may not be able to save her life after saving Tom's. Should I stop her? She'll be furious.

Then that plume of smoke rose in her brain again. Her logical side said, *Leave them. We have enough problems. Nobody knows about them. They'll die soon and won't create more havoc in the Family.* But it was clear her spirit, the part of her connected to the universe of souls, was guiding her in a different direction on all of these issues—Tom, Jazz and the people under that smoke—and regardless of what her logical brain thought, her heart of hearts was never, ever wrong. No matter how much it frightened her, she had to try to help them, she had to let Jazz lead, and she had to figure out how to release herself completely to Tom. She buried her face in Latifah's mane and began to sob.

THIRTY

Her heart rate increased as she came to a realization. Latifah noticed, causing him to become agitated.

"You know what we have to do, don't you?" The horse snorted. "Yeah, I'm sure it's a dumb idea too."

They rode at a comfortable pace east along the rise. They stopped and waited for the tiger to stride out of the woods. He jogged alongside them. She was in no hurry. She sensed the quiet all around her. Only the rustling leaves dared to break the silence. She fell into the rhythm of Latifah's hooves as they rode past the place where the bamboo was, out of the shorter grasses and into the very tall grass to the east, just north of the dead zone. They rode toward the thin pillar of smoke in the distance, lit by the faint glow of the fire through the trees. She slowed their pace even more.

The edge of the northern wood in which the camp was located arced and stopped abruptly about 50 yards to their south. The dead zone appeared to continue well beyond it to the east. Sarah dismounted around an outcropping of trees so that Latifah wouldn't be seen but would be close enough to come get her if needed.

She and the tiger crept silently into the woods, moving low to the ground. The light from the fire danced through the trees around them. The two skilled hunters slipped from shadow to shadow, shifting their eyes left and right, sensing even the slightest movement or presence. To her surprise, there was none, not even tiny woodland creatures.

From behind a bush near its edge, Sarah scanned the small clearing. The group, no more than 20, were all asleep except one man, who paced back and forth on the far side of the fire. Tall and gaunt, he'd eaten little since the Storm. *How many of them are close to death? We can handle a small group like this, but will we?*

The man stared into the fire, a sorrowful gaze of hopelessness. She was shocked as she recognized him. *Fuck, fuck, fuck. It's Robert, my goddamned husband.*

The tiger understood only the fear and hatred. He crouched to attack and glowered at Robert. She touched him. *Not now.* They backed out of the woods with the same stealth. Sarah stood with her right arm around Latifah's neck, frozen in place, legs weak, holding on as if for dear life. *Now what?* She was quivering and cold. The tiger rubbed up against her leg like a house cat, and Latifah nuzzled her face. Their concern offered a troubled warmth, as she rested her left hand on her feline brother's soft head, stroking it absentmindedly, her mind adding yet another worry to her already overwhelming list.

She took a deep breath and gathered herself. *Don't you guys worry. I'll figure this out.* She mounted her horse and returned at an easy pace. A gentle spring rain fell, and although the night air was chilly, the water felt good rolling down her skin. She stared through a small break in the clouds at the stars in the sky, briefly sparkling through the mist. Latifah took the opportunity to bend to the grass. The tiger gazed up at her. He was concerned for her, but he wanted to head home to his family. All of this made him uneasy. She nodded to him and he to her, then he trotted off toward his home. She watched as her huge friend disappeared in the darkness of the eastern woods and could feel his joy as he returned to his family.

Again, as they walked onward, her brain and heart were at war. *These people need us, and badly. They'll die without help. But the last thing I can deal with is Robert, with his jealousy, his rage.* Her thoughts volleyed back and forth in her mind. *He's a violent man, but at least now he won't be drunk. He'll ruin everything.* She and Latifah stopped in the middle of their grasslands, and she lay against his neck, emotionally spent and physically exhausted.

Goddamn Robert. How the fuck did you get here? How the fuck did you survive? Why the fuck did you survive? If she did nothing, told no one, Robert and the other people wouldn't survive long. Her heart was clearly telling her to save these people; ignoring them was simply not an option. *How does unconditional love work in this scenario?*

Even though she knew in her heart what she, what they, had to do, she was not ready to go back to the compound and do any of it. Latifah's mane felt good against her face as she lost the battle to remain awake.

THIRTY-ONE

As the sun brightened the overcast sky nearly straight over her, Sarah sat on Latifah amidst the prairie of beautiful wildflowers in a steady rain in her first seriously bad mood since the Storm. The internal battles between her mind and soul had raged within her all morning. Should she tell the leadership, or anyone, about finding the group of people? Or that the group of people included her husband Robert, whom she hated with every fiber of her being? The man who'd beaten her for years, raped her multiple times, who'd shot her three times, who'd made her drag her children away from their only family, who'd vowed to kill her as he escaped from jail.

If the Storm hadn't come, she would've uprooted her girls once again. That man, whom she'd been sure she'd escaped from for good when the Storm rolled through, who'd caused damage to her psyche that was preventing her from loving the greatest guy on the planet; the man who'd tried to rape Jazz and had chased both girls around their house, threatening to hit them; that asshole, that putrid asshole, was still alive and he was here! Did she have to tell them about that?

If it was only him to consider, she'd leave him to die in this new world, but it wasn't. There were 20 or so other people in his camp who were in dire need of rescue. They'd die if left to their own devices, and death for some would come sooner than later, perhaps even before she and the Family could get to them. Even though she knew in her heart of hearts that she was going to tell Ms. Watson about the group and organize a rescue party, she had not moved from this spot for hours.

Too many questions. *How could I tell Tom? How will Robert affect Jazz and Janie and their relationship with Tom? How will Robert deal with Tom? How will Robert interfere with her status in the Family? No matter what, he'll upset the perfect balance and harmony we've finally reached.* She could see no scenario where any of the answers to these questions were positive.

But there was something else, perhaps someone else, gnawing at her, driving her decision to save them. She had no idea what it was, but the universe of spirits did, and she trusted them more than anything else. She thought about traveling there by herself, killing Robert and then rescuing the rest, but that would never happen. She should have let the tiger kill him for her, but she knew better, even then.

Why didn't I kill him back in Virginia when I had the chance? She leaned down onto the back of Latifah's neck, tears flowing down her face and onto his sleek coat. "There's only one option, isn't there?"

Latifah snorted, indicating even he knew what the right thing to do was.

"OK, you're right. Damn!" Sarah took a deep cleansing breath, which didn't help, then sighed, "Let's go."

Latifah ambled toward the barrier gate. The rain was light, and the Family was bustling as usual.

Sarah slipped off Latifah and headed back to the chiropractic treatment area to talk to Tom before she mentioned this living nightmare to anyone else. The compound was greenest around the edges but was becoming worn in the middle, especially around the cooking stone. The shaded path to the creek was also worn. The rain made the compound muddy. She sloshed and smushed her feet in and out of the mud, enjoying the feeling of it squishing through her toes, delaying the inevitable. She attempted to sense anything positive from nature around her, even on a chilly, rainy day like this. There wasn't much, but her crappy mood blocked any positive spirits.

Missing dinner, nearly an entire night's sleep, breakfast and now lunch was taking its toll on her. Neither Tom nor her girls knew where she'd been. It was as though her mood, perhaps reflecting a negative glow, repelled others as people shied away. She didn't know or care. She wanted to be left alone, and she guessed that somehow her abilities conveyed that desire.

As she strolled toward him, Tom rose from beside the patient he'd been treating and started jogging toward her. He expected her to run and jump into his arms as she usually did, but this time she stopped in her tracks. He increased his pace. Her emotions ran wild: Tom, love, Robert, Jazz, snakes, new people, balance, Robert, pain, trauma, Tanya, self-doubt tearing at her insides. She began to shiver. Her heart raced. Tom sped up, and when he reached her, she broke, crying uncontrollably and falling into his arms. He swooped her up and held her close.

"What's wrong? Sweetheart, what's wrong?"

She couldn't speak. She held onto him for dear life. He carried her to some richer grass and sat down with her in his lap, her legs and arms wrapped around him as if letting go would mean certain drowning in a sea of desperation. No conflicted feelings existed within the embrace. Just pure warmth, strength, love and safety.

Others began to gather. None of them had ever seen their leader in such obvious distress. Ms. Watson came running, having been alerted, with Molly close behind. Jazz and Mark rushed from the river and Janie from near the infirmary. Everyone stopped within about 6 feet of them, creating a huge circle that soon included the entire Family. This was the last thing she wanted.

Erika pushed through the crowd and put a hand on Sarah's shoulder. "Oh my. There's a darkness in Sarah's soul. Someone dangerous is alive. 'There are others. We have to save them.' I have no idea what that means, Sarah."

Sarah looked up from Tom's shoulder. Erika was extremely concerned, and the same look was etched on the other faces surrounding her. She felt relief that the story, however cryptic, was out. A weight was lifted off her shoulders.

"Oh my god, Mom, it's Dad," Jazz nearly screamed. "Dad's alive and here!"

Sarah could only nod through her tears. She slipped off Tom's lap and sat back on the wet grass, her legs still on either side of his waist, her hands on his shoulders. She met Tom's eyes and matched his love with as much intensity as she could muster. "Tom, Robert's alive." She curled to her knees and held out her arms. Jazz and Janie ran to her, but even Janie knew better than to jump on her. The embrace was gentle. She whispered to them, "Daddy is alive. I've found him."

She could feel that they were deeply conflicted. They both looked at Tom, who was also struggling with the news, and then at their mother. Sarah, summoning all her emotional strength, hugged her daughters close, gave Tom a loving look, slid the girls to the side and stood to address the Family. They took a few steps back. Joe brought her a log to stand on.

"When Jazz and I ventured out to where the bamboo is growing, I saw a slim plume of smoke on the eastern horizon, the sort of pillar that comes from a small campfire. Although much smaller than ours, it worried me. I couldn't figure out why, other than it meant more humans. I didn't alert anyone. I was distressed but didn't know why. Yesterday afternoon, I needed to get away to think. Then last night, Latifah, the tiger and I went to investigate." There was a murmur through the Family.

"When we arrived, the tiger and I snuck to the edge of the woods surrounding their encampment. There are about 20 or so humans. They were sleeping, so I'm unsure how many are alive. They're in desperate straits. We have to go and rescue them as soon as possible.

"There's one problem for me, personally. One man stood guard when we arrived. That man was my husband in the old world, Robert, who is a violent, angry man. A vengeful man. A brutal human being who never respected me. When we bring him here, it must be expected that he'll treat me in the same manner as he did before the Storm.

"You all know me. You know that my heart belongs to one man, and that's Tom." It came out so easily, naturally, fluidly like it was reality, meant to be. This came from the universe of spirits, and she turned to him with a smile that radiated from deep within her. *I do love him. He is different than Robert. He's different because he loves me for me. For who I am. And I love him for who he is. That is the differ-*

ence. I loved Robert for what he could do for me, and he loved me for the same reason.

Overwhelmed by this realization, she dove for Tom and gave him a huge hug and passionate kiss. "I'm so sorry I doubted you, doubted us. I love you. I love you with every fiber of my being. I will love you forever, and Robert is not going to do anything to interfere with that." The Family members sighed.

Tom had tears in his eyes. "I love you too, sweetheart. I'm sorry Robert is alive. We'll do whatever we have to, as your Family and me as your life partner and lover, to make this as easy for you as possible."

She fell into his arms. *He called me his life partner. Life.* Nothing had ever felt better, and she melted into him. It was several seconds before she was ready to let go. What was out there, outside Tom's warm embrace, was horrible, but she was their leader, and the Family needed her. She kissed him again, dried her eyes and stood to face the Family. Tom stood beside her, his arm around her waist.

"Robert was not a good father to Jazz and Janie, either." She regarded her girls, seeing anger in Jazz's countenance and confusion in Janie's. Sarah squatted down and wrapped her arms around them, hugging them closely before standing back up. They moved next to her, and Jazz snuggled into the safe crease between Tom and Sarah. Tom removed his arm from Sarah and wrapped it around Jazz to let her know he was there for her.

"Tom has been a wonderful father to Jazz and Janie in this world. I'm afraid of how that'll play out when we bring Robert here. So that's why I've been in such a piss-poor mood this morning and why I stayed away with Latifah." She now addressed Ms. Watson, Erika and Joe.

"OK, all that stuff aside, there are 20-something people out there who need our help or they'll surely die. I'm not sure how they've survived so far. We'll take all three horses, and I'll ask the elephant to join us. Marsha, can we create something to carry any people who can't walk? It's probably about 8, maybe 10, miles from here."

"Absolutely. No problem." Marsha consulted her team, all of whom nodded. "We'll start building the travois we were planning to make to haul bamboo, but it'd be easier with bamboo."

"We're not getting bamboo between now and whenever we leave. That's too much. Jazz needs some time to deal with her father coming back and has plenty of other things to do around here. Right, Jazz?"

Jazz nodded without conviction. Sarah could sense that she was overwhelmed by the intrusion of her father in their tranquil world.

Marsha gave in. "OK. I think we can put something together with the wood around here. What d'ya think, Jake?" Marsha's team and Jake's wood-gathering team came together to discuss options.

Sarah continued, "We need to think this whole rescue through in detail. We need to bring food and meds with the intention of feeding and treating them there. Do we help them build their strength before we bring them here? Or should we try to bring them here all on the same day?"

She was back on the log and noticed the crowd spread out a little as Family members broke into many conversations.

"Why do we have to bring any of them back?"

"Twenty more mouths to feed."

"Twenty people who will be useless for days?"

"More revolutionaries who aren't Family."

These comments came from several people followed by assents to these concerns.

"How many are sick?" asked someone.

"What if they have some disease that wipes us all out?"

"Yeah, they'll use up all our medical supplies," rose a voice from the back.

"What if they're all as negative as Robert? We're bringing another Tony right into our midst. We already fought that battle and lost some good people."

"Yeah, do we have to bring them all? Can we, like, interview them to see if they'll fit in? They have to understand our culture." That came from one of the eight youth who had been rescued in the melee with the teenagers.

"I agree. How do we know that these people aren't like those kids who attacked us, or the revolutionaries? We don't want either."

Prejudice was so ingrained in the human psyche, she thought as she listened to more comments with similar self-protective sentiments. Of course, these were precisely the issues she'd been wrestling with herself.

This group was widely diverse, with people of every shade and hue of brown, from freckly and pale to tan to Sarah's golden brown to very dark. Different nationalities and ethnic backgrounds were represented, and numerous accents and dialects could be heard. In the old world, some of these people wouldn't have included the others in their circles. Here, they're all Family. Others, no matter who they are or what they look or sound like, are outsiders. The fact that Robert, as described by Sarah, came with this group did not help matters.

It was time for Ms. Watson to take command, so Sarah helped her up on the log.

"Family, Family. May I remind you that nearly everyone here came to us from out there? Sure, we've all been here a while now and have developed relationships and bonds. We've created a culture, but each of you, when you arrived here, had to adapt to it. You had to learn how to live in this situation with these people, the vast majority of whom were strangers. Now, they're Family.

"We're going to help these people. You all sense it deep within your hearts. Despite these valid concerns, we are going to help these people."

After a few minutes of murmuring, everyone nodded in agreement, and Ms. Watson continued. "Now that that's settled, all the concerns you've mentioned need to be addressed in the plan. This is a much more dynamic adventure than anything else we've tried, but we have experience. We've herded revolutionaries to the far reaches of the western fields. We'll be going in the same direction as the bamboo but farther. We have tools and weapons and can build structures that will help us."

"And," came Claire's voice from within the group, "we have animal allies to protect us!"

Sarah could feel a sense of comfort settle over the Family. Ms. Watson's superpowers were surely responsible.

Ms. Watson closed the Family meeting by concluding, "We'll take all of today and tomorrow to plan for this rescue. These strangers will have to make it on their own two more days so we can make sure to do this properly. We'll also need to gather the resources required to accomplish this: enough food, enough medicines, building the transports. So, in addition to everything we normally do, we have these things to do.

"The leadership will meet and talk this through. Please, all of the crew leaders, come forward and let's meet right here. Anyone who wants can stay and listen."

She could feel the rain letting up as many of her Family members streamed by, taking her hand briefly or patting her on the arm and giving her their unconditional support in this. Tom stood behind her with his hands on her shoulders as Jazz and Janie stood on either side. They were all greeted with support.

THIRTY-TWO

Over 20 people, mainly the middle-aged adults from the 70-plus total Family members, assembled in front of Ms. Watson. This large contingent of leaders was great for organizing the operations within the camp, but Sarah was concerned it would be too cumbersome for decision-making.

Ms. Watson passed the baton to Sarah to lead the meeting. This was obviously her mission, as most of the Family's adventures were.

"OK, as I mentioned, I estimate there's about 20 people. The only one I could see reasonably well was Robert, and he was gaunt and looked terrible. We should assume they all look like that. I didn't see any spears or other weapons, which doesn't mean they don't have anything, but given Robert's appearance, we can assume they're getting by eating greens and probably bugs. Throughout our relationship, Robert never learned how to live in the wild. I bet he regrets that now. He used to say that 'humans camped when they had no other option, and now we have air-conditioned houses and television.'" Several people laughed. "That being said, something had to have rubbed off on him."

"Mommy," Janie chimed in, "I taught him about greens that could be eaten and even a little about mushrooms. Remember my book on plants? He read that to me at bedtime sometimes when I was little."

"OK, so hopefully they didn't eat any of those bad mushrooms. That's a relief. There may be others who've camped and might know a few other things. Obviously, someone got a fire started."

"Should we worry they're violent?" someone asked.

"We have to be prepared for anything. We'll bring spears," Joe said.

Rhonda spoke next, "We can gather greens along the way, but how are we going to transport meat that far? If we're going to stay there for a few days, how are we going to feed everyone, including ourselves?"

"How many are we going to send?" someone wondered.

Erika answered, "We should bring at least 30, I would say. One for each person there and others to help. We'll bring all three horses."

"And the elephant," Sarah reminded.

Ms. Watson chimed in, "OK, does 30 of us sound right? That's a pretty large contingent of our most productive Family members. They could be gone for a few days."

Sarah added, "The journey alone will be dangerous and take most of a day at the pace we'll be able to sustain. Latifah and I did it in about three and half hours but took almost four to get home, moving at a horse's pace."

"There'll be predators and stuff—snakes, large cats, hyenas and who knows what else," Joe mentioned. "We'll need to be prepared and alert."

Ms. Watson summarized, "This will be a dangerous mission. All 30 will have to volunteer."

There was discussion in the ranks about this. "Man, this is a lot to consider," a woman from her left said. Sarah recognized her friend Caroline. "I don't know if we can figure this all out today and then get it all put together tomorrow."

"Well, I'm going," Sarah declared. "Ms. Watson is not. No kids, not even mine. No one who is elderly, obviously. Some of the older teenagers could be considered, but basically only those of us who are strong enough. We need specific skill sets. No one needs to decide right now. We'll have direct conversations with folks after we get other things figured out. Everybody on board?"

"So how long will this take? Does it have to be more than one day?"

Sarah waited to answer as people discussed among themselves. "Since the camp is maybe 8 or 10 miles from here and, assuming we don't run into anything along the way, walking at 2 miles per hour, average for a group, plus breaks, that'll be about a four- to five-hour walk minimum. If we leave right after breakfast, we can get there around early to mid-afternoon.

"The problem is we have no idea what we'll find when we get there, or how Robert or the others will react. With all these variables, it's difficult to determine how long we'll need to be there to get ready for the return trip. Assuming they have a bunch of starving and weak people, we'll need at least the rest of that day to feed them and give them some of their strength back. I'd say we stay overnight and try to return the next day. Hopefully, that will be possible."

Erika jumped in, "Well, I'm clearly going. If the team stays close together and makes noise, we should scare any predators away, including the big cats. Sarah will ride in front on Latifah and keep an eye out. Someone will ride the draft horse too."

"I'm goin'," Gus volunteered. "I'll ride Big Gus up front—that's what Janie named him."

"Good. Of course, she did. You have a namesake then." Gus smiled under his bushy beard.

"Thanks, Gus." Erika nodded to the cowboy. "I'll ride Sergio in back."

"I'm going. No way I'm missing this party," Randi announced as she stepped forward.

"Of course." Erika smiled. Randi was becoming her right hand.

Ms. Watson slipped through the crowd, talking to people, calming fears. Erika, the captain, took charge. "Marsha, why don't you head out and get started on those travois thingies? Rhonda, you should stay here and find food for the Family while we're gone," Erika continued. "Marshall and Samantha, will you join the group to be our hunters? We can spear hunt some game if there's any that direction. Your expertise with spears could come in handy in other ways as well, but let's hope that won't be necessary."

"We'll need something big to smoke overnight and take with us," Marshall said, thinking aloud to his hunting partner.

Samantha agreed, "Yeah, we're headed out to the west river fields for elk. We saw a wounded one wandering around out there we should be able to put out of its misery."

"OK, get on that. We'll talk about tomorrow this evening." Samantha and Marshall left. "Olivia, will you join us as our medical officer?"

"Sure. I'll create some packets of meds for various things and prepare some extras for here while we're gone. Mandy can come with me."

"Great." Erika was on her game. Sarah nodded her consent, and Olivia rose and left.

"Joe, we need a good guard crew." Erika seemed to be ticking off a mental list. "Can you gather some volunteers? Your best-trained team."

"Sure. I'm in, of course. I'll get a team of 10, including me. Don't you think that should do it?"

"Sounds good. So, we have me, Sarah, Randi, Joe's ten, Marshall and Samantha, Gus, Olivia and Mandy. How many is that?"

"18," Tom replied.

"OK. Twelve more. We need people to relate to the rescued folks. Talk among yourselves and let me know by the end of the day if you want to volunteer for this. It's a long walk, and we'll probably be helping people walk back here. We can put people on Latifah, Sergio, Big Gus and—what do we call your elephant, Sarah?"

"Nothing. Elephant. Animals don't have names. Elephant is fine."

"Right, OK. He'll also be able to pull some people behind him."

"The elephant is a female. Big, strong and female, like you and me. Just so you know," Sarah noted, and Erika nodded with a wink.

THIRTY-THREE

Ms. Watson spoke up, "What else will these people need?"

"Something to drink," Erika answered. "We should bring some clean water in bladders."

Amy offered, "Herb and I'll take care of that and, of course, preparing the food for transport."

"We'll need water for us and the animals as well," Sarah added. "There's a small creek on the north side of the rise, but that bends into the northern forest a little short of the bamboo. I didn't see any streams once you get out east of the bamboo."

Erika was thinking. "We need about a quart of water per person per day. Assuming this takes 2 days and we take 30 people, we need 15 gallons of water just for the Family members. We'll need about that, probably, for those we're rescuing if they're as famished as we think they may be and some for the animals. So that's like 50 gallons of water. Can we even carry that much water? Do we have enough bladders or whatever for that much?"

Amy looked at Herb and then back to Erika. "We're on it. We'll talk to the Seamstresses and see what they can craft. We can make it work, with maybe a little help from Sarah."

"Of course. This doesn't mean you have to go with us," Sarah noted.

"No, we're definitely not. You guys have a grand time. Herb and I will stay safely in the compound feeding those still here, thank you very much."

There were giggles in the crowd, and Amy and Sarah shared grins.

"We're in for sure. All three of us," said a burly man, representing the three guys who had hauled rocks for the fires that first day. They'd developed a reputation for showing off their bodies and flirting with all the prettiest women, but they were strong, worked hard and would be assets to the team. "We can haul a lot of shit, Sarah. You can count on us. I think we know a few others who'll join us too."

Ms. Watson returned from the crowd and stood on the log.

"Excellent. Glad to have you," Erika said then returned the floor to Ms. Watson.

Ms. Watson was anxious to get this going. "OK, everyone has marching orders. Get all of this planned and figured out today. We'll get it prepared and built tomorrow. The team will head out the morning after. There's lots of regular chores, so let's get back to Family matters." Ms. Watson stepped off the log and marched through the crowd.

Erika added one last bit as the Family began to disperse. "We have a lot to do around here. Talk to me if you have some ideas or want to join us on the trip. Help out as much as you can. Thank you for all you do around here."

Sarah said to Erika and Tom, "That went well." Sarah and Erika shared a quick hug before Erika headed off to put the plan into action.

Sarah knelt and took a hand of each of her girls and asked Jazz and Janie, "How do you guys feel about this, about bringing Dad here into this Family?"

"Mom, it sucks. He is not my dad. Tom is ten times the father Dad ever was. I reject him and hope he dies before he gets rescued." Jazz radiated hatred. She tried to run off, but Sarah held her hand tight.

Janie had been only five when they'd left, and Sarah wasn't sure what Janie's memories were of her father. "Hon?"

"Mommy, I don't know. We haven't seen him in a long time. I hardly remember him. Things are so nice here. What if he messes everything up?"

Sarah had no answers. These were the same feelings she'd been wrestling with. "I don't know, girls. I don't know."

"But Mommy, I understand. We can't let all those other people die just because we might not like Daddy. That's selfish." Janie, though silly and fun-loving, was often wise beyond her years.

Even Jazz nodded, her head lowered, then they both fell into Sarah's arms. Tom stood above them, present but not part of the discussion.

"It'll be OK," Sarah said without much conviction. She coaxed Tom to join them, and he wrapped his arms around them all. Sarah continued, "Things are very different. No way he hits me now. I'll knock him into next week." She felt Jazz giggle a little. "He hasn't had a drink in forever for him, so he's sober; there's no alcohol for him to drink."

Jazz joked, "I know some really tasty mushrooms he might love."

Jazz and Sarah shared a little laugh. "Now, now. Let's see how this goes. No stresses, like there were in the old world. No booze. Perhaps he's tolerable."

"Yeah, maybe. We'll see. If not, I'll get the 'shrooms and you knock him into next week. Agreed?" Jazz was only sorta smiling, and Sarah wondered if she was even joking.

"We'll see, honey, we'll see." Sarah and then Tom released them; Sarah kissed them and patted them on their fannies. "Now, you guys have things to do to keep this Family we love healthy and secure, so off with you. I'll be down to help make more spear points, just in case we need to take him out before he gets here." Sarah backtracked, "No, that's not what I mean . . . in case there's trouble."

Jazz grinned.

As she wandered off, joining Mark on the way to the river, Tom's face conveyed concern as he looked down at Sarah, who was still crouched. "Honey, that the death of their father makes you and Jazz happy is probably not a good way to begin this reintegration."

Sarah nodded as she rose but couldn't help but feel that sharing some levity with Jazz during this time of uncertainty had to be good.

She watched Jazz walk hand in hand with Mark. "I'm glad she has someone to help her deal with this, to support her," she said aloud to no one. Lingering back, Sarah studied Tom, now standing a couple of feet away, before sidling up to him as seductively as she could. She threw her arms around his neck and said, "Hi." She could feel his spirit again. She could sense his heart, feel it, entwine with it again. Hers sored, and she poured her love into him. She had no idea what to say, but she wanted to make sure he felt her love before she broke the next bit of news.

"Sarah, this is huge news for me, you realize."

"I know. That's why you're not going."

"What? Of course, I'm going." he released her, but she held on.

"Tom, sweetheart, you're the love of my life. I feel that like never before. You know that. Robert is dead to me, and even though he's not actually dead, which sucks, he will not come between us. Do you understand?"

"Yes, but—"

She shushed him and continued, "Jazz and Janie aren't going either. I need you to stay and take care of them, emotionally as well as physically. Jazz, especially, needs you right now. I know she needs me, but I obviously have to go. More importantly, I need to deal with Robert alone, without you or them confusing the issue. It needs to be me and him, one on one, except that I'll have 29 armed supporters and a tiger behind me, will be atop a horse, and possess the strength of a black bear and a Bengal tiger. So, I feel like I'll have the upper hand this time."

Tom didn't smile. "But what will the Family think if I don't go with my love in this difficult adventure?"

"I'll take care of that. They'll understand." She paused and gazed into his eyes. "It'll be OK. This is the right thing to do; listen to your inner heart." After giving him several seconds, she could feel him succumb. "I'm sorry for all of this. I had no idea he'd be out there. I think if I'd known, I wouldn't have ever gone in the first place or even mentioned it, but what are the chances?"

"That plume of smoke worried you."

"That's why I went alone, with Latifah and tiger. I led this Family into a battle that killed Hector, injured others and nearly killed me. I could've kept everyone inside and let the crazies die from the poison. The barrier was strong enough. But I led us out there. Then I took too long to take on Tony, until that became a battle and people died, including almost you.

It's bothered me ever since. I wasn't going to do that again. I wanted to check it out to make sure it'd be pretty safe to take others."

"That stuff was not your fault."

"I know. Down deep, I know. But still, it bothers me. So, I checked it out by myself. Of course, Robert's presence pisses me off, but there's something else driving me back there. There's more than Robert; we have to go save the other people."

"I know. Of course, we do. Of course, you need to lead the Family. It's your duty. I understand why you went last night. That was smart. You did the right thing. And running into the melee of zombie teenagers was right. You saved those eight kids. And this is right. And now, I understand I can't go tomorrow. It sucks, but I understand."

She wrapped herself tightly around him again. He hugged her gently. "Can I get a little kiss?" she cooed. He bent his head down and kissed her. Not passionately, but loving and tender. She never felt that from Robert, ever, even in the beginning, and Sarah greatly appreciated the tenderness. She could feel how conflicted he was between what he felt the Family would expect of him and what they both knew in their hearts was right for him and their relationship. At least now, they were on the same page again. Her heart was smiling.

He released her, and she settled from her tiptoes to her heels. "I have some patients to care for, and you have a lot of planning and preparing and stuff to get done. I'll see you at dinner." He kissed her on the forehead and left for his clinic.

As she watched him go, she thought, *Robert is NOT going to come between us. Even if I have to kill him, he is not coming between us!*

THIRTY-FOUR

The next day was incredibly busy but invigorating for everyone. People were buzzing with excitement and trepidation over the adventure. Sarah had been out many times, as had the hunters, but most everyone else had not been outside their safe grasslands or nearby woods. There were more than enough volunteers, and she was pleased Erika had to turn many down.

She met with Amy, Herb, Bobbi and the Seamstresses and guided them through the process of cutting, preparing and sewing up 50 half-gallon skins to hold water. Bobbi knew how to waterproof the skins. Although not happy with parting with so many of their precious hides, she understood the importance of this venture and the great need to carry water, food and tools. Each water skin had a strap that could go around someone's neck and be tied shut at the narrow opening. Once they were able to cut through bone, Sarah planned to add a small ring to each opening to support it, but that would come later. These water bags would be invaluable for the adventure and in the future.

Sarah also talked them through the creation of woven nets to serve as bags to carry food and helped with designs for saddles and straps for the travois. The Seamstresses were busy making bandages, rope, small pouches to hold medicine and berries, and sandals for some of the newer travelers. Ol' Mac and his team were working on spears, knife handles, parts for a smoker they would take with them and other devices. Janie and her team were gathering plants for Olivia, Mandy, Bethany and Franklin, who were preparing ointments, salves and berries and wrapping them in the pouches crafted by the Seamstresses. Amy and Herb filled similar pouches with dried meats, fresh greens and herbs, and fruits, loading them into the food nets.

Sarah, Tom, Jazz, Mark and Janie enjoyed a wonderful family lunch out in the grass away from the crowd. Wanting this meal and the next to be special, Sarah was more present than usual.

Janie launched into a story about catching nine rabbits, the ones they were eating. Sarah listened carefully and asked questions. Tom was amazed and smiled appreciatively at her. She usually spent about five minutes at lunch and was off tending to the needs of the Family. Sarah scooted over into Tom's lap and snuggled against his strong chest. Then she grabbed Jazz and guided her oldest into her lap. Tom wrapped them both in his arms. Jazz, smiling, pulled Mark over and held his hand as Janie chattered on about this and that, waving her arms and getting up and sitting back down as she acted out every aspect of her morning.

She and Roger had quite a show prepared for that evening, but "that's, like, a complete secret," she confided, even as she danced and sung small snippets. *What an entertainer.* Sarah, enjoying the time with her little family, sunk deeper into Tom's body as Jazz slipped out of the embrace to cuddle with Mark.

THIRTY-FIVE

The afternoon was more of the same. Sarah was active, building, hauling, using her Bear strength to move things others could not. She brought in the elephant to fit out for her travois, then thanked her as she trotted back to her family.

Sarah sensed a commotion in the western wood, coming from her bear. Carmen and Candy shouted from the riverbank, "Sarah, something's attacking mama bear and the cub. You have to help them."

Sarah and Erika raced across the falls and into the woods, armed only with knives, dodging trees as Sarah sensed the way to the female bear, who was in obvious distress.

"There!" Erika screamed.

"Hyenas! Damn, I thought they were gone from here," Sarah yelled back.

The four hyenas Janie had encountered had cornered the female bear and her cub against a concave rock face. The male bear arrived with them, coming up behind the hyenas who were stalking forward. Sarah skirted past the male, leaping onto the cliff, bounding along a tiny ledge, vaulting over the female and landing on the dirt between the hyenas and bears. Erika rounded behind the hyenas as the male bear moved in from his side. Sarah was coordinating their counter, pouring anger into the four beasts, whose fangs were bared, heads low, preparing their powerful jaws for attack. They'd met Sarah once before, and they were not backing down this time. She had no idea what had provoked this attack, but these hyenas meant harm. The mama bear pushed her cub behind her and prepared to defend him as only a mother can.

Four on four. Here we go.

The hyenas launched their attack as one. Erika hurtled forward, landing on the back of the smallest one, forcing her knife into its neck and knocking it to the ground. It tried to turn on her, snapping monstrous jaws at the air, but Erika rolled, wrestling the beast on its back above her, its feet flailing in the air, as she stabbed the hyena repeatedly.

Sarah took the largest, who led the attack, thrusting her palm down into the top of its nose, much as she had to Robert all those years ago. She shoved the hyena into the ground, plunging her dagger into its heart and twisting until she felt its life drain away.

Her bear had taken on the one closest to him, ripping across its hindquarters with a huge claw, knocking it into the rock wall; the hyena yelped. The big black bear dropped on it, pinning it with one powerful paw while tearing into the overmatched animal with the other, avoiding its jaws. Erika left her limp prey to come to his aid, slashing the hyena's neck.

The fourth headed for the cub, but his mother was ready. She reared up and came down on the body of the hyena with tremendous force, sinking her teeth into its hide. Sarah abandoned her kill and dove toward the hyena, digging her knife into its heart and twisting until it slumped onto the ground.

The three young guys who ran together arrived with Joe, driving spears into the dying beasts, ending the skirmish. Sarah had a small gash on her leg, Erika bled from her side and arm, but the female had sustained the worst injury—a nasty wound to her belly that would kill her slowly and maybe the unborn cub. To everyone's surprise, Candy and Carmen rushed up to the female. "Sarah, you have to save her and her baby," Carmen screamed, pressing her hand to the wound.

Sarah moved Carmen aside, put her hands on either side of the gash and guided her Elephant spirit into it. The wound closed, and even though they'd seen her do this before, all present stood agog. The female turned to her cub, gathering him into her arms.

Sarah sat back in the dirt; Erika joined her, sweat pouring off both warriors. The big male licked her on the cheek, and Sarah decided now was a time for a favor. Sarah communicated that she'd be away and would appreciate it if he'd watch over her Family while she was gone. He agreed and then joined his family. Candy and Carmen had deepened their connection to his mate, who also agreed, which helped Sarah feel better about going on the rescue.

Joe and the three big guys carried the four hyenas back as Sarah and Erika, bloody and tired, led the group across the falls.

"Mom, what happened?" Jazz asked. She and Mark were still standing on their rock, waiting for them to return.

Erika launched in, "Oh, we just saved the bear family from these four hyenas. That's all." The men emerged from the woods behind them.

The story traveled through the Family while Sarah and Erika were cleaning up. Jazz and Mark stood above them. Tom slid down the bank. "What now? Are you *trying* to get yourself killed?"

Sarah smiled, reached over and grabbed him, dragging him into the river with a deep, passionate kiss. "Just part of a day's work, sweetie. Right, sis?"

"Yep." Erika put an arm around Sarah. Tom watched with an exasperated smile.

After she'd cleaned up, Sarah gave Erika a hug, and her sister jogged back to the preparations. Tom kissed her and headed out of the river. Sarah bounded up the falls and took Jazz's hands.

"Mark, can you give us a few minutes?" Mark nodded and left the river.

Sarah and Jazz shared with each other their negative feelings about Robert, resolving only to give the situation a chance, as they finished a few points and knives. The conversation hit a lull, and Jazz gave her the eye that she wanted to be alone with Mark, who'd returned through the woods.

When Sarah reached the top of the riverbank, she surveyed the compound; all was well, and people were busy. She considered what else she could help with, and while there were certainly options, she'd provided instruction, lifted the heaviest items and started so many processes that the Family now had it covered. It was late afternoon, and she decided she was due something just for herself.

"Hi," she said in her sultriest voice to Tom as he finished up with a patient. "Let's go to our spot. I'm going to be gone, and I want to make sure I leave you with only one woman on your mind." He chuckled.

"Shouldn't you be helping get ready for tomorrow?" Tom asked, hoping the answer was no.

Sarah looked around and saw that Erika had things under control. She returned her gaze to Tom's. "Nope. They got this." He picked her up, she wrapped her legs around him, and the two lovebirds headed to the river. *Now was the time.* She knew she could finally live up to her promise to Daffodil.

She kissed him with such sensuality that he had to stop walking to handle it. "Now mush, boy, we got things to do over there." In the back of her mind, she feared that this might be the last time they could make their escape for a while. She had no idea how Robert would change their world, and while he wouldn't come between them, he'd almost certainly try to make her life miserable.

They made love in the beautiful warmth of the sun and rolled over in the grass. She stared up into the sky, absorbing the feeling of him next to her. She reached over and delicately caressed his taught abdomen. *That asshole is NOT going to ruin this. No way.* She took a deep breath, calmed herself and turned on her side to face him.

"Tom, no matter what happens, you know I love you so much. I'm not going to let Robert and his inevitable crap come between us, but he'll try hard to."

"I know. We'll get through this. I can handle myself. If he gets out of line, I can take care of him. It's best I not go because he might not make it back if I did."

"He might not make it back either way." She laid back and stared at the sky. They were silent for several minutes as she absentmindedly trailed her hand up and down his body. She touched his penis, by accident, but it brought her back from her thoughts. She caressed it, and he became aroused again. He rolled toward her and grinned, and she returned a sexy and mischievous smile. He rose above her in a plank, and she caressed his muscular arms. He was showing off, and she loved it. She wrapped her legs around him, forcing him down on top of her. He spent a long time gliding along her body—her breasts, her legs, down to her feet then slowly he rose between her legs. She laid back, closed her eyes and let him love on her. He was amazingly talented.

It was all about her, but it was not all about her. It was about how much he loved her. She gave in to him. He wanted to do this. Her heart beat quickly, electricity pulsed through her body, her breath bated, her eyes rolled back in her head, her toes curled, her back arced, her entire body quivered in pure bliss. He stopped at precisely the right moment and hovered his body over hers, allowing her to revel in the gradual descent from utter ecstasy. Then he shifted his weight to one side and held her in his arms. She was in heaven.

After several minutes, she opened her eyes. With Robert, she'd escaped to her spiritual universe when he forced himself on her. Earlier with Tom, she went there to expand the experience. This time she remained in this world, his world, their shared world, and it was every bit as magical. She rolled to her side and kissed him. Now she wanted him inside her. She moved on top of him and guided him in. She whispered, "Slow and steady," and he complied as she moved in sync with him. His shoulder muscles bulged as she moved her hands over them, wet with sweat. She felt the strength in his chest as she caressed it, feeling him slide in and out in a steady rhythm. Her hands found each muscle in his abdomen. Sarah slid her hands back to his chest, passion boiling inside her. She closed her eyes and took a deep breath, centering herself on the feeling in her loins as it rose, warm and loving.

This was lovemaking from her soul, not from her body. It was deeper and more special. She could feel his soul dancing with hers, caressing her, and as they reached orgasm together, their spirits fused as though they were one. They *were* one. They were more than soul mates.

She settled her full weight on top of him, and she could tell he was relishing the feeling. She felt weightless; they were weightless. The sun, the breeze, the wonders of nature all around them joined with them in this moment. Tom felt it as well. Their breathing aligned, senses combined, their souls frolicked in a revelry she'd never felt before. This was an unbreakable bond, formed in the hottest forge. She didn't want to separate from this position ever, and as they laid within their own universe, time stood still.

Finally, she broke the spell. "Tom," she whispered into his ear. He moved his head and gazed into her eyes. "So, who was the blond hussy who you let kiss you the other day?"

Tom had to think for a few minutes. "Tanya? Is that what got you all freaked out?" Tom gathered her into his arms and smushed her into his chest. He held her for a few seconds before he released her and said, "Honey, Tanya is lost here. More than most, maybe. She's a lesbian. She believed she was the only one. She's not, of course. She was frightened to approach any other woman for fear that she'd be ostracized. I guess she grew up in a small Missouri Bible Belt town and had just gotten up the nerve to leave and live her life in St. Louis when the Storm hit. Luckily, she heard the children sing and made it here. She's shy and a loner. Doesn't make friends easily. She felt trapped, so I was trying to help her. She has zero interest in me."

Sarah tilted her head back to look at him.

"Oh, and I have no interest in her or any other woman, Sarah. NONE. Ms. Watson told me that Tanya was a massage therapist. Of course, Ms. Watson would know this. She brought Tanya over and introduced us. We talked. I hooked her up with a couple of clients. She did great. That helped her feel more comfortable.

"Aaaannnddd, you won't believe this, but once I uncovered the core issue and told Ms. Watson, she told me that she, herself, is a lesbian, *and*, despite how she behaves, Carmen down at the river is as well. Ms. Watson introduced them yesterday. I don't know what happened, but I think they'll make a good couple, don't you?"

As her mind began processing this news, Sarah leaned back from her lover and gave him a sheepish smile. "I'm sorry, Tom. All the craziness with Robert came flooding back when I saw you with her, so pretty, and

I hadn't even found him yet. Then she kissed you. I remembered how fast I let myself become sucked into Robert's life, to believe I'd fallen in love with him, and then the disasters that led to. I didn't care that he cheated, but when I really cared that you might be, well, that created a whole bunch of emotions I couldn't handle." Sarah wrapped her arms around him and sunk into his strong chest. "I'm sorry, honey. I'm a mess. This probably won't be the last time I'm weird."

"It's fine, sweetie. I love you. And now you have your own huge Family that's all yours. No one's sucking you into it. No Mother, I guess, except for Ms. Watson, but that's not the same." Sarah smiled. "No one tricking you or me into love. Our souls are intertwined so tightly that we almost feel like one." He tilted her chin up and gazed deeply into her eyes. "At least, I feel that way."

Tears streamed down her cheeks as she melted into him and sighed. "I do. I do feel that way. I need to trust it's right this time. I've put a lot of trust into things that turned out to be horrible lies in my life." As he wiped the tears from her cheeks, she beamed, staring into those bright blue eyes, and said with more conviction than she'd ever said it, "I love you, Tom. I do."

"I love you too, Sarah."

They kissed a long warm romantic kiss, the kind written about in fairy tales but never really happens. She was never going to let go of this. She felt Daffodil, Asha and her mother smiling down on them. All the negativity that had flowed into her when she discovered Robert and all the fear his presence had created were gone from her soul.

She was ready. Not through anger and fear, but from a place of love and power. She knew she—they—could take on anything Robert could dish out.

Love was power. The depth of love she now knew existed, that she now enjoyed with Tom, gave her power no man could overcome. *It was time.*

THIRTY-SIX

"Y ou're feeling better," Erika noted with a smile.

"You don't know the half of it," Sarah quipped.

"Sounds like you two had quite a time up there," Ms. Watson said.

"Shirley, it was amazing." She paused, needing to share. "I, maybe for the first time in my life, let someone love me. I completely let Tom in. When we made love, it wasn't just physical, it was spiritual. Our souls made love. Our souls, I don't know, became one. Shirley, I feel free. Robert no longer scares me. Nothing scares me anymore." Sarah grinned. "Except snakes."

Ms. Watson smiled and placed her hand on Sarah's shoulder. "Good. I could sense your trepidation with Tom. Glad you worked it out."

Sarah, Erika and Ms. Watson spoke for several minutes, Sarah baring her soul to her dear friends—summarizing her history with Robert, fears of his return, how her love grew with Tom, how amazing it is now. It wasn't in her personality to do this, normally, but her sisters listened patiently, and oddly, no one else gathered around them. It was as if Ms. Watson had enveloped them in a bubble.

The cry of "Come and get it or we'll throw it out," broke the bubble. Everyone filed through the dinner line. Janie bounced past, waved to her mom and sprinted to her friends in line. "Famished," she yelled over her shoulder.

Sarah smiled at Ms. Watson, who headed over to orchestrate the line, which, without Tony's ruffians, ran quite smoothly. Erika stood and offered her a hand, which she took.

"We've all got your back, sis. You know that, right?" Sarah hugged her.

Sarah found Tom, ran and tackled him, holding him up with her Bear strength, then jumping into his arms, kissing him all over his face in front of everyone. She whispered, "I love you so much, and I'm hungry."

"Me too, on both counts." They smiled that wonderfully mushy smile of two people head-over-heels in love.

She winked as she slid down to the ground; they walked hand in hand toward the line. This time she joined the middle of the line with Tom. People beamed at them, happy to see their hero strong and confident again. When Sarah was jubilant like this, the Family was in wonderful spirits. The elk tasted exquisite. Rhonda had bagged a deer, which was also prepared. Lots of meat was being seasoned and smoked for the two-day adventure.

Ms. Watson spoke briefly. Candy and Carmen related the story with the bears and told everyone that the bears were there for them while the group was away. Sarah spoke to the Family about the rescue mission, assuring them that she was prepared to face Robert, that the Family was ready to help these poor people, and that Tom was staying back to care for Janie and Jazz and also so she would have the opportunity to deal with Robert alone. The Family understood. She was thrilled that there'd been no emotion, no fear, not even hatred in her message to the Family as she spoke about Robert. He was, in fact, just a man. A man who might make trouble, like any of the others they were about to bring back here, but she was certain she was ready for him. She slept like a baby that night.

THIRTY-SEVEN

Sweat slipped down between their bodies as she awoke. She rolled onto her back and let the beads flow down her sides. The skies were sprinkled with clouds but nothing ominous. *It's going to be a warm one. A long trip in the sun on a warm spring day. Not the best of options, but better than others.* The sun was not yet above the trees on the horizon.

"OK, sweetheart," Sarah said as she rolled on top of Tom, "we have to get up. I need to get this show on the road. I'm going to miss you so much."

She kissed him, a long and sweet romantic kiss; when they'd separated and stood, she gave him a peck on the lips as though she were off to the office. She transformed from vulnerable lover into powerful invincible leader ready for anything.

The place was teeming with people all listening to Erika, Amy, Ms. Watson and Marsha as they prepared for the journey. Sarah walked out onto the hill at the end of their maze of hillocks and called in her elephant without a sound. Within minutes, she came loping up beside her and followed her to the group. Sarah connected to the elephant and conveyed an understanding as to what they were about to do.

The elephant ate as Tom and Sarah helped secure the harness and travois sled to her back. Others did the same with Big Gus. Sarah and Tom then helped load supplies. They relished working together and smiled uncontrollably as they did. Sarah carried the hides of water, loaded into one big net, which no one else could budge. Everyone was given a spear, a small water bag and a leather necklace adorned with a rabbit's foot. The Family lined up on both sides of the corps preparing for the journey.

Sarah paused atop the large mound in front of the gate, and everyone faced her, ready to follow their leader. The scene could have been out of a 1950's epic about ancient Egypt or Rome. All they needed were trumpets to announce the procession. They even had big horses and an elephant. Ms. Watson and Erika strode over and greeted her. They took positions on either side of her—Ms. Watson on her right, Erika on her left.

Ms. Watson nodded toward Mark, who stepped forward. As he'd been asked to do, he raised a spear into the air and then presented it to Sarah.

"Did you make this?" she asked. The boy nodded. "Even the tip?"

"Yes, ma'am." Mark beamed from ear to ear. "Every bit of it. Jazz helped a little with the tip, but I did everything else," he explained. "It's like 5 or 6 feet long. I whittled the handle with some help from Ol' Mac. The hard part was the end. It's carved into the head of a tiger."

"I can see that. Well done."

"Ol' Mac kinda helped, but I did it all. Then I used some berries to stain it in tiger stripes here and then wrapped the middle, where you hold it, in some dog-skin leather we still had."

"This is magnificent. Well balanced. Powerful. I can feel the strength in this spear." She nodded to him. "Well done, sir, well done. Thank you very much." Pride radiated from his face.

Jazz appeared from behind him and wrapped a new leather belt around her waist. A beautiful sheath was attached to it. A delicately carved and painted handle protruded from it, also with the stripes of the tiger. Sarah gripped it and slid the blade out, a wonderful long flint knife.

"This is gorgeous." The knife glistened in the sun. About 10 inches long and sharp as any metal blade, it was mounted on a wooden handle carved with stripes and a tiger head at the base.

"Mark carved that tiger head as well, Mom. He's pretty good at that stuff," Jazz complimented.

"Jazz did the rest. It's perfectly balanced. Isn't the sheath colored beautifully? Black stripes." Sarah was speechless. She pulled Jazz and Mark into an embrace and hugged them for several seconds. The entourage behind them applauded. "Thank you so much. These are beautiful. So wonderful. Honey, I'll miss you very much."

"Be careful, Mom. I'll miss you too. Dad's probably a complete mess, but maybe he's healed." Sarah was impressed by her attitude. Perhaps she'd reached an epiphany as Sarah had.

"I hope so, sweetie." She kissed her as Janie joined them. Janie presented her mother with a necklace. Specially made for her, it was adorned with two rabbit's feet and the canine teeth of the hyenas she and Erika had slain. Sarah bent down and allowed Janie to put it on her.

"This is beautiful, honey."

"Those feet are from the same rabbit, a big one. Jazz made us a drill to cut a hole in those teeth. I made all the holes and strung this for you." Then she addressed Erika, "I made you one too." It was smaller and had fewer teeth and only one rabbit's foot, but Erika cherished it. She dipped her head so Janie could put it around her neck and gave her a small hug.

"Thank you very much. This is fantastic," Erika said, holding the necklace up so she could inspect it. Again, the Family clapped.

Sarah said, "We'll treasure these always. I'll miss you two. Take care of Tom for me, will you? Make sure he doesn't get into any trouble."

"Sure, Mommy. Me and Roger are going to make a big production for you guys when you return. Be safe."

"I will." She hugged her and gave her a big kiss. She also kissed Tom one more time as her girls stood beside him. Sarah waved to the Family staying behind, who all cheered the rescue party waiting for her. She sensed Latifah coming, pivoted, ran and leaped just as Latifah arrived from the valley. She grabbed his mane and landed fluidly onto his back.

"OK, everyone. Gus!"

"Head 'em up and move 'em out," he bellowed from the big draft horse at the front of the parade.

"Let's get this show on the road," Sarah yelled as loudly as she could. Everyone cheered as she and Latifah galloped to the head of the team.

Gus got Big Gus and the elephant moving forward with their heavy loads. Erika rode Sergio forward to meet up with Sarah.

"Howdy, pardner," Erika said as she pulled up alongside Latifah. "Sure am glad that elephant agreed to help. There's no way Big Gus could've pulled everything."

Sarah nodded.

"You know Janie named your elephant this morning."

"Really? I'm shocked," Sarah said in mocked amazement. "So, what's the poor thing's new name?"

"Bubbette, adjusted from Bubba when she learned the elephant was a female."

Sarah grinned and shook her head. The two chatted as they led the rescue party out of their grasslands. The group moved slowly. It took longer than it should have to reach the rise that led east toward the bamboo and ultimately the encampment.

"I'm going to ride ahead a little and see if I can see that plume of smoke," Sarah said. "If the rain put their fire out yesterday, they may not've been able to get it lit yet, but it'd be easier to find them if it is." Sarah pointed east to where the smoke should be. Even on a good day, they wouldn't be able to see it from where they stood, and today was very breezy. "It'll probably be a while before we can really see it, but it's worth a try."

"Agreed. I'll keep moving the troops along." Erika reversed Sergio and rejoined the procession as Sarah rode off to find evidence of the encampment.

Sarah and Latifah trotted at a gentle pace, and the tiger emerged from the darkness, jogging beside Latifah. She let him know she was happy to see him.

When they had nearly reached the bamboo, she saw it. Thinner than two days ago, but smoke arose from the horizon. *Wow, that's a long way off at our current pace.* She asked the tiger to hang out while she returned to see if she could speed up the group.

"I can see the smoke," she announced. "I guess that means they're still there. Any chance we can move along a little faster?"

"These sleds is heavy, ma'am. Maybe you can talk to Big Gus and Bubbette. We kin all walk faster, but they don't seem ta be movin' very quick," Gus answered.

She connected with both animals and they picked up the pace, as did the other Family members. At least the loads would lighten as they took breaks, drank water and eventually ate lunch. After about two hours, they rested to take advantage of the water in the creek to their left along the northern forest. The tiger stayed well out in front, and most of the time, Sarah rode out there with him, tuned into the new world, searching for danger of any sort.

She worried about what could be going on back at the compound. She was well out of range now, which bothered her. She and Ms. Watson had instructed the remaining Family members to stay within the safety of the barrier as much as possible, but she knew things had to be done outside it. They were armed, the bears were around, and some strong folks were still there. Nonetheless, she worried about being this far away. Those hyenas were not acting like typical hyenas. She wondered why and what other animals may be behaving differently now, like her own tiger.

THIRTY-EIGHT

With some more urgings from Sarah, the group moved a bit faster. They passed the peninsula that marked the location of the bamboo, which Erika pointed out to everyone with pride. She also pointed out the dead zone. The bleached bones rose above the grasses within it, and Sarah could hear disgusted exclamations and a few expletives from the Family as they noticed them. Sarah was well in front. A thin green path ran through the dead zone. *Odd.* She sensed a commotion to the south but couldn't see anything. She, Latifah and the tiger were all on edge, focusing their energies in that direction. Whatever it was, it was coming their way.

She saw the clouds of dirt and grass first. *That's a herd of something.* She turned and rode quickly back to Erika. "Take everyone down to the north side," she instructed, indicating the northern forest, "but tell everyone not to get too close to it. Start making noises. Talk loudly. A herd of something is coming. The problem may not be the herd but whatever's chasing it."

She galloped back to the tiger. The dust cloud continued toward them. They weren't tall animals, whatever they were, remaining below the height of the grasses in the dead zone. She watched as the first animals emerged at full stride from the green path. Strange, ugly pigs. Two different kinds. One looked warty, and the other had huge curled fangs. The hogs turned left as they saw Sarah, Latifah, who was jittery, and the tiger, who was not. He lowered himself into the grasses. Sarah steered Latifah back down the hill behind the tiger as far as was safe.

143

Twelve wild pigs rumbled out. A jaguar burst from the grasses and took down a trailing animal. Then the tiger shot forward and, in a matter of a few strides, toppled another near the back of the group, killing it immediately. The tiger then rose and faced the jaguar. The jaguar was female and, Sarah realized, pregnant.

Unfortunately for the wild pigs, the two cats were not the only predators in that stretch. Sarah watched as Marshall and Samantha, much farther west than her and the two cats, crept up the rise. Samantha pointed to the animal that would be their target. They rose and, in practiced unison, released their spears with tremendous force. Both struck the poor hog and dropped it on the spot. Within seconds, the two humans were upon it, slitting its throat before dragging it back down to the rest of the entourage.

The panicked herd turned right and raced down the rise behind the Family and into the dense northern forest. The jaguar stood over its prey. The tiger looked at Sarah, who nodded, and he picked up his warty-faced hog and carried it into the woods for his family to devour. The jaguar grabbed her kill and dragged it north across the rise between Sarah and the rest of the caravan and into the forest.

Erika had kept the Family silent during the three kills. They were not silent now. They were excited to have witnessed the event and were all a bit shocked at how calmly Sarah had watched as two huge predators made kills not 20 feet from where she and Latifah stood.

As she arrived before them, she asked, "That was cool, right?"

The fact-filled portly man, who'd been a psychologist, noted, "Those were two different types of wild hogs, both from the Zoo. The ugly ones with the bumpy faces are Visayan warty pigs, and the ones with the big curled teeth are babirusa. That's what Samantha and Marshall killed."

Gus cleaned the babirusa. Despite his better judgment, he threw the entrails to the dogs, who tore them to shreds in seconds. He stored the meat on the elephant's sled, under the large hide of water. "Hopefully that'll keep it cool."

They were falling behind schedule, but then, what schedule? They had all day to get there and all day to get back tomorrow.

"Alright, everyone, let's make sure the horses and elephant are all watered up. Then let's get back on the trail. We have a long way to go still, and at this rate, we'll not get there before dinner."

After a short break, Erika and Gus tried to drive the animals harder, and with a few communications from Sarah, they responded. Everyone was excited, so they, too, moved at a quicker pace, pushing ahead. Along the way, the tiger returned to her side. "Glad to have you back, ol' friend. Everyone like the meal?" He met her gaze and sent positive feelings in her direction. She'd provided him another benefit, even though she was getting credit for something that she had nothing to do with. Or maybe she did—who knew, these days. She'd take the chit, nonetheless.

After a while, the sun not quite directly above them, they stopped again, this time for lunch. It consisted of dried elk and deer, some greens and berries Sarah had found nearby, and water. It was not a lot, but it was enough. The animals grazed and drank. Sarah allowed them about a half-hour break and then asked everyone to head out again. It was probably at least another two hours to the camp at the rate they were moving.

With the sun high in the sky, the day was warm. Few had been this exposed to this much sun. The walkers were tiring, the breeze had died, and the heat was becoming oppressive. The grass was higher, making walking increasingly difficult. Everyone took to following behind the travois being hauled by the large animals, as they knocked down the grass. Still, few complained. The pillar of smoke was getting closer, and the adventure was still new and full of interesting moments. Five white-tail deer popped out of the forest behind them, two fawns among them. When a Family member yelled and everyone looked, the deer thought better of it and darted back to safety.

Erika rode behind. Randi had hopped on behind her. Erika was also listening and trying to sense any danger, teaching Randi how to do the same. The two were exploring her abilities, although neither was as connected to this new world as Sarah. Erika and Sarah were connected with each other and didn't need to be close to share information, like risks of danger. So far, there was nothing new.

THIRTY-NINE

Finally, as the sun was a good distance into its descent, creeping into the western sky behind them, they approached the outcropping of trees near the encampment. Sarah stopped. With a finger to her mouth, she pointed out the safe spot behind the trees to Gus. She rode back to the group and asked them to be quiet as they arrived. She, Erika and Randi dismounted, and Erika gathered the security detail.

Sarah, Erika, Joe, Olivia—who brought some medical supplies—and the three guys who were always together, whose names she couldn't remember, headed to the spot where the tiger was gazing into the woods, waiting. Randi stayed to protect the entourage.

"OK," Sarah said in a whisper, "they're through these trees about 20 yards or so. Be very quiet. Erika, Joe, follow me. You guys spread out a bit, several yards behind Erika and Joe, and watch our flanks and rear. Got that?" They all nodded. "OK. When we believe the situation is right, we'll call you forward. I may want a show of force." She lowered herself below the underbrush and waved them forward.

She and the tiger crept in together, just as they had a couple of nights before, but now there was daylight. As they approached the clearing, she could see emaciated people loafing around a small fire. These people were no threat. She waved the tiger back a few paces into the woods. He could still support them if things got dicey, but they didn't need to frighten these poor people.

146

She stood upright and entered the clearing. Erika, Joe and the three young men followed. Two men with sticks staggered forward as best they could. When Erika and Joe stepped toward them with their superior weapons, the men stopped.

Sarah, adorned with the necklace of hyena teeth, her large spear and the glistening long knife hanging from her belt, spoke first. "We're here to help. We're here to rescue you, if you're in need of assistance. I'm Sarah; this is Joe, Erika. We have many others with us, including a tiger, three horses and an elephant." The three guys arrived behind her with Olivia. "We have food, clean water and medicines."

"Sarah?" came the weakened voice of Robert from somewhere among those lying on the ground. He rose to his feet, a shell of his imposing former self. "Sarah." She approached him carefully, and he started toward her.

"Robert, you look terrible," she said calmly. He had a cut on his arm that was clearly infected.

"Sarah." He said to the others in his group, "Everyone, this is my wife. I'm so happy. How are the girls?"

"Robert, I'm not your wife. Please stand back." Sarah, without taking her eyes off Robert, addressed the three guys. "Run back to the group. Bring everything. Bring it quickly! Erika, accompany them." Her captain nodded, and they all took off in a sprint through the woods. The tiger strolled into the camp and laid down in a nice warm spot in the sun, cleaning himself like a housecat. There was a collective gasp. "Don't worry about him. He's harmless. Well, sort of. If you mess with me or my Family, then he is anything but."

The Family members hauled in water, medicines and food, including the fresh babirusa meat. The three young men were a godsend as they did, as promised, carry a lot of stuff.

A faint voice from the back of the small clearing tentatively said, "Joe?"

"Who is it?" Joe asked as he walked cautiously in that direction. Then he saw her. "Trudy! Oh my god, you're alive." He sprinted toward her. "Olivia, come now. She needs you." Olivia left Robert. Sarah followed.

There was Trudy, struggling against death, lying in the shade of a willow. Joe removed his water bag and gave her a drink. She gladly accepted it. Olivia knelt beside her.

"She's bad off, Sarah. Looks like a broken ankle, at least. Mostly, like everyone else, she needs food. They'll need to take it in a little at a time though."

Olivia handed a pouch of berries to Joe. He took one out, held her head gently and offered it to her. She took it and ate it. He gave her another. She took that one as well.

"Slowly," Olivia reminded him. "With water."

Erika assigned one person to each of those around the camp, including Robert. Olivia handed out water bags and pouches of food and instructed them to feed the residents slowly. "Water first. Not too much. One or two berries next. Then a little more water. Then give them a minute to get that down. Then a small amount of protein. Let them chew it and swallow. Make sure they chew it well. Give them a chance to assimilate the food. They should start to recover, but it'll take a while." Olivia kept up the mantra as she moved around the camp with Mandy, beginning to triage injuries and ailments.

When Erika discovered that Joe had found Trudy, tears welled up in her eyes. Sarah noticed, but Erika waved her off and began checking on the residents. They all suffered from malnutrition, dehydration and exposure, which was made worse by injuries and a few other illnesses.

Several people who appeared to be very ill had been separated from the rest. Three of them were dead. A young couple approached Sarah, thin and exhausted like the rest. "Those people have some nasty disease. It's killed quite a few of us." Sarah called Olivia and Erika over. The couple repeated what they'd said and provided Olivia some additional information.

Olivia said, "It's probably influenza or tuberculosis but could be worse. We need to keep the sick separated and get the dead out of here."

Erika ordered the three young men to carry the deceased out to the grasslands, which allowed Erika time to collect herself outside the camp and deal with the end of her relationship with Joe. Sarah, seeing her friend in emotional distress, followed them out. Erika spied a ravine and guided the guys over to it.

"Any water in there?" she asked.

"Nope," the largest man said as Sarah arrived at Erika's side.

"Alright, toss the bodies in." After the job was done but before they returned inside the camp, Erika huddled with them. "Do not tell anyone that we threw their friends into this ravine. We do not have time for proper burials or pyres or whatever. Do you understand?"

They all nodded. "Yes, ma'am."

Once back inside the camp, Olivia had the boys move the other severely ill a bit farther away from the others. She then checked to see if anyone else was suffering from the same symptoms.

Gus had built up their small fire into a stronger blaze. The boys washed in water Gus had heated at Olivia's direction for that purpose.

A team detached the travois from Big Gus and Bubbette so they could graze freely. Guards were stationed by the animals to protect them.

Sarah found Gus. "Can you run the camp for a bit? I need to check on Joe and Trudy before looking for some water. It's amazing that Trudy's alive. She was in Springfield, Illinois, and made it this far trying to get back to him and Joe Jr."

"It's a miracle, fer sure. Jus' hope she lives to see her boy."

"Well, we'll make sure she gets to our home. She may not be able to walk for a while, if ever, but she'll see Joe Jr."

"Gotta feel for Erika."

"I hear that. I can't imagine what she's going through right now. Must be tough. She wants to be supportive, but if Trudy survives, that pretty much ruins her relationship with Joe."

Sarah and Gus stood lost in thought for a few minutes. "OK, Gus ol' boy, you run the show around here. Erika and I are going to see if we can find a body of water and maybe spear some fish, and we'll search for some edible greens, perhaps mushrooms or flowers. We need to get everyone fed tonight. I'll have the hunters head out and see what they can find. I'm not sure what's around here, but maybe they can catch something fresh for breakfast."

She strode over to the young couple, who were already feeling better. "Where do you guys get water?"

"Down that way. By the way, how'd you find us?"

"We'll discuss all that later. Eat. Get your strength back. We'll talk once we get your group back to our compound, OK?"

The couple smiled at Sarah. "Thank you so much."

"Of course." She touched the woman on the shoulder and smiled. "You two will be fine, but I have things to attend to so we can keep as many of you alive as possible. It's a long way back to our place, and we've got to get you all as ready to travel as possible by morning. Lay back and rest. Eat and drink and get your strength back." They obeyed.

She noticed Robert slinking in the shadows, staring at her, taking food and water from a young man assigned to him. She shook him out of her head and turned to find Erika.

FORTY

Erika was standing in the shadows watching Joe and Trudy. "How are you doing, girlfriend?" Sarah put a hand on Erika's strong shoulder as they observed the lovers.

"Joe's thrilled he's found her. I guess he's scared to death at the same time. He loves her so much, and I knew it as much as anyone." Erika paused. "Trudy's elated. Her trek'll be worth it."

"It's a miracle," Sarah noted, patting Erika on her shoulder.

"She'll see her son tomorrow." Erika gazed into Sarah's eyes. "Her strength came back fast as she was filled with joy and hope from seeing us. I feel really good about that, Sarah, I do."

The two stared at the couple for a few seconds. Trudy's leg was broken and bent. She couldn't straighten it. Erika had been listening as Olivia treated her. "She injured it falling on some rocks on our side of the Mississippi River. She swam the fucking Mississippi, Sarah. She was so exhausted that she passed out right there. Two of these people found her and carried her here. I guess she hasn't moved much since she's arrived. Olivia says she also has some bed sores and some infected scratches, but she's treated those, and Joe's lifted her up off the ground to alleviate the pain from the sores."

"Yeah, but sweetie, how are you?"

"I don't know. Happy for Joe and Joe Jr., of course. Sad because our deal is ended, whatever it was. Not sure how to feel really. He never let me in, so . . ."

"Sorry about this. I had no idea."

"Are you kidding? Look at them. This is every Christmas that ever happened anywhere, all rolled into one moment for them. It is joy beyond joy. Joe and I were . . . well, we were fun. But he never stopped talking about Trudy. He named his spear after her. He prayed for this moment. I get that. We had fun. We had our time. But this is wonderful. It's the way it should be."

Sarah put her hand on her dear friend's back and led her away from the reunited couple. Erika began to cry. Sarah guided her through the woods and out into the grasslands near the animals. "Wanna ride?"

"Sure."

"Gus has got the camp under control. We can do some reconnaissance." Latifah strolled over. "The two of us, together on Latifah, like the old days. I'm still driving." Erika cracked a smile. Sarah vaulted onto Latifah's back and reached a hand down to Erika. She took it and heaved herself up behind Sarah. Wrapping her arms around Sarah's waist, she snuggled close, and they headed out at a walk.

"It's weird. I prayed with him that this day would come, that Trudy would survive and that he'd find her. All the while, of course, I hoped it wouldn't come true. I don't know if I love Joe. He fits me, that's for sure. We fit. In lots of ways. We run the compound together. We're both former military. We're both physical people who love to challenge each other. He makes me feel strong." The tears resurfaced, and it took a couple minutes before she could continue. "Now, no matter what happens, that's gone. I'm not sure what our friendship will look like. Can we be friends, run the camp, do the stuff we used to do?"

Sarah listened. There were no easy answers. She leaned back into her friend and grabbed her hands and pulled Erika closer. Latifah stopped. Sarah twisted her body and slid up on Latifah's neck to see her friend. Then she flipped her legs over and faced Erika, took her in her arms and hugged her. Sarah let Erika cry it out, whispering support into her ear.

Enveloping her with positive energy, Sarah's soul warmed Erika's. Gradually, they merged. Sarah poured more positive energy into Erika. After several minutes, Erika's tears slowed and then eventually stopped.

Their embrace became warmer, softer, more personal between the two of them as they pushed Joe out of Erika's heart.

Sarah lifted Erika's head up so she could face her. This time Sarah originated the kiss. It was sweet and meaningful. The closed-lip kiss signified more than a friendship between the two women. Since that first kiss, they'd shared a bond like sisters. This kiss solidified it.

Erika's soul let Sarah's all the way in, and the sisters' spirits entwined. The loss Erika experienced was not gone, but she felt better, and both knew they could safely rely on the other.

"Ready to head back, sis?" Sarah asked.

Erika smiled. "Sure. Got a lot of new Family members to feed back there. Let's quit lollygagging and get to it, shall we?"

"I think we shall."

Sarah swung her leg over Erika's head and spun around on Latifah, who'd lifted his head from the grass. As he headed back, Sarah contemplated that she could have ridden him backwards, but Erika's arms around her waist felt nice.

"Let's sleep together this evening around the fire," Sarah offered.

"Sounds good."

Suddenly, a commotion from the ravine interrupted their peaceful ride. Sarah guided Latifah, against his wishes, over to where the men had dumped the three dead refugees. A pair of hyenas were tearing the bodies to shreds, crunching through the bones with their powerful jaws. Crows and ravens circled overhead, diving in and grabbing bits and pieces of flesh when they could. Several buzzards arrived, approaching from multiple directions. The hyenas seemed not to care. The vultures, too, began to rip at the flesh the hyenas had tossed aside in their frenzy.

Latifah reared back as rats appeared. Thousands of rats chased away the birds and even overwhelmed the hyenas. The two humans and their horse moved about 20 yards from the ravine atop a small hillock where they could easily see, but were safe from, the onslaught. The hyenas dragged one of the bodies away from the rats and ripped large pieces off before running south into the tall brown grass of the dead zone to consume their meal. The vultures sat patiently on the edge of the ravine. The crows and ravens continued to dive in, feeding opportunely on scraps. Within a matter of minutes, it was over. The scavengers left the scene as quickly as they'd arrived.

Sarah and Erika craned their necks to look into the ravine. There was nothing left. Nothing. No bones, no skin, no evidence whatsoever that a human body, much less three, had been lying in that ravine.

"OK, so that explains why we haven't seen any dead human bodies. I'm surprised there are still bones back there in the dead zone," Sarah remarked.

"That was fast. Fuck." Erika swallowed. "Remind me not to die around here."

FORTY-ONE

After leaving Latifah with the other animals, the women spent some time hunting for edible vegetation and talking, mostly about men. There wasn't much in the way of greens or flowers around this camp. There were no berries and only a few wild onions.

"No wonder they're starving," Sarah said.

They headed back into camp, tossed Gus their paltry haul and strode across to the other side in the direction of the water source the couple had mentioned.

"Hey, you," called out a female voice, weak like the others but urgent. "Don't go in there. It'll kill you."

"What'll kill us?" Erika asked.

"The beast."

Sarah exchanged a look with Erika, who shrugged her shoulders, and the two headed into the woods. They found the small shallow creek. No fish except minnows. It was difficult to even draw water from, though it was clean and clear.

Erika gave up. "Let's head upstream. Maybe there's a pool in that direction."

Sarah nodded in agreement.

Wading slowly, they listened for anything and sensed the world around them. Sarah and Erika both realized they'd left camp without any spears. Sarah withdrew her long knife, Erika her shorter one. They crept up the stream bed.

Sarah sensed it first. Then Erika. It was to their right, further upstream. They crouched in the creek bed and watched. They were downwind, so whatever it was wouldn't smell them easily. Possible prey.

The family of raccoons couldn't have been cuter as they followed their mother down to the water. The four little ones played while their mother washed something in the creek. Raccoons were fastidious about cleaning their food before eating it. The women grinned at each other.

"Better than watching hyenas and rats tear a human corpse to pieces."

"Nice image, Erika."

"Just saying."

Suddenly, the mother raccoon spun and bared her teeth, uncertain where the threat was coming from. The little ones instinctively moved behind her. Then Erika and Sarah saw it. A cougar slipped quietly from the underbrush up the bank from the raccoon, facing down the much larger predator. She had to defend her cubs, who cowered behind her except for one. That precocious youngster stood, fur raised to make him look larger, teeth bared.

Sarah shook her head and asked Erika, "What is it with men?"

The two stood upright, knives out, and faced the cougar. They focused on him until he began to back down. Erika sent positive energy toward the mother raccoon, letting her know they were there to protect her. Sarah rose out of the stream and began to approach the cougar. The cougar was unsure but was not backing down. Sarah met his eyes. She felt the cougar. He was hungry. This raccoon, or at least one or two of her pups, were to be dinner.

Erika moved quickly behind the raccoons and above them to flank the cougar then said, "Mr. cougar, you picked a bad time to try to catch your super cute dinner." The mother quickly moved her young back and into the brush behind the two women as the cougar swiped a paw with long claws at them, but he wasn't close enough to hit either of them.

They had no desire to harm him, and they conveyed that as best they could to the cougar, but he was not getting his evening meal from the mother raccoon and her family. At least not this evening, not on their watch.

Sarah sensed the moment and, taking a page from Janie's playbook, growled at the cougar. He turned and reluctantly slipped away into the underbrush. They knew it was partly due to them, but largely because his prey had vanished. They high-fived each other and looked down at the measly creek.

"This is worthless. No wonder these people are almost dead. There's nothing to eat around here. At least nothing easy to kill," Erika said.

"OK. Let's head back and eat some pig. I've never eaten whatever-it's-called hog, have you?"

Erika shook her head. "Never even heard of it." They made their way back down the creek. Sarah could feel the cougar shadowing them from somewhere above them in the woods. Erika saw him and screamed. Sarah twisted in time to see the cougar pounce at them from the high side of the creek. Sarah ducked to the side beneath the cougar and, with a blood-curdling scream, drove her long knife up into the chest of the cougar. The cougar's back claw scratched her arm, but she didn't notice as the cougar's momentum yanked her precious knife from her hand.

After Sarah's attack, Erika sprung with a menacing cry, landing on the far bank and plunging her knife deep into the struggling cougar's side. The cougar fell hard, bleeding profusely, but he regained a wobbly balance and prepared for another attack. Erika dove at him and slashed him viciously across his face, again drawing a spurt of red blood. The cougar refused to back down, and both women fearlessly faced off against the predator, prepared for another assault.

"Come on, you fucker, give me one more rip at your sorry hide," Erika screamed at the startled cat.

The flash of orange was more than welcome. Tiger flew from the woods behind the cougar, camouflaged by the dappled sunlight. He landed on the weakened cat, gripping its head in his powerful jaws. One twist and the cougar slumped to the dirt. The tiger stood over the carcass and nodded to Sarah and Erika. They smiled at their friend and nodded back. The tiger had no interest in the cougar. He turned and leaped back into the forest. Unlike humans, this was not a repayment or a balancing of the scales. They were friends, or more like allies. The mutual relationship was not easily definable in human terms. Sarah sighed in relief as he disappeared into the dappled rays of sunlight in the woods.

"Sarah, we have to get you back right now. You have some pretty deep cuts, girlfriend."

"You know, for someone so connected to this world, I sure get my ass kicked a lot." She touched the wounds. "They're not bad, not too deep. He grazed me. I'll be fine with a little of my own magic." Sarah winked.

They headed back when Sarah yelled, "Wait! That cougar is *not* getting my knife." She released Erika's hand, jumped onto the bank to the cougar and flipped the body over. The knife was fine. She ripped it out of the cougar's belly and said a final farewell to the dead cat, "Take that, you furry male bastard."

Erika smiled. "OK, Miss Badass, let's head back."

Sarah laughed and bounced back down to Erika. "I want that hide, though. That'll be nice. I'll start to tan it tonight. Get your boyfriends up here to get it for us."

"And I want those claws for our necklaces."

"I get the ones that cut me. I want my blood still on them. You can have the ones from the other paw."

"You bet. Come on now, Rambo, let's get you down the hill."

Blood was streaming down her right leg from a cut she'd sustained on a rock in the creek and down her left arm from four evenly spaced claw marks. Those four would be badges of honor, turning into scars she'd wear proudly.

Having heard their war cries, everyone was already staring at them as they entered camp. Sarah walked in by her own power, and the two stood tall and strong. The three guys were flirting with one of the prettier girls from the Family who was tending to two girls from the group being rescued.

Erika yelled, "Boys, keep 'em in your pants—if you had any." They and the girls blushed. "Just kidding. But before you continue your flirting, there's a dead cougar up the hill. Go get it and bring it to Gus to cut up for dinner. Then we want the hide and those claws—all ten of the front claws. You guys can share the back ones for your efforts. Got it?"

"Yes, ma'am," the three answered in unison.

The two girls from the new group were astounded. "You killed the beast?"

One of the young men answered for her, "They do it all the time."

"They killed four menacing hyenas. Their teeth are around their necks," another said.

"Defeated a horde of over 40 vicious rebels and a crazy evil wizard and drove them off the face of the earth!"

"Well, we kinda helped," the first added with a grin. "C'mon, boys. Let's get that cougar."

"So, one little cougar is child's play for those two," the third man stated as the three stood.

"Do not fuck with those women," the three said, almost in unison.

Sarah and Erika smirked at the much larger young men. "Shut up and go get the cougar, would you, please? Olivia, would you mind tending to my insane friend here?" Erika ordered. The three trotted off into the woods and up the hill, as much to impress the girls as anything else.

Olivia jogged over for a look. Sarah complained, "I'm fine. He barely got me. Give me a moment." She also wanted to do this in front of the new group. She closed her eyes and focused her Elephant spirit on the wounds. Within seconds, the scratches on her leg disappeared and four claw marks closed up, leaving only the scars she'd wanted.

As Sarah came out of her trance, healed and strong, Erika asked, "How many times do I have to save your life, girlfriend?"

"What, *you*?"

"I saw the cougar first."

"It's my knife that's all bloody," Sarah protested. "Go test it. That's cold red male cougar blood."

"I got the beast twice, and he didn't disarm me!"

"Whatever. It sure was fun though." Everyone stared in awe as the two hugged and shared a kiss.

"Sure was. Let's do it again real soon." Erika patted Sarah. "Gotta check on the guards out front." Sarah nodded and decided it was time to talk to Robert to set a few things straight before they headed to the compound.

Gus announced to the crowd, "Ya'll get used to it. Like the fella said, do not fuck with Sarah and Erika. She's our leader, and them girls is just the right amounta crazy, if ya ask me. Jus' glad they's on our team, tell ya that right now!" He smiled broadly, and the two women returned the smile. They loved their reputation as badasses.

FORTY-TWO

The rescued were awakening from days of hopelessness, hunger and pain. The physical aspects of their suffering, though somewhat better, were still very real, but the presence of this new band of healthy, strong and positive-minded rescuers and their two powerful female leaders had provided what they all desperately needed most—hope. That turned out to be the strongest medicine they'd brought with them.

Gus was making a soup from bones of the wild pig in a tough hide that Bobbi had specially tanned to handle hot liquids. He'd brought with him a frame he used in camp to hang a similar bag near the fire. He'd re-assembled it and filled it with water and the bones. It'd be a rich, healthy broth, filled with iron and other minerals from the marrow, that'd be easy for the group to handle. Ol' Mac's team had carved a couple of ladles, a couple of bowls and some spoons from hickory over the last few days to solve the soup-eating problem back home.

Sarah shifted toward Robert, whose eyes displayed complete disbelief and a touch of fear. She could see him considering his words. "These people are amazing, Sarah. How'd you do it?" Robert asked.

"Yeah, I'm the leader, but this is a great team with numerous bright people in our Family. We're at the site of the girls' school. Of course, it's no longer there, but it's a perfect little sanctuary. We're flourishing."

"I can see that." He paused. The young men returned, struggling with the huge cougar. The large gashes in its chest and underbelly were

161

no longer bleeding. There was almost no evidence of the tiger's finishing work. "And you killed that cougar?"

"Well, I had help. Erika and tiger."

"That cougar's been a scourge on our camp. He's killed at least five of us over the last several days. We're frightened to leave the camp area to try to hunt. We're even afraid to get water or try to fish or pretty much anything."

"What've you been eating?"

"Mostly beetles and grubs. Luckily, there's plenty of those. They have some protein and moisture that barely kept us alive. We maybe had another day or two before we'd all be dead. I can't thank you enough for saving us." Despite his demeanor, a menacing undercurrent emanated from him, as a touch of sarcasm marked his words. Sarah contemplated, *He'd probably rather have died than have me save his sorry ass and show off my strength in front of these folks.* The thought made her smile inside.

"You're welcome," she responded. "I do have a question. How is it you're here and not dead back in D.C.?"

He looked at her askance, then grinned and said, "Well, simple really. Remember the guy who flew us to Wyoming?"

"Sure."

"When I escaped, he was ready with his plane and flew me here. We arrived a bit ahead of that Storm, and he dropped me off. Not sure what happened to him."

In a long pause, she considered asking how he knew where they were but decided it no longer mattered.

"So, you found us?" Robert asked.

"Yep. A couple of days ago, Jazz and I were cutting down bamboo culms, and Jazz was communicating with the snakes that live there when I saw your plume of smoke on the horizon. I didn't want to expose Jazz to whatever was here, so we headed home."

"Jazz talks to snakes?"

"Communicates. Animals don't talk. Like I communicate with the tigers, bears, the elephant and the horses. Samantha and Claire, who's back home, communicate with the dogs. It's a weird new world, Robert. Weird new world. We have lots of allies. It's good to have allies." She watched him closely as this sank in. She needed him to realize how completely outmatched he was. She could feel how angry it made him that she, of all people, was saving him from certain death. She relished the advantage and wanted to ensure it stayed that way.

"So anyway, late that night, Latifah, which is what Janie named my horse, and tiger and I rode to this camp. Through the darkness, I saw you in the firelight. I have to say, I panicked, given the way we left things in the old world." He nodded. "But I rode home, and we spent all day yesterday getting everything together. We have four horses, soon to be five. One's a draft horse and two are riding horses. The fourth's a pregnant mare. There was no way the draft horse could handle everything we needed to bring, especially all the water. That's when I enlisted the elephant to help." After explaining this so matter-of-factly, she could see Robert's head swimming.

"How many are you?" Robert asked.

"We brought 30. There are about 70 or so total. Molly can give you the actual count when we get back if you want the details."

"Seventy. How the fuck do you feed them all?"

"Years of learning and practice. You know how much my parents taught me and how much time the girls and I spent in the wilderness. You could have joined us, you know."

"Yeah." He sighed heavily. "I could've done a lot of things better. That was a long time ago."

"OK, about that. As far as I'm concerned, you and I are no longer a couple or anything other than the parents of the same children. Do you understand? This is not up for discussion."

She could see him processing. "But, Sarah, you're my wife. We never divorced. You're legally mine." Her Tiger spirit roiled inside her, and she nearly exploded at the idea that he could own her now or ever, but she pushed it back down, took a breath and continued.

"I've found the love of my life in this crazy new world. His name is Tom. I wouldn't let him come because I didn't know how you'd react. He's a great guy. You'll meet him tomorrow. The girls love him." She contemplated her next words. "Robert, you need to know this, and I'm not sure what you remember from those days, but here goes: They're not looking forward to seeing you. Especially Jazz. I don't know if you remember, but like you did to me so many times, you tried to rape her one evening, in her own room, on her bed. Luckily, you were too drunk to do it, but she pretty much hates you. You need to be aware. There's a lot of reconciliation that needs to happen with Jazz."

He stared into the ground. "I never raped you! You're my wife. A husband can't rape his wife. Sex is what they're supposed to do." He was somewhere between anger and depression, but too weak to explode as he would have in the old world.

"Robert, you held me down against my wishes and forced yourself on me. In any book, married or not, that's rape. And you tried to do it to your own daughter. And she hates you for it."

He breathed deeply. "I don't remember doing that. If I did, I was plastered, and it wasn't my fault." Sarah glared at him and he recoiled. "OK, fine. Thanks for letting me know." He sat silently for a couple minutes then looked up into her eyes. Those once seductive brown eyes had no effect on her. "Sarah, I realize I don't have to tell you this, but I was fucked up back then. I had affairs, lots of them. I know I beat you and tormented the hell out of you." No remorse showed within those eyes, either because he didn't really care or was too hungry and dehydrated to feel anything. Either way, she felt absolutely no desire to comfort him and didn't.

"Well, your admittance is a start. When we get back, you have to promise not to create problems for me, the girls or Tom or anyone else in the Family, or I will straight up take you out." She said it with a calmness that caught him off guard. "You are much easier to deal with than a cougar. So, do you understand and agree to these terms?"

"Sure." It wasn't convincing, but she didn't care.

She almost wanted him to act up, to do something stupid so she could tear him apart or throw him to the dogs or something. Again, she settled her insides, took a breath and said only, "Good." She patted him on the head in a condescending way and walked off.

Robert stared at the dirt in front of him. Sarah couldn't gauge how he was accepting this information.

Olivia appeared. "Time to change your dressings, Robert." He winced as Olivia removed the leather bandages. Sarah took a peek and shivered at the green, yellowish and gut-wrenchingly disgusting gash on Robert's bicep, a few inches below the scar left from the time she coldcocked him into the glass coffee table in their old house. *Some form of poetic justice? Maybe he'll finally die from that?*

FORTY-THREE

Next, Sarah sought out Joe and Trudy. An athletically built woman with sandy blond hair, Trudy, though emaciated, seemed much better, more lucid, and they were talking incessantly. She was telling her story of returning to them by swimming across the Mississippi when Sarah arrived.

"We're going to have some amazing new stories to tell around the campfires in the coming weeks, Sarah," Joe said.

"I bet. How's the patient?"

"OK," Trudy responded as she snuggled into Joe's chest. "Actually, wonderful. I never dreamed we'd find each other again. I can't walk, and I figured I would die right here."

"Well, let's see if we can do something about both those issues," Olivia announced as she joined them. "We're going to try to straighten that ankle. If you ever want to walk again, we'll have to fix it. You're no longer going to be a world-class sprinter, but perhaps we can get you back on your feet. You may need a crutch or a cane, but we can see if we can get you walking someday, perhaps soon."

"She'll always have me to lean on," Joe said.

Trudy smiled up at her devoted husband.

Olivia said solemnly, "Trudy, this is going to hurt like nothing else you've ever experienced, including childbirth. It may cause you to pass out. We have no anesthesia, so we're going to try our own unique way to see if we can get you through this. You willing to try?"

Trudy glanced at Joe, who nodded reassuringly. "These women know more about this world than I ever knew about the old one. You can trust them."

Trudy took a deep breath, turned from Joe to Olivia and nodded, closing her eyes tightly.

"That's OK, Trudy." Sarah touched her, and she opened her eyes. "First, I'm going to take you out of your broken body so you can handle the pain better. Is that OK?"

"What?"

Olivia explained, "Sarah here is going to help guide your soul to hers and out of your body when we do this. Your soul is really you. Your body is the machine you live in and operate. That's what's broken and where the pain will be. Does that make any sense? Your body will still feel the pain, but you won't. Well, not until your soul returns to your body, but by then, the worst will be over."

Trudy, still uncertain, shot Joe a doubtful look. Joe said, "Trust them, honey." That seemed to calm her fears.

Sarah instructed, "Just clear your mind and relax, and I'll guide you through this." Trudy nodded. The three young men now stood behind Olivia, ready to assist.

"This takes a lot of force. Jack and Michael, please stabilize Trudy's lower leg: Jack below her calf muscle here, and Michael just below the knee, there. Hold tight, and when I say three, pull back gently to counter the force I'll be generating in the other direction. Got it?"

The two nodded.

"We have to keep her leg as stable from the ankle up as humanly possible. Got it?" The two young men nodded again and took their positions.

"Zach, you're with me. You have to help me pull. We do not yank. We pull firmly and gently until we get the ankle back in place. Then Sarah will work her magic and get the bones as close to mended as she can."

"I don't know if I can do that," Zach replied squeamishly.

"Zach, this is not a request. Now get on your knees and do precisely as I say."

"Yes, ma'am." A crowd was gathering around, even those from the new group who could move, including Robert and the girls the three men had been flirting with. That helped solidify their courage.

"OK, Mandy?" The skinny dark-haired woman who worked with Olivia came forward with two solid sticks and some leather bands to create a makeshift splint.

Once everyone was in place, Olivia gave Sarah a nod, letting her know it was time to begin. "OK, Trudy, you're going to have to focus with me. I need your spirit, your soul, to connect with mine and do as I guide it. Do you understand?"

She shook her head, eyes terrified.

"Trudy, you'll feel me arrive. Just let me in." Trudy met Joe's eyes, who smiled encouragingly, then Trudy nodded. Sarah took the lotus position at Trudy's left side, facing her.

Sarah then said to Joe, "Joe, hold Trudy tight. Love her with every fiber of your being. Pour your love into her like a pitcher pours water. Fill her to overflowing and keep on pouring. Release all negativity, fear, apprehension and concern. Trudy will be wonderful. Trudy *is* wonderful. Close your eyes and love her with everything you have. Do not doubt along the way. If you feel something weird happening, focus more love into it. You will feel as much of Trudy's pain as you can handle—the more the better, much as I did when Tom was dying." Joe nodded his assent. "It won't last days like that did, but it will help her handle the pain when she has to go back into her own body. Are you willing to do that?"

"Yes, absolutely. I'm excited to do it. I know it will hurt, but I'd do anything for my Trudy. It'll be OK, honey. I'm here. We can do this together."

Trudy was frightened but looked at him with such love and gratitude, Sarah believed they were both ready.

Joe told Trudy, "I love you with all my soul, and I'm happy to absorb your pain. I'm ready. I love you, sweetheart." He addressed Sarah, "I'm ready."

She spoke softly and slowly to Joe and Trudy in a voice that seemed to resonate from within, "Close your eyes and breathe deeply together. Feel each other's spirit. Joe, pour your love into Trudy, warm and soft and gentle. Trudy, let it flow into your soul. Feel it warm you and enwrap itself in your spirit.

"Take another breath, together, an even deeper breath. Trudy, soak in Joe's love. Hold it. Feel it penetrate every fiber of your being—deep and warm and perfect. As you exhale now, let all the negativity, doubt, fear, pain and apprehension flow out of you, out into the air. That's wonderful. Now one more, even deeper breath together and hold it. Become one. Let his soul enter your body and feel it beside yours, entwined with your spirit. Good. Now let your breath out slowly. Let any remaining doubt, fear or apprehension leave you with this breath."

Sarah could feel the warmth and positive energy from the exchange.

During the next part, Sarah did not speak. Her soul entered and touched Trudy's soul. It took a moment for Trudy to release herself to Sarah, but Sarah could feel Joe guiding her, his love powerful and strong. As she had with Erika during the revolution, Sarah guided Trudy's spirit slowly out of her body, remaining connected to Joe's loving soul, still there to protect her.

Olivia sensed it was time. "Alright," she whispered. "Ready?" Jack and Michael nodded. Then Zach nodded. Olivia took a deep breath. "On three. One, two, three." Olivia pulled and Zach mirrored her, adding much-needed strength. Jack and Michael held her leg steady. Trudy's body and Joe's body writhed in pain, but Sarah sat calmly, focused on protecting Trudy's soul. The crack rang out through the camp and startled nearly everyone.

"OK, we're past the hard part," Olivia whispered. "Keep holding boys. Zach, you're still with me." Olivia guided the foot and ankle back into place, feeling for the right position, angling the separated appendage gently back and forth until she felt it settle into place.

Sarah sensed the leg and brought forth her Elephant spirit, lending it to the healing process, connecting bones, stretching tendons, restoring cartilage. It wasn't perfect, but it would hold, and Sarah was weakening. She knew after healing Tom that this was going to be tough for her.

She heard Olivia say, "That's it. It's in. Mandy, now please." Sarah held onto Olivia's soul, feeling Joe still pouring love into her, enduring the excruciating pain as Mandy attached and tightened the splint. "Good, done. Thanks, Mandy. All of you can return to your own bodies now."

Sarah released Trudy back into her body where she was greeted by Joe's spirit. Then she felt Joe's spirit slip back into his body, though Joe and Trudy's spirits remained as entwined as hers was with Tom's. Joe was sweating profusely, his eyes still closed, as focused as he'd ever been in his life.

Suddenly, Trudy gasped and her eyes shot open. "Holy fuck, goddamn, that hurts." And then she smiled and grimaced at the same time. She patted Joe's leg, and he opened his eyes. "I love you so very much, sweetheart. I love you so much."

"I love you too," he responded, exhausted and breathless.

He'd taken in the pain and a lot of it—more than Sarah had expected he could. *Love is strong medicine indeed.*

"I know." Trudy's voice was soft and comforting. "I could feel it. I could feel it everywhere, even when I was with Sarah." She pushed herself up and kissed him passionately. She put her hand around the back of his head and refused to let him go. Olivia sat back and let out a long breath. So did Jack, Michael and Zach. Sarah was spent. Trudy looked like a woman who'd just gone through the pain of childbirth, but in the same way, both Joe and Trudy grinned from ear to ear.

Olivia examined the leg, which was quite red and swollen. "It's badly damaged, and I think several if not all the ligaments are in bad shape, but it's in place now and should start to heal. Sarah did a nice job. We need to elevate it, give her plenty of fluids, and when we get back, get it into the cold stream. We'll get it massaged, and Tom can work with her and see what he can do to help her gain some movement, but that won't be for a few days."

Olivia and Mandy stabilized the splint on Trudy's ankle and lower leg then wrapped it tightly in ropes and leather. They then produced a flat piece of wood, which was set under Trudy's foot to support it. Four straight sticks ran up from each side of her foot and around behind her heel. These were tied together with leather, rope and sinew. "That foot is not going to move until we get home," Mandy said, proud of their handiwork.

Trudy winced a few times as they put it on and adjusted it, but she and Joe were soon jabbering like school kids, and she was eating and drinking as he held her in his arms. *Strength against time, and time doesn't matter,* Sarah thought, missing Tom's comforting arms and wishing he'd come. However, she knew they'd made the right decision.

FORTY-FOUR

Sarah was instinctively drawn to Erika, who was helping Gus prepare dinner. They'd assembled a small smoke house that Gus had brought with them. Long slices of meat were hung within it. Smoke billowed up to cure the hanging meat for the next day's trek.

The dried meat they'd brought was still being fed to those being rescued. Sarah could see their strength growing. They were talking to the Family members, amazed at all the stuff that was happening. Sarah was a bit impressed as well, partly at the level of planning they'd put into this excursion, but also by the shear level of technology they'd developed in such a short period of time.

These people think this is amazing, wait until they get to our home. She thought about the luxuries they had there: massages, chiropractic care, the best doctor in the world—as far as anyone knew—two beauticians to do your hair, actors and singers and storytellers. She might as well add elephant rides, for crying out loud. *It'll be a shock, but a good one.*

Olivia drifted among the group with Mandy. Weak and feverish, the four who were very sick struggled to keep anything down. Olivia had Jack, Michael and Zach, who more or less worked for her now, build a small fire and move them to the far side of it, away from the rest of the group, fearing that whatever they were suffering from could be contagious. Erika stationed a couple of guards nearby to protect them though, instructing, "Don't touch them." The two guards had no interest in doing so. Erika patted them on their shoulders and headed toward Sarah. Olivia reported to Sarah and Erika that she was pretty sure at least two of them wouldn't make it through the night. The other two, she felt, would be lucky to endure the trip home.

Erika asked, "Should we even bring them back? What if they infect the entire camp?"

Olivia added, "Sarah, we should quarantine all of these folks, perhaps outside the barrier, until we know what we're dealing with. Heck, we could all become carriers, at least those of us who've been dealing with the sickly here."

Sarah took a deep breath. This was her hard decision to make. "I don't think we can bring those four back, whether they survive until tomorrow or not. It's too dangerous to the Family. And I agree, we'll have to quarantine them outside the barrier when we get home. About the rest of us . . . Olivia, what do you think the chances are that we'll get this?"

"If I'm right that it's the flu, then probably pretty small. We're all healthy and strong, and while we may get the sniffles and low fevers, some of which we already have back home, we shouldn't die from it like these extremely vulnerable folks have or will. They're all older and were more susceptible before all of this happened, so, again, if it's influenza, then even any of the others here who've been infected should come through it OK."

"Well, what else could it be?" Erika asked.

"Not sure. Tuberculosis maybe. The options are long. Bacterial, viral, fungal. Anthrax poisoning is one, but it's not contagious. There's anthrax all around, and if they're eating bugs, they could get it that way. They're exhibiting flu-like symptoms, so there's a gazillion possibilities, some worrisome and others not so much. I can't take blood, and even if I could, I couldn't analyze it. Heck, I don't even have a stethoscope to listen to their heart and lungs, and I'm not putting my ear on them."

"OK. We'll figure this out, but we aren't bringing those four home with us," Sarah confirmed.

"Maybe we can leave Robert to care for them?" Erika joked. The three women shared a smile.

Sarah and Erika called the two young cross-country runners over, and they all left the clearing. "OK, you two, time to do your thing. You need to head back home and tell Ms. Watson that we'll be bringing about 14 new people back tomorrow. Tell her we may need to create a quarantine space for them to live outside the barrier, just until we see who is and is not infected with whatever those four people have. We'll probably get out of here around mid-morning. We'll move slowly, I'd guess, so it'll be late afternoon at the earliest when we get back. We'll be running low on water. I think we're OK foodwise. Have her create some water bags and station a couple of guards near the bamboo stand to wait for us. There's a creek there. We'll have some thirsty folks and animals by then."

"We need berries," Olivia added as she joined the small meeting. "Most of these people have scurvy, which means they need vitamin C. They're responding nicely to the berries we have and will be fine, but we'll use them all up soon, and I haven't seen any source for more around here. It'd be great to get more into them as soon as possible tomorrow, even if it's on the last leg of the journey."

The girls nodded. Each girl had her own water bag and a small bag of berries and dried meat. "Here, take my berries," one offered. "I won't need them for the trip home, and if we save someone, all the better."

"Yeah, take mine too." Both women also had their necklaces and a belt with a knife.

"Need anything else?" Sarah asked. They shook their heads. "OK, we're sending tiger with you to protect you." She noticed the apprehension in their eyes. "It'll be OK. Now, I'm going to call him shortly. When he arrives, stand straight and look right at him. Take a deep breath and let any negativity, fear and doubt leave you with the exhalation. Do it again if you need to. Project only positive energy. Confidence, courage, love. Got it? Can you do that?"

They were clearly not sure. "Let's practice," Erika suggested. "If I can do it, you can do it. Sarah's a different critter altogether, but you and I, well, we're human." The girls giggled a little, and Sarah frowned in mock disapproval.

"Now, stand up straight. This is to show your respect. Look the tiger in the eye. This is to show you're an equal and not prey. Convey positive power, courage and especially love to the tiger. This is to convey that you're a friend. Animals have only two energies: positive and negative. They don't name feelings like we do. So, doubt, fear and anger are all the same to them, got it? Love, courage and confidence are all positive energies, and again, all the same to the tiger. He wants to feel those emotions, those energies from you. Make sense?"

Without a word, they nodded.

"OK, how quickly can you get back?" Sarah asked. "Let's assume it's ten miles."

"It's 9.8 miles," one of the girls corrected her.

"I don't care how you know that, but how fast can you run . . . 9.8 miles?" Erika repeated as Sarah smiled.

They conferred together. Then the same young lady answered, "64 minutes, max."

"Probably 56," the other girl noted.

It unnerved Sarah at how precise they were. "OK then."

"That's pretty fast," Erika said.

"Yes, ma'am. We're part of the state champion cross-country team."

"We were both training for an iron man triathlon that was to happen in May."

"We ran at least 10 miles a day."

"Twenty at least twice a week."

"Three days if we had the time."

"Back then we could average 5.73 minutes a mile over 20 miles."

"We added 8 minutes because we haven't really trained the same way."

"And for the terrain."

"We usually run on roads, but we've run plenty of nature trails."

"Great for the cardio."

"We've been working with the hunters."

"We usually run messages back and forth for them."

"I'm Tabitha."

"Jennifer."

"Or Tabby."

"Jenny."

"Hell, they talk fast enough. I'm sure they can run fast too," Erika said with a grin.

"OK, Erika, help Tabby and Jenny get focused. I'll call tiger."

"Wait. One more thing." Erika turned to the girls. "This is very important. Tell Ms. Watson that Joe has found Trudy. Tell her that she must swear everyone to secrecy about our relationship. Do you understand? This is critically important. Joe and I are friends. Colleagues in the leadership. Ms. Watson will know how to handle it. Do not forget this part. Tell her and no one else, and keep this a secret. Please do not forget this part."

"Yes, ma'am," they said in unison.

"Jinx!" they also said in unison. The exchange reminded Sarah that before this crazy Storm, these girls, so vital to their Family now, were typical teenagers.

"OK, now I'm going to call for tiger."

"Deep breaths. No fear. Courage. Let all the negative energy out." Erika observed them as they focused on their mission. "Good."

Sarah thought about the tiger and soon he came loping out of the woods. He'd obviously been sleeping. He seemed strong and in a good mood, which was always a good thing.

The four women stood straight, and Sarah nodded at the tiger.

Erika whispered, "Now focus. Feel the tiger's soul. Feel his spirit. Let him feel yours. Nice, even breaths."

Sarah could feel them connecting with the tiger, at least enough for this trip. Sarah conveyed what she needed then nodded to the tiger. He lowered his head very briefly. He waited for the two girls to come to him.

Erika whispered to them, "Walk over. Don't touch him. He's not a pet. He's a powerful, independent spirit who happens to be a valuable ally. Once you get to him, simply start your run. You ready?"

They nodded and walked toward the tiger. When they reached him, he headed west and led them home. Sarah thanked him. The girls picked up the pace, and the tiger increased his speed. He seemed to enjoy the run through the grass. They stayed on the path the animals had beaten down a few hours before. Sarah and Erika watched as the two girls and the tiger faded into the distance over a small hill.

FORTY-FIVE

"They'll be fine. Come on." Erika pulled Sarah toward the camp. Sarah wished she could have gone with them. She wanted to run and jump in Tom's arms and hug her girls. She noticed Latifah watching her, ready to take her home. It helped her refocus her energies. She had work to do, so she followed Erika back into the camp. *The responsibilities of leadership.* She trotted forward and flung her arm around her best friend and kissed her on the cheek.

"What was that for?"

"I don't know, sis. Do I need a reason?" The two headed back into camp, both feeling stronger and more ready to lead and get home.

Another of the sick people had died, just as Olivia had predicted. The body was carried unceremoniously by the young men to the ravine and dumped in. When they returned, Sarah and Erika greeted them.

"Where are the other three bodies we dumped there like an hour ago?"

"Beasts ate 'em—hyenas, rats, vultures, ravens, crows—bones and all," Erika said without emotion.

"It was amazingly efficient," Sarah said. "So, it's a good way to get rid of whatever killed them."

"Speaking of that, you all should go wash well," Erika added. "We don't know what killed those poor people."

The two leaders then headed over to help Gus. They took the thick soup around to their new Family members. It seemed to help a great deal, both to hydrate and to add needed nutrients. And it was warm. It took a while to get soup to everyone who needed and wanted it and to each Family member who had come on the journey.

When everyone had eaten, Sarah and Erika took one bowl and one spoon to the three sick and dying patients at the back of the camp. The first threw up his spoonful immediately, collapsing back down to the ground.

"He won't live much longer," Sarah whispered to Erika as they moved to the next patient. The other two took a few spoonfuls; one barely kept it down, but the other soon gagged and threw it back up. Sarah and Erika returned with the utensils.

"Gus, we need to sterilize these before we use them again. Can we produce some boiling water to soak them in?"

"Hard to boil water out here. Guess'n I kin try."

"If you're not sure, let's just not use them. We can pack them up, take them home and clean them back there," Sarah suggested.

"Don' think we need 'em anymore. Let's jus' do that."

"OK, Gus, ol' boy, do that." Erika patted him on his hairy back and then looked at her now sweaty hand. Sarah chuckled and backpedaled as Erika came at her behind Gus's back with that hand.

The smell of wild pig and cougar roasting over the fire wafted through the camp. Sarah could see the delight in the eyes of the residents. Gus bellowed, to the surprise of the newbies, "Come and get it or we'll throw it out. Where the hell is Herb?" he joked.

Sarah and Erika stepped forward. "We'll serve." They handed out eating baskets to the Family members, who then took them to their charges. Many were now capable of walking and wanted to get up and move around. Robert was among them. Joe picked Trudy up and carried her to dinner.

"We have reservations at a lovely place over here," Sarah heard him say to her. Trudy swooned. They were extraordinarily cute.

Maxy, the young fisherman's mother, mixed the greens Amy and Herb had packed with berries and flowers and a dressing of herbs and rabbit oil that Amy had made. It was delicious. They parceled it out as equally as possible. Mandy took some to the three patients, but none were interested in the salad.

The meat came next. Everyone got a good-sized piece of pig and cougar. Many of the new members were anxious to eat that menacing cougar. Predator was not as tasty as herbivore, but that didn't matter to those who'd feared and hated the beast. Sarah needed the respect and support of this new band that she presumed had, until recently, belonged to Robert, so she served the cougar. They nodded their appreciation to her as they passed.

Olivia saved the remaining berries for those who were still dealing with the effects of scurvy.

Sarah patted her on her back. "Good job out here. They're all looking so much stronger."

"They seem like good people, Sarah. I think they'll fit in," Olivia added.

Sarah responded, "Hope so."

Sarah had two fires constructed out by the animals to keep predators away. Erika stationed three guards by them for additional protection. The remaining bones from the cougar were, with great ceremony, fed to the dogs, who served to protect the larger animals. Many of the new Family members who'd lost friends to that cougar stood and watched as the dogs gnawed on the last vestiges of the beast.

As they did at home, all gathered around the fire after the evening meal. Sarah led the meeting.

"First, I want to welcome our new Family members. I am thrilled to have found you. I'm even more thrilled to have found Joe's beloved wife, Trudy. Joe Jr. will be beyond happy." Everyone cheered.

"We're so pleased to have you and are looking forward to getting you all safely back to the compound. We sent our messengers back to camp with the tiger. They'll be expecting us late tomorrow afternoon. Our goal is to sleep well tonight and have a light breakfast, which Gus is already preparing. Big hand for Gus." They all cheered Gus.

"I want to get out of here as early as we can. We have a lot to load up for the journey. It's about a six- or seven-hour trek. We don't live around the corner. It was a long way here and will take most of the day to get back tomorrow. We'll stop for water. We'll stop for lunch. Again, we have that covered. Right, Gus?" He nodded and she continued.

"We have a group set to meet us most of the way home with more water and some snacks. Probably berries, but who knows. They'll make sure we get home safely.

"OK, let's see. Who are we? Most of you have met me. I'm Sarah. I've been dubbed the leader of the Family, but we are led by many. You'll meet our co-leader, Ms. Watson, who is a people genius, which I am not. And Molly, who is masterful with the kids.

"We have great leaders who run the cooking crew, of which Gus is a founding member. He's also on our hide and cowboy crews." Gus tipped an imaginary hat. "We have a wood-gathering crew; bowhunters; engineers, who made the sleds, or travois, to haul our supplies, among many other ingenious inventions; a manufacturing team, who we affectionately call the Seamstresses, who made the baskets and ropes; and the wood carvers, who made the bowls and spoons we ate soup from along with many other things.

"My partner and soul mate, Tom, runs our chiropractic and massage area. Doc, obviously, and Olivia run the infirmary. We have beauticians, trappers, fishers, gardeners, pharmacists, chemists, performers and a whole host of other experts to make our lives easier.

"My daughters—well, Robert's and my daughters—Janie and Jazz are also leaders despite their young ages. Jazz has several responsibilities. She leads our team of stone cutters. All the points you see on our spears, all our stone tools, are made by or at the direction of Jazz. I'm on her team as well. It's not so fun to be bossed around by your daughter, but she loves it." There were several chuckles.

"Jazz will also be on our bamboo team. We work with nature to take only what we need and what nature wants to provide us. That's worked out well for us so far. Jazz communicates with the poisonous green snakes who live in the bamboo stand where we'll get some of our building materials. Jazz created the saw to cut the bamboo, and it's magnificent.

"Janie, our youngest, gathers our edible plants, from fruits to greens to flowers to mushrooms to herbs for seasoning and medicines. That lovely salad is courtesy of Janie and her crew. The dressing was made by Amy, our head cook.

"Janie, and this will come as no shock to Robert, is also the resident clown and one of our fine performers." Robert smiled and shrugged. "Roger leads our entertainment.

"Erika, of course, along with Ms. Watson, is my right hand. Ms. Watson is sort of the Family mother. Erika is my best friend and sister. You'll see the three of us together a great deal. Erika's essentially head of operations. She organizes the work teams, keeps track of everyone and works closely with Joe on security. Joe runs our security force, leading the guards and shoring up our other defenses.

"Marshall, over there, and Samantha, over there, are our spear hunters. They downed that weird pig for our dinner tonight." There were several cheers.

"So, bottom line, before I bore you all to tears, I am the de facto leader, but this is not a ruled group. We, and you are included with us, are a community. We are a huge team dedicated to the survival and joy of one another in this crazy new world. We love one another, which is the driving force behind our successes. We welcome you into our Family, but please take time to understand how we work. Talk to your assigned Family member. Think about where you'll fit best. Everyone works. We try to allow you to do so in a way that best fits your abilities. There is no prejudice. Everyone is valued for who they are. We don't merely tolerate differences, we embrace them. So, talk that through.

"Normally Ms. Watson explains all this, and she'll do that tomorrow, I'd imagine. Let's get some sleep so we can get up early and be on the road as soon as we can. Agreed?" Murmurs from the crowd indicated consensus.

"Oh, and one more thing. We have several allies. A few you've met—the tiger, horse and elephant. The tiger escorted our messengers back to our compound earlier. He provides security to us as long as we safeguard his family. A family of bears lives in the woods to our west. Same deal. We protect them and they protect us. They come down to our pool every morning to fish and drink. We have dogs that protect our front entrance.

Some are traveling with us. They also hunt with Marshall and Samantha. We have four horses. Three are with us. One is having a foal soon.

"I know you've had your differences with animals around here, but we've found that it's much better to become allies with your neighbors. Erika and I tried to reach a peaceful accord with your cougar, but he had other plans, which resulted in him becoming dinner. We killed him out of necessity, not choice. Please respect our friends both on the way home tomorrow and in camp. I'll go over how to behave around each when we get out there tomorrow morning and when we get home. Note, these are *not* pets. We do not own any of them. They are not part of the Family. They do not come into the compound, except the horses and on rare exceptions. They're all independent, positive spirits with whom we are allied. Do you all understand that?" Of course, she knew they didn't. "I know, it's different, but so is everything else." She paused for several seconds. There was remarkable quiet.

"Any questions?" She waited again, and this time there were murmurs throughout the camp.

"OK, hearing none. Let's get some sleep. I, for one, am exhausted. Find someone to cuddle with for warmth, and I'll see you all in the morning."

She found Erika, and they chose a place outside the camp, near the entrance and close to the animals. They spent the next hour preparing the pig and cougar skins to be tanned by Bobbi when they got home. When they were done, Erika wrapped them in a carrying hide that had been full of water.

Erika had guards stationed around the perimeter of the camp. Erika and Sarah would take the third shift, the most dangerous one, when predators who hunt at dawn would be out.

Sarah lay down and patted the ground in front of her. Erika lay there, and Sarah wrapped her top arm around her and slid up tight against her back. Erika reached back and laid her hand on Sarah's hip. They were asleep in minutes.

FORTY-SIX

Sarah and Erika watched as Michael, Jack and Zach carried another of the sick out of the camp to be tossed into the ravine for the scavengers. They were relieved this death happened while most were still sleeping, during the final shift change.

"Wash well, boys. We don't want you or anyone else to get whatever killed those people," Erika reminded them as they passed back toward camp.

"Yes, ma'am."

"We don't want to get nothin' either," Jack said.

"Good. Thanks," Erika added.

"Sure. Any time. See you in a few." And they disappeared into the darkness of the woods. Erika had also released the two guards stationed out by the animals, and they also headed inside.

"You good out here all alone?" Erika asked Sarah.

"Sure. I'll be fine. I could use some alone time really. Not from you. Just from running everything. It gets tiring, and it'll be a very busy day."

"Yeah, I understand. This has been a stressful trip. Robert's strange, kinda scary." Erika took a deep breath and stared at the starry sky. "Finding Trudy and losing Joe. Dealing with all this death and sickness."

"Fighting the cougar was fun." Sarah hoped to bring her focus to something positive.

Erika looked back at Sarah. "Boy, did I need that!" she said with a smile.

"Damn straight. Me too. It was nice to release so much tension on that big male bastard."

"Alright, girlfriend, take care out here. Holler if you need anything. I'm going to take my post."

Latifah wandered over as Erika set off through the woods.

"How are you, ol' buddy?" she communicated to Latifah. She stood with him for a few minutes, absentmindedly stroking the soft hair of his mane. They watched the sunrise together, though the horse had little interest in it. Soft warm colors spanned the sky, pushing back the darkness and promising new warmth and a trip home. She connected to the natural world around her. Birds singing, insects buzzing in the trees. Rodents scurried about in the grasses. A hyena couple were not far off in the brown grasses, rising and caring for their young.

Suddenly, the three young men burst through the woods. They were carrying another of the sick and apparently now deceased. Although she'd made it through the night, barely, she died before the trip home. They passed Sarah, carrying her limp body down to the ravine and unceremoniously tossing it in. They backed several feet up the hill and watched as the scavengers arrived to devour her. It didn't take long. The birds, vultures and ravens arrived first. This alerted the others. The two hyenas emerged from the grasses, tore off an arm from the carcass and were gone.

The boys were reveling in the destruction of a human corpse as though they were watching a Fourth of July fireworks display, slapping each other and pointing. Then the rats arrived by the thousands and covered the ravine. The birds dove for bits and pieces. Within 15 minutes, the body was completely gone. It was amazing, even still. The three boys walked back, talking about what they'd seen as though a ballgame had ended.

"Not a word in there about that! Understand?"

"Yes, ma'am," they all responded.

"Hey, while you're here, why don't we get the travois sleds mounted on the draft horse and elephant?"

"Sure."

"Should I get Gus?" Zach asked.

"Go in and wash off really well. Get that dead person's germs off you. Have Erika send out a couple of guards to relieve me out here, and I'll come in and we'll figure it all out. Let's do that."

"OK." The three jogged back into the camp area. Within about ten minutes, a couple of young female guards appeared from the woods with their spears.

"What are your names?" Sarah asked, determined to be better at this.

"Mary," answered the tall and sinewy one.

"Connie." She was shorter but muscular. Both had brown hair and eyes.

"OK, Mary, Connie, there's a family of hyenas out that way, but they shouldn't bother us. Still, keep an eye out. Watch the grasses for movement. This is prime hunting time for big cats, but I didn't sense any. Can you two connect at all into the nature in this world?"

The two twenty-something women shook their heads.

"Alright, lesson one. There is energy all around us." Sarah went through the same spiel Erika had gone through with the two young runners, but this lesson related to the broader expanse of nature. It took a few minutes of breathing and letting go before they began to get it.

"OK. Focus on everything around you. Connect with the horses, elephant and dogs. Feel them. Connect with them. Feel the birds, rodents, lizards, insects and snakes all around us. The simpler the animal, the more neutral their aura and the harder they are to sense. Insects are the worst, but they have a spirit. You can keep the ones that want to bite you away with the power of your soul, if you know how. We'll get to that later. Now your goal is to sense anything big and menacing, like a lion, cheetah or hyena. Got it?"

Mary and Connie nodded unconvincingly.

"Confidence. Power. Love. Positive forces. No doubt or apprehension. Those are negative energies. Focus. You can do this. I'll be back soon. See with your eyes but sense with your soul."

Sarah patted them both on the arm and headed back to the camp. She glanced back and saw the women talking about the lesson.

Olivia met her at the entrance of the camp. "The last of the sick is awfully close to death. He can't eat, is barely coherent, and his fever is through the roof. He's showing the final signs of this disease, whatever it is. If he's like the others, he'll be gone before we leave."

"I hate to root for death, but we can't transport him back with us. Have the boys bring him out front near one of the fires. Make him as comfortable as possible, but the real objective is for him to die here before we take off—ideally before any of the Family head out there. We've been dumping these bodies into a ravine, and it takes the local scavengers about 15 to 20 minutes to make them disappear, and they are not quiet about it. So, I'd rather folks not be out there when he dies and is put in there."

"I know, it's gruesome." Olivia cringed.

"Got that right." Sarah was conflicted but knew the right thing to do. "I feel inhumane or something, but I know all that's left is an empty machine. The soul of the person is long gone." She reflected quietly. "So, let's get the sick guy out there. No accelerating the process, but he'll be closer to his body's final resting place so we can move him quickly and get on our way."

"OK. I'll get the boys on it right away."

Sarah saw Olivia round up the three guys and lead them back to where the last dying man lay. Within minutes, they were carrying him out through the woods to the area where the animals were waiting to be loaded up.

"Over here," Olivia instructed. "It's out of the way. We don't need anyone infected. Now go wash again."

Most of the Family members were up, and Gus had begun feeding them as Sarah, Olivia and the young men returned to the clearing.

Breakfast was cold dried wild pig and cougar along with the remaining greens, which were beginning to wilt. The people with the worst cases of scurvy received the few remaining berries. It wasn't gourmet, but it was edible, healthy and gave everyone strength for the journey.

Erika oversaw the packing of their gear. The entire Family was involved, along with quite a few of the new members. Olivia returned outside to the sick man. Mandy was wrapping up their few remaining medical supplies. They'd gone around the group early that morning and changed dressings one last time. They were out of the juniper salve, bandages and most everything else.

"SAAAARRRRAAAAHH!!" came the scream from out front. It was the combined voices of Mary and Connie, the two guards.

"Erika, boys, with me now!" All five sprinted out to see what was going on. Many in the Family followed at a slower pace.

"They're coming. Look! There are thousands of them," Mary shouted as Sarah broke through the brush and onto the beaten-down grass at the entrance to the camp. Rats. Thousands of rats were coming at them, toward the dying man, from the direction of the ravine. The two hyenas were waiting at the edge behind them.

"Fuck. They smell the sick guy!" Erika screamed. "They sense death and are coming for their share. OK, boys, pick him up. We're headed to the ravine. When we get close enough, throw him in."

"But he's not dead yet," Olivia protested.

"How close?" Sarah demanded.

"Pretty close. Based on the others, pretty close."

"We can't bring him home with us. We have no idea what he has. We can't leave him here. He's drawing those scavengers to us. We have to sacrifice him for the greater good," Erika reasoned.

"Hold on. Give me a second with him." Sarah ran to the man.

"A second's all you've got," Erika urged.

Sarah entered the lotus position and did her best to connect with the man's soul. It was afraid. She calmed it, allowed it to realize that death was not the end but a new beginning. The man's soul settled, and she guided it out of its body and released it to the universe of spirits. The man's body was dead.

Olivia ran the short distance to him and put her hand on his neck. "No pulse. OK, he's dead."

Erika yelled instructions: "Pick him up, boys."

Sarah stood and faced the oncoming carpet of rats. "Erika, with me!"

Erika sprinted to her side. The rest of the Family was streaming out of the woods. The boys stood beside the man behind the two women. Olivia retreated a few paces.

"We need the Storm," Sarah said.

"What the fuck is that?" Erika's voice was strained.

"I have some of the power of the Storm inside me. It's what allowed me to defeat Tony. It's unpredictable and I can't always control it, but I think *we* can. I want to share it with you, and I think we can make it a part of our spirits and control it with love, together."

Zach screamed, "Do whatever right now because they're almost here, and they look hungry enough to eat all of us."

Sarah took Erika's hands and engaged with her soul, already entwined with Sarah's. Her Bear spirit released the Storm into her and guided it equally within each of them. Erika gazed into Sarah's eyes as the two absorbed the Storm spirit, felt its power soak into them, using the love they shared to fuse it with their combined spirits as an intensity neither could grasp welled up within them. When Sarah and Erika turned toward the rats, they appeared larger and glowed bright red as one.

"Grab the fucking body," Michael screamed to his mates.

Sarah and Erika focused the intense spiritual heat of the Storm at the rats, controlling it together. She shot a look of gratitude to her sister. Fear flowed from the Storm spirit into the simple souls of the rodents as the women screamed at them, the same blood-curdling scream they'd delivered to the cougar. They advanced on the nearly unbroken field of rats before them. The rodents in front stopped in their tracks, but the rats behind marched forward into and atop them until they felt the fear hit them. Some sat up. Others turned immediately.

The two women marched forward, in complete control of the Storm's power, and the pack of hungry rats began to retreat. The men followed with the corpse.

The vultures and ravens took off in near synchronization from tree branches and rocky outcroppings, cawing in protest. The rats ran over one another in their efforts to escape, backing up, zigzagging and scampering into and up the far side of the ravine.

Soon the humans were within yards of the edge. "Now!" Sarah screamed as the women parted. The young men rocked back and tossed the body in. "Back," Sarah ordered in a lower voice. The boys sprinted to the others as Sarah and Erika settled the Storm spirit within themselves. The rats, interested only in a meal, backtracked and ran into the ravine, descending from all sides upon the corpse.

FORTY-SEVEN

Sarah and Erika slowly backed up. After taking several deep breaths to regroup their spirits and gain control, they finally faced the Family.

"And that's how you get rid of nasty pests," Erika announced, breaking the tension. Several people laughed.

Robert stepped forward accusingly. "You killed that man! He was alive, and you threw him to those beasts."

Sarah replied, "You're wrong, Robert. He was moments from death, but I connected with his spirit and guided it from his body, and it went willingly. When they picked him up, he was dead. Those beasts, as you call them, were simply following their natural instincts. They sensed death and were on their way here to find it." She shifted her attention to the entire group that had gathered.

"My job as leader, why I am the leader, is to protect the entire Family from danger. I didn't want to sacrifice that one sick and dying man, but there was no way I was going to allow thousands of rats, a hyena couple and a bunch of birds to descend on this Family. You, my Family, come first. There are others whose responsibility it is to care for each of you individually. It is my job to make the very hard decisions required to protect the Family as a whole. That being said, when the men tossed that body into the ravine, his soul was gone. The body was empty."

Erika stepped forward. "Sarah's nearly sacrificed her own life, more than once, saving this Family."

"Yeah," said Lizzy, who Sarah proudly remembered was one of the girls saved from the zombie teenagers. "I'm alive today because of Sarah. So are my friends back home."

One of the three big guys interjected, "Dudes, we told you not to mess with those two women."

"Yeah, we're with them," Michael said.

"We're at your service, your majesties." The three knelt before Sarah and Erika.

"Rise, you goofballs. Thank you for your service. I know that was tough. Now, go wash again then tell Gus we can toss that water." Sarah once again addressed the Family, "OK, the show's over. We have a ton to do to get out of here this morning. I want to be on that road out of this godforsaken place in an hour. Got it? One hour." Then she hesitated. "Not that I have any way to measure an hour, but dammit, you know what I mean."

The Family chuckled, and she and Erika smiled in relief. Robert was not happy and stormed back into the camp, his young assignee scampering in after him. The others proceeded more slowly, each new person paired with a Family member.

Sarah took a deep breath and centered herself. "Erika, this is our power and our curse to share now. We must use it wisely and control it well. It's getting stronger. It doesn't come from my animal spirits but from that crazy Storm."

"It's dark and scary, but also so alluring," Erika acknowledged.

"We're back and that's good, but I fear that this can take control of us. We need to be careful. The darkness from that Storm acts strongly on our spirits. Meditate with me."

Sarah took the lotus position, and Erika did her best to follow suit. She couldn't make her feet do what Sarah's did, gave up and sat cross-legged. Sarah waited patiently for her to get settled.

"Close your eyes." These were the last words spoken out loud. Their spirits easily connected as they settled into deep meditation. Sarah guided them away from their bodies into the universe of spirits. The experience was peaceful, serene, warm and sensual. The souls of the two women swam together in harmony. Sarah searched for and found the Storm spirit, deep within herself, strong and vibrant. Erika was there, feeling it with her. It was the more positive side of the Storm, the part that had brought nature back to the earth, but it had done so with a vengeance and with general disregard for human life.

She and Erika's entwined souls embraced the Storm spirit. Together they were strong enough to allow it to interact with, rather than be controlled by, their souls, to become a part of their combined spirit. Her confession to Tom beside the raging fire in the eastern woods had released so much darkness from her soul. The battle with Tony had released the last remnants of the evil side of the Storm from within her, but she'd retained this portion. She wasn't sure that had been a good choice, if it had even been a choice. Robert's presence was creating more negative energy. That darkness and conflict was what the Storm fed on.

Sarah worried that perhaps she had endangered her sister by sharing it. Erika did not have the Bear to control it if it ran amuck. But she knew in her soul that it felt good and right for it to be shared with Erika. Together they could control it, use it for good, to protect their Family.

It seemed as though they were there for hours—floating, sensing, enjoying the bliss of seemingly total consciousness—when the universe of spirits guided them back to reality. The powerful spiritual energy of the Storm, now shared between them, settled comfortably into their collective souls.

Sarah, returned to her body, opened her eyes, as did Erika. The air was sweet. The sun was warm. The tension was gone. It had only been minutes.

"It's now ours." Sarah reached across and took Erika's hands. "I couldn't control it without you, without your love and support. We share that awesome power now, and we must use it for good, which we always will." They stood, hugged and kissed, and then headed in with the others to get ready for the trip home. The Family was still filing through the woods back to the camp. Other than the two female guards, who seemed stronger somehow, no one had even noticed them sitting in the grass.

"You can do that too, you know," Sarah said to Mary and Connie over her shoulder. The two began talking, occasionally glimpsing at Sarah and Erika as they faded into the woods.

FORTY-EIGHT

"I hope those scavengers are done by the time we're ready to load everything," Sarah said as they walked. "We don't need the loud crunching of bones as a backdrop."

As expected, the battle over the corpse took about 15 minutes, all while the entire Family, save the two guards, were in the camp packing. By the time they were back out in the clearing to load up, the scavengers had done their efficient, instinctual job.

Four older people who'd be unable to walk the whole way, although they were feeling much better, were helped onto the sled behind Big Gus. Olivia wanted to keep them separated as they were most likely to be vulnerable to the illness. They'd ride on the empty hides that had held supplies on the first half of the journey.

Joe would ride atop Bubbette on a hide with Trudy in his lap. She could rest her leg on the back of the big animal, which would be a lot more comfortable than being carried by Joe. Plus, as brave as he wanted to be for her, there was no way he could carry her all the way back to the compound. He was conflicted about sitting while others walked, but he wouldn't have left Trudy for the world. They'd been separated for too long, and he was mad at himself for giving up on her. Now that he'd found her, she'd be his sole concern until she was healed. Everyone reassured him that they agreed with his decision. Erika had let him know that she'd cover his security duties until he was ready.

"She's awfully nice," Trudy said.

"She's a great colleague and friend. You'll get to know her better, but she's pretty busy around the compound."

"She was pretty busy around here."

"Sarah and Erika have a lot on their shoulders. I try to support them in any way I can. You'll like Ms. Watson too. They really run things, those three."

"I'm sure you're wonderful too, honey."

"Awww, Joe is the most wonderful," Sarah mocked. "Now, get up on that elephant. We've got to get moving." Everyone laughed. The elephant helped Joe up first and then basically lifted Trudy up with her trunk. Joe guided her from atop the animal and helped Trudy get situated.

Sarah mounted Latifah, and Erika mounted Sergio. They rode around to make sure everything was in order.

"OK," Sarah yelled, "Gus!"

"Head 'em up and move 'em out!" came the familiar cry from the front of the caravan.

Gus got the draft horse and elephant moving forward, side by side, dragging the grass back and flattening it in the other direction as they plodded forward. The Family streamed along behind the two big animals. Sarah felt like she should raise her spear in the air and part the Red Sea or something. Instead, she rode out ahead then stopped to sense the world around her. *Nothing, and nothing was always good.*

Erika arrived beside her a few seconds later. "Gonna be a long day."

"Yep. I need a blade of grass in my teeth or somethin', doncha think?"

The two rode side by side, about 30 yards ahead of the two pack animals, scanning carefully for anything that could cause them more headaches. Erika had her guards stationed around the Family. She put the two female guards they'd worked with that morning in the far back and had instructed them to practice tuning into the world around them. They'd excitedly agreed.

"Apparently they sensed the rats before they saw or heard them. Good sign, eh?"

"Why is it that only women can do this?" Sarah wondered out loud to Erika.

"Hmmm" was Erika's only reply.

Sarah continued, "Jazz can talk to snakes."

Erika nodded.

"It's Samantha and Claire who communicate with the dogs. Marshall just treats them like pets." The two trotted in silence for a while, thinking but coming to no conclusion. Sarah finally spoke again. "Maybe men are just stubborn. Oh, by the way, what are the names of those three guys who've been helping us? I've heard them tons of times but have totally forgotten already."

"You suck so bad. Oh my god. They've been doing things for you for days and this entire trip, and you have no idea what any of them are called?"

She sighed. "Nope. Not a one."

"The bigger guy, the blond, is Jack. Quite a hunk, don't you think?"

"Yep. Nice body. Nice, uh, accoutrement. The three of them are sort of hanging out with those three young girls, the two new ones and Dana, who came with us."

Erika rolled her eyes. "How do you know her but you don't know those guys?"

"I don't know. I don't. I can't remember the guys, for some reason. I don't connect to them in any way. I think that's the issue. Of course, I want to. I try to. I care about the Family, the whole Family. Tom and Ms. Watson help me with their names. I'll get them all eventually."

They rode quietly for a while.

"OK, so what're the names of the other two boys? Just their names, no extraneous info."

"Michael and Zach."

"OK. Remind me later when I talk about them at the fire tonight."

"You bet." Erika laughed and Sarah joined in.

"We'd better ride reconnaissance and make sure the coast is clear in front, to each side and behind. I'll head forward several hundred yards. You take the north side over near those woods," Sarah suggested as she pointed, "and then back to make sure we're not being followed. I'll check out the tall grass to the south. Good?"

"Good. I'll get the girls to tell me what they've sensed around us; see if they're making progress." The two women rode out on their respective missions.

FORTY-NINE

After several minutes, having noticed nothing untoward, Sarah and Erika met at the back of the traveling group.

"We're moving at a snail's pace," Erika noted.

"It's been about an hour. Things look good out in front. Time for a break, a drink for everyone, and then we'll get some of the new folks up on mounts so that we can move more quickly. You and I can walk with the rest."

"Awww." Erika faked a pout then smiled. "On it, boss."

Erika took charge. "Everyone, let's take a quick break here. Olivia, check out all the wounds and whatever. Let's get everyone a drink. If anyone needs a little dried meat snack, we have some. Ration it, though. That's all we have. Sarah and I have checked out our path, and it seems pretty safe right now, so we're going to get as many of our new brothers and sisters up on mounts for the balance of the journey. We need to pick up the pace."

Sarah, wanting one last review before giving up Latifah, rode far out in front of the group along their intended path before returning.

Five of the fourteen new Family members were already riding: Trudy and the four older folks. The latter got up and moved around during the break. The remaining nine were divided up: the two women who the young men had been flirting with were helped by Michael and Zach onto Latifah, and then they helped a father and son onto Sergio. A short man and a tall woman, both emaciated like the others, were helped up onto Big Gus. The young couple Sarah had spoken with were lifted onto the elephant and helped up by Joe. Robert stayed off to the side and, when asked by Gus, refused to ride. Sarah couldn't care less, and anyway, they didn't really have room for him.

Once everyone was ready, Sarah took a place at the head of the procession alongside Gus. Erika followed in the back, still focused on the environment for any possible issues. Sarah said to Gus, "We're going to have chiggers worse than I've ever had chiggers."

"Still early. Still colder'n 60 at night. Ain't no chiggers."

"Well, if there is, I'll talk to Amy, Bethany and Franklin about making a vegetable oil and peppermint oil infusion. It'll help with itching."

"Fine with me. Ain't gonna be no chiggers." Sarah nodded. Gus was in a grumpy mood. Probably tired. It'd been a long trip for everyone, and Gus had worked his tail off.

The progression moved much faster and without incident. After about two hours, Sarah stopped the group again. The travelers drank the last of the water and finished the remaining food. Sarah and Erika guessed that they were less than halfway home. While the others rested, the two women mounted their horses and rode another perimeter to make sure nothing was stalking them. They neither sensed nor saw anything of concern.

"I hope Ms. Watson sends someone out with water to meet us in the next hour or so," Erika noted. "The sun's pretty harsh today. No breeze. It's downright hot, and we're exposed to the sun's rays. The sooner we complete the journey, the better. The troops are hanging in there but wilting. At the rate we're going and with all the breaks these folks need, we have at least three hours left. Hopefully we can move a little faster. Without more water, the rest of the journey will be tough."

Sarah gazed out over the grassy horizon. She sighed, "Yep." Trying to stay positive, she gifted her sister with a hopeful smile.

"Let's get on with it then." Erika patted Sarah on the shoulder.

The two dismounted so the new Family members could remount. The sun high above, with no clouds to block it, was bearing down on them. While the Family worked in the sun a good part of each day and were comparatively used to it, the new members had been living in a shaded grove in the middle of the woods. Many were already sunburnt.

"Olivia, what kind of hides do we have that aren't being used? We need to get something on top of these new folks. This sun's hard enough for us, but they're burning up." The two rustled through the sled behind Bubbette.

The water hide was pretty big but was wrapped around the cougar and pig pelts. They removed them and rolled them up carefully, and Michael and Sarah threw the water hide up to Joe on the elephant. Joe did his best to cover Trudy and the riders behind him, but it didn't completely do the trick. They were sitting on a hide to avoid the uncomfortable hairs on the back of the elephant. Respite from the sun was now more of an issue, so the riders agreeably removed it, which was rather amusing to watch, and then added it to their cover.

Michael mumbled to Sarah, "I'd rather walk in the hot sun than sit naked on that elephant's back." Even though he was quite tan from all his hard work in the sun back at the compound, his shoulders were getting red.

Olivia and Mandy took apart the portable smoker and passed out the deer hides to the riders on Latifah, Big Gus and Sergio. The hides didn't cover them completely, but it was all they had. Robert's skin was bright red, but he belligerently declined a small hide for his shoulders. *Still a macho dick. He hasn't changed, no matter how he's acting around the others.*

Erika happened by and saw that Sarah was watching Robert. "Such an ass."

Sarah nodded then addressed the group. "OK, everyone set? We have no more water and no more food, but we're pretty sure that members of the Family will meet us with some soon. So let's push on as fast as we can, and we'll be able to get through this."

The response was anything but enthusiastic. "OK, Gus."

"Head 'em up and move 'em out," he said without energy.

Sarah stood off to the side as the two pack animals gained momentum. Gus led them forward. Joe was doing his best to keep Trudy comfortable. She was sitting in his lap rather than on the elephant. *That's a very good man.*

Olivia had cut and gathered some leafy branches from a tree not too far from their path that she'd placed on the four older people lying on Big Gus's sled. *Good idea.* The Family rescue party she'd led out on this successful mission trailed behind the animals. They were a strong and proud bunch. She saw that Erika had separated Jack from his two comrades, and they were engaged in friendly conversation at the rear. She was a few years his senior, but he didn't seem to care. The other two men and Dana were engaged in a lively conversation. Olivia and Mandy circulated among the group, checking on people.

Randi had joined Mary and Connie in the back, and all were working on connecting to nature. The male guards were paired off and chatting, some dragging their spears behind them. Overall, they seemed in good spirits.

Sarah waited as the entire procession passed. Several people waved at her. They were doing their best to move faster. The allure of home was rising within them. The women in the back stopped what they were doing and nodded in deference to their leader. They paused for her, but Sarah waved them forward.

Sarah fondly watched her receding Family. *What a strong group they'd put together.* She couldn't have been prouder. They'd saved 14 people who were days, at most, from death. Now most were getting better and stronger. While riding, they were tired but chatting. Robert walked alone on the north side of the procession.

Erika gestured to her from the back of the pack, yelling, "Are you coming?" The big guy she'd taken a fancy to was right beside her.

"Yeah." Sarah jogged up to her dear friend and gave her a hug. "We did it, girlfriend. We're going to make it back with 14 people we saved from death. I was just reveling in that."

They walked in silence for a while. Sarah could sense that Erika wanted some alone time with Jack.

"You two have fun back here; I'm heading to the front to make sure we're not flanked by anything. Erika, you got it back here?"

"Sure." Erika glanced up at the young man. "Don't we, big fella?"

"Absolutely, Sarah."

Sarah smiled broadly and jogged past the Family, the horses, travois sleds and pack animals and around front to Gus, intentionally sticking to the southern flank to miss Robert.

"How's it going?"

"Goin' fine, ma'am. Movin' along right nicely now. I reckon we're past halfway, maybe a bit farther."

"You're probably right."

Sarah fell in step beside him, but neither spoke. She was staring at the horizon, hoping against hope that she'd see a few guards with water and refreshments. Even the strongest Family members would soon languish in this blazing sun.

"Hot one, ain't it?"

"Yep," she agreed then, without warning, ran ahead toward the horizon. Without knowing the reason, she had sensed it was the right thing to do. About 30 strides out, she saw Tabby and Jenny, the two cross-country runners, gliding like gazelles through the grasses in front of her. The tiger was keeping up with them.

Sarah stood tall, as was their custom, and greeted the tiger.

"You're almost there. Maybe 24 minutes," Tabby began their back-and-forth way of speaking.

"Probably less."

"Depending on your pace."

"Based on that," Jenny said, pointing to the lead animals, "I'd say 21 minutes."

"OK," Sarah interjected, "let's say less than half an hour. Half an hour to what?"

"The Family, but not that long, for sure," Tabby said.

"They're all waiting." Jenny was smiling. Neither was breathing heavily.

"I think if you get to that rise, you'll see the smoke."

"What smoke? Smoke from what?" Sarah asked.

"The barbecue," Tabby answered.

"Everyone's there."

"Yeah, we have water, tea, lots of meat and berries and greens—all prepared or being prepared."

"We're beside a nice pool in the creek for the animals to drink from and others to wade in to cool down."

"Under some shade near the bamboo."

"Almost everyone's there."

"Oh, that's wonderful. Well done, ladies. Run around to the others and tell everyone. They need a big dose of good news right about now." The girls ran off, bounding around the various animals, conveying the news in their teamwork staccato style.

Sarah yelled the now ten or so paces back to Gus, "Can we pick it up? What do you think?"

"You talk to these beasts. Tell 'em what to do. I'm not doin' much 'cept kinda walkin' 'em."

She knew he was right. Although she and Erika had not figured out the reason men couldn't communicate with animals, that did seem to be the case, and it irritated Gus, who considered himself a horse whisperer. She engaged the two pack animals. They were tired. She communicated what was ahead and asked if they could increase their speed. They obliged, and the procession began moving at a good pace. The Family, spurred on by the news, had no problem keeping up. A few moved from the back to the sides but soon decided fighting the high grasses was not worth it and moved back.

The two runners returned to the front. The tiger had remained beside Sarah while they delivered their news.

"Any messages for the Family?"

Sarah thought carefully. "Nope. Tell them we love them and will see them as soon as we can get there. Oh, and have the children sing." The girls were off. Sarah thought about joining them. They were truly relishing the opportunity to just run and run fast. They were born to run, but Sarah was tired.

The faint voices of the children, singing a song she'd grown to love, rose in the air. She turned to observe the group behind her. *Now we'll see who's Family among the newcomers.* She saw all the original Family members perk up and peak around. Of course, they heard the singing. Trudy heard it. The father and son and those riding the horses heard it. She jogged around back. Two of the four older folks heard it, but she wasn't sure the other two, both by far the oldest, could hear at all. The couple on top of the elephant behind Joe didn't seem to hear it and were confused at the delight shown by Joe and Trudy. *We'll have to watch them, but at least their spirits are positive, and they appear to be trying to hear it.* Joe said something, then all of a sudden, recognition crossed their faces. *Perhaps they just hadn't known what to listen for.*

She ran around the elephant to get a look at Robert. He was walking alone, head down, with no reaction whatsoever. *Nothing.* She watched for quite a while. As the others became increasingly animated, he trudged forward, his arm limp at his side and his skin crimson. *What a shocker. Robert isn't Family.*

They crested the small rise on their path, and sure enough, she could see the pillar of smoke blowing north in a rising breeze. Her heart leaped. She knew her girls and Tom would be there, waiting for her. It'd only been one night away, but it seemed like forever. She skipped out in front of the cavalcade, staring at the horizon as it beckoned her.

The tiger stopped and veered toward the south.

"Aww, damn. Now what?"

She hadn't sensed danger, which was odd. Of course, she was preoccupied with getting back home. She tuned into the tiger now.

The female tiger and the two cubs emerged from the thick brush. Sarah grinned as the male tiger rubbed cheeks with his mate as the two cubs romped around their feet chasing a butterfly like two kittens.

Sarah bowed her head to the female, who acknowledged her in return. Together, the five jogged to the top of the next small rise.

FIFTY

S arah stopped in awe. There they were—the rest of the Family, all except for the General and probably the Seamstresses, who would've stayed with him, and probably some guards. Even the little children were there, running about in the shorter grasses among the sweet-smelling wildflowers and clover in the shade of the wood on the south side of the east-west passage. Guards flanked all sides, standing ready to protect.

The procession was coming up behind her. Sarah sprinted ahead. Here, the grass was shorter, softer and easier to run on.

Joe yelled from atop the elephant, "There they are!"

The entire rescue team behind the pack animals cheered, emerged and began to jog toward the Family. They helped the riders down off the horses so they could run as well. Erika and Jack gathered the hides strewn in their wake and tossed them on the travois behind Bubbette.

When the awaiting Family became aware of the oncoming parade, they returned the cheer. She saw Janie and Jazz and Tom, carrying Joe Jr., running toward her. She broke into a full sprint to meet them. The elephant, Zach, Jack and Michael helped Joe and Trudy down, and he carried her toward their young son, who was screaming like a kid who had received a puppy for his birthday, running with delight toward his parents.

Sarah jumped into Tom's arms and kissed him deeply and then jumped down to hug her daughters. "I missed you guys so much." She paused and connected to Jazz, "Your father's coming. He's admitted to me his mistakes and promises to apologize to you. Keep an open mind but be wary at the same time."

"OK, Mom. I'll try." Sarah could feel the growing trepidation within her. "You OK?" Jazz asked.

"Oh sweetie, I couldn't be better." She gave her daughters another big hug and kissed each of them on the head. Just then, Robert emerged from around the big draft horse.

He was walking as quickly as he could toward them. Jazz froze. Janie suddenly took off through the grass. As she approached, Robert knelt in the grass and let her run nearly full speed into his arms. He winced from the injury to his arm and sunburn but wrapped his other arm tightly around her and kissed her over and over. Holding Janie's hand in his, they walked slowly toward Sarah, Jazz and Tom.

As he got close enough, Jazz said remotely, "Hello, Father."

Robert burst into tears and fell to his knees. "Jasmine, I'm so sorry. I had no idea what I was doing. I don't even remember it, but I'm sure it happened. I love you, and I would never have done that if I hadn't been soused all the time. I'm so sorry. I know you may not be able to accept that right now, but I'll do everything I can to make it up to you." Tears streamed down his cheeks.

Jazz looked up at Sarah, who said, "Honey, what does your heart tell you?"

After a deep breath, Jazz stepped toward her father, who reached for her. Jazz stopped abruptly. "Not yet, Dad. I'm not ready for you to touch me yet. I'm sorry."

"No, sweetie, I'm sorry. And I understand. We'll take our time." Robert was smiling, his right arm wrapped around their youngest. "At least I'm here, sober, and that's not going to change. I'll do whatever it takes."

Sarah stepped in to break the tension. "Robert, this is Tom."

Tom extended his hand. Robert stood up and took it. "Tom, it's nice to meet you. Sarah's told me a lot about you." Robert squeezed Tom's hand hard, staring directly into Tom's eyes, more threatening than conciliatory. "You're a lucky man," he said without the slightest sincerity.

The tiger, who was only a few yards away with his family, growled under his breath at Robert. Robert's glare continued as he released Tom's hand. Tom stood erect and strong, maintaining eye contact. The standoff lasted seconds, but the gauntlet had clearly been thrown down.

"Robert," Olivia broke through the tension, "we need you to see the doctor about that gash." Robert held Tom's eyes for another second before Janie pulled him off to follow Olivia.

Without speaking, Sarah let her tiger know that she appreciated the warning, but for now, Robert was weak and being as civil as she could have expected, and she'd like to keep it that way.

Reunions were happening all around, and each rescuer introduced their charge to the rest of their new Family. Erika and Olivia kept those newcomers who Olivia feared may be infected, those with slight fevers and more difficulty keeping food down, away from the group. They were sad but seemed to understand. "Could just be the heat and exertion," Olivia reported to Sarah.

The elephant and the horses drank thirstily from the stream that ran in the shade of the northern forest. The elephant sprayed himself and then others with his trunk. The Family, new and veteran, along with the children, laughed and danced in the shower, refreshing their hot skin. The newcomers and rescuers took turns stepping into a shallow pool to cool their feet and legs. Some even settled into it to cool their entire bodies. A gentle breeze had picked up, and some clouds were forming off to their southwest. Sarah could feel the impending rain in the air.

Big Gus and Sergio greeted the mare, who'd been enlisted to drag everything out. Latifah found some shade and tall green grass. The Family dined on nicely seasoned and cooked elk, deer and turkey meat, a vibrant salad and baskets of berries. They all lounged around in the shade and mingled with the newcomers. Olivia, Doc, Mandy and the team attended to the few deemed ill and to the numerous infections Olivia had begun treating the day before.

"Eewwww," Sarah and Tom heard Janie squeal when Doc removed Robert's bandage.

"This is a dangerous infection," Doc said.

Sarah and Tom strolled over. Jazz didn't follow but wandered off with Mark. As Doc examined Robert, Sarah wondered to herself if she wouldn't prefer if he died from this infection.

"This is going to hurt a great deal." Doc washed the wound with some warm water. Robert screamed in pain, tears welling up in his eyes as they met hers.

"That, unfortunately, was the easy part." Doc scrubbed the wound with a rough hide. Robert again cried out. Others were gathering around, but Sarah noticed that none of the newcomers had come.

"What's that?" Robert asked about the brownish paste the Doc squeezed out from a bladder. "The stuff Olivia used was bluer."

"This is a lot stronger. It has juniper berries like that one, but this also has crushed mustard seeds and peppermint leaves. Your arm is seriously infected. Let's hope it's localized to the arm, but I can't tell if it's migrated. You have the early stages of gangrene. That means your skin is dying. What we need to do before it infects more is cut it out. We'll treat it with more antibacterial paste and sew it up. You'll likely faint before we're through. That's tough, but if we don't treat it, you'll lose that arm, and perhaps your life," he emphasized.

"Can I do that thing Sarah did for the lady with the bad ankle?" Sarah was shocked that Robert didn't know her name. Unlike her, he was gifted with names. She was beginning to realize that Robert hadn't been a leader after all. In fact, perhaps he wasn't well liked there. No one walked with him and no one came to his aid now.

"What thing?" the Doc asked.

"I'm sorry. Sarah can only do that with other women," Olivia lied, "and we don't have a man with those capabilities. It's a unique skill, and like most unique skills, it's pretty limited. I'm sorry. You'll have to handle this on your own." Olivia clearly didn't like Robert any more than Sarah did.

"We're here, Daddy," Janie offered.

"I know. I'll try to be strong for you, but if I pass out, will you catch me?"

"Of course." Janie jumped in behind Robert.

"Alright then, Doc, do what you need to do. I kinda like that arm."

"No guarantees. We're pretty primitive here, but it's the best we can do. Bite down on this so you don't bite your tongue." Doc handed him a leather guard, which he put in his mouth.

When the Doc applied the poultice, Robert screamed as it burned his already delicate skin. Then he passed out.

"Is he OK?" Janie asked.

The Doc felt his pulse in both arms then laid a hand on his forehead, which was quite warm. "He's hanging in there. No warmer than he was when he got here. Not sure we got this in time, but we'll do what we can. Mandy, can you bring some wet skins, please?"

FIFTY-ONE

Sarah and Tom decided Robert was in the best hands possible and returned to the party. They both received a nice basket of food. Even Sarah wolfed down the marvelous meal. As they were seated with others in the rescue party, the newcomers streamed by to thank her for saving them. Most were feeling much better since their issues had largely centered on a lack of food and water. With plenty of both over the previous 24 hours, they were all feeling invigorated. The few with minor cuts and abrasions were healing well. Enjoying the shade and guided by their assigned Family member, most were now settling in smoothly with their new Family. They were gaunt, but then again, most of the Family members, while healthier, had also lost a lot of weight since the Storm.

The clouds gradually covered the sky, and it started to rain gently. Ms. Watson stood in the middle and declared the barbecue a success, welcomed the newcomers and thanked everyone. The entire Family helped to pack things up and got the procession going again. The new Family members all walked, even the older ones, and Joe carried Trudy the rest of the way back to the compound.

The tiger family, who'd remained nearby during the picnic, nodded at Sarah and sauntered back into their woods. The two runners had shared some of the Family's food with them.

As they walked back, Janie was with her little group, chatting and laughing; Jazz was holding hands with Mark; Sarah was arm in arm with

Tom, feeling blissful; and Erika and Jack were walking and talking. Doc and Olivia had determined that the few who appeared ill could be monitored and treated in the infirmary, and so none were quarantined outside the barrier.

Everyone seemed happy and at peace . . . everyone except Robert. He was unconscious and alone on the sled behind Big Gus. His wound was now sewn up and bandaged.

The procession still took over an hour, but it felt like only a few minutes.

Her heart soared as she walked through the gate amid her now larger Family, sharing love and holding hands with Tom, smiling from ear to ear. *I—we—can handle Robert.*

FIFTY-TWO

Fists rained down on her as Sarah struggled to defend herself. Blood swirled. Bourbon filled her nostrils. "You're mine, bitch! I own you!"

Sarah woke with a start; sweating, heart racing, she jumped up to a ready stance. Her head pivoted back and forth. Where was he?

Tom, startled, said, "What?" She was shaking, and he pushed himself quickly to his feet. "Honey, what's going on?"

One of the night guards jogged over. "Everything OK?"

Sarah's heart settled, her eyes cleared, and she came to her senses. The night air was cold against her wet skin. Tom grabbed her and held her.

"It was a nightmare. I haven't had one that specific in days, since before the battle with Tony. Tom, Robert was beating me, and I couldn't do anything to stop him." Her eyes welled up with tears. "Tom, I can't have him here. I need him gone. He's bringing everything back. I don't think I can handle it."

Tom had no idea what to say, so he held her tight. "It'll be OK, honey. You can handle him."

Eventually he guided her back down to the ground, still in his arms. Memories flooded into her consciousness. She couldn't sleep, even though her body was exhausted. Tom whispered calming words, trying to soothe her. After a time, it began to work. Sarah let him in, let him calm her with his love, molding into his body, feeling his warmth and, finally, dozing off.

Though she avoided Robert, each of the next three mornings, she awoke in terror. Sarah had kept herself busy as she attended to the affairs of the Family, helping to assimilate the newcomers and preparing for the first foray out to bring back bamboo. The rescue had used a lot of resources that needed to be restored; hides needed to be repurposed and food replenished.

Even as her love with Tom strengthened, Robert's presence was stressing Sarah emotionally. Robert had recovered quicker than expected and was gaining strength. He'd joined the wood-gathering team, and though his arm was in a sling and he was still in obvious pain, Jake said he worked hard and pulled his weight. He was gaining allies and friends in her Family, which she resented. Although she didn't complain, her body language told the story.

At Tom's and Ms. Watson's suggestion, she left in the late morning the second day back with Erika on Sergio and tiny Randi riding on Big Gus, which others found comical, but Sarah was not in the mood. They traveled on a reconnaissance mission to the west, gaining an understanding of the terrain, checking on the status of the many grazing animals, locating the small herds of horses and cattle, and showing Sarah how they were keeping track of and now helping the former revolutionaries. It felt good to be away, but all the while, she worried what Robert was up to back in camp. Janie was spending time with him, but Jazz would not go near him.

When they returned, late in the afternoon, Sarah spent time with Jazz and, of course, the ever-present Mark down at the river making points and knives. They also planned the trip to bring home bamboo. Amid this work talk, Sarah tried to bring up Robert, but neither wanted to talk about it. They shared an unresolved anger and couldn't come to discuss it.

She dined with Tom. Jazz spent time with Mark, and Janie was spending more time with Robert, which bothered Sarah. One more thing. All the joy she had felt just a few days before, after realizing how much she loved Tom, was drained from her existence. She was quiet, withdrawn and a bit distant with everyone. She chose not to speak at the evening campfires, asking Erika, Randi and Olivia to tell the Family about the rescue and what they found in the western fields. She barely paid attention to Janie's performances.

After waking up to another nightmare and being calmed by Tom, she needed to get out of the camp. She enlisted Gus, who Sarah was bickering with for no good reason, to bring in the herds of horse and cattle they'd found the previous day. Erika and Jazz joined them, with Jazz riding behind Sarah on Latifah part of the time and on Sergio behind Erika the other. The troop brought in the horses in the morning and the cattle in the afternoon. They'd work on teaching more Family members to ride, and Gus would teach a group to care for the cattle and learn to milk the cows, several of which were pregnant, but Sarah had no interest in either at the moment. Marsha led efforts to expand the barrier to create a pen for the new animals in the fields next to the river, just north of their barrier. Sarah was also apathetic about that project.

While she'd been away, Robert and Tom had gotten into a brawl. It was resolved by the time she'd returned, but Robert had stalked off out of camp without shaking hands with Tom as ordered by Ms. Watson.

"He attacked me from behind while I was working on a patient. I flipped him over, and we stood facing each other. He growled that he owned you, and I told him he was full of it; no one owns anyone here. Then he came at me, and I smacked him on his wound. That knocked him to his knees. By then, the cavalry came and broke it all up. We haven't seen him since."

"Damn him. Are you OK?"

"Fine. Not even a scratch. I told you I could handle myself."

As they hugged, she realized that Robert didn't affect her like Tony did. He wasn't evil from the Storm. Her skin didn't crawl when he was around. Instead, her blood boiled. He was mean and brutal, and she knew it personally. She could not quell the hatred she felt for him.

"I thought I was over it," she lamented as she walked with Tom out in the grasslands after dinner. "I thought I could handle it, but he simply cannot stay here. I can feel it in Jazz too. I don't know what to do, but he has to go."

"What if you gave him a chance, some time? See if you gradually get over it."

Sarah turned on him like he was defending a murderer, which, to her, he was, "He shot me, Tom! Three times! He put me in the hospital two other times! He raped me more times than I can count, and he tried to rape Jazz! He beat me, tormented me, and I barely made it out alive! He's a mean, horrid, despicable man, and he needs to be kicked out of here! That's all there is to it. It's him or me."

"I'm sorry, honey. You're right, of course. He attacked me, and he's a total jerk. Problem is, I don't know what to do."

They walked and held hands. Sarah stared at the grass, not feeling a thing around her. Her chakras were blocked, clouded, dark.

After a bit, Tom broke through her stupor. "Do you remember this place?"

Sarah looked up. It was the little pool Tom had taken her to heal. This was where their love affair began, where she'd made love with him the first time. He picked her up and held her in the way he'd carried her out here that warm spring day. He walked into the pool and laid her in the same place. He began to caress her in much the same way, talking to her, calming her, reassuring her of his love and her strength.

She relaxed and settled into deep meditation. She soon left her body and entered the universe of spirits where she'd found so much peace and solace in her life, including during her time with Robert. Peace and joy surrounded her, and she could feel the souls who love her emerge.

"Honey, he's just a man, and a weak man at that. You need to forgive him. It's the only way you can escape this."

"Mom, how can I? You know what he did to me. What he did to Jazz. What he did to Janie, though she obviously doesn't remember much. How can I forgive him for that? He was supposed to have died or at least be stranded halfway across the country."

"Hatred is the worst of the negative emotions," her mother's spirit warned. "It is the only one that can block your powers, your strengths. Your positive spirits cannot get through it, and you know it in your soul. I know you hate him. I know he deserves it. I know Jazz hates him. I know that you empathize with her. But you cannot let her go out to deal with those snakes with this much hatred in her heart. If you can't do it for yourself, your family or your love for Tom, do it at least for Jazz."

Sarah knew her mother was right. It was the only way. "Thank you, Mom." Sarah came out of the meditation and settled into the cold water running over her body and the feeling of Tom's strong hands. While her heart knew she was right, her mind struggled with her mother's advice.

"Tom?"

"Yes, honey?"

"I spent some time with the spirits just then."

"I could tell." Tom sat back and waited for Sarah to tell him whatever was on her mind. *He's so good at listening,* she thought. *That's another thing I love about him.*

"My mother tells me that I have to forgive Robert." She paused to let that sink into her own soul. Tom didn't say anything. "I have to forgive him or I'll lose my powers. If I lose my powers, Jazz can't communicate with the snakes, and if she can't do that, then we can't get bamboo. Claire can't relate to the dogs. I wouldn't be able to summon my spirits to keep the Family safe." Saying it out loud seemed to help herself process it. Tom began massaging her feet, which he knew she loved. "So, I obviously have to forgive him. I'm just not sure I can, Tom. I'm not sure he deserves it."

"You're not forgiving him for Robert, honey. You're forgiving him for you. It doesn't even matter if he accepts your forgiveness. It's about clearing your soul, not absolving his. That's for someone or something else to do."

She thought about this and realized Tom was right. "Coming out here was a great idea. You're right. I need to do this. I need to forgive him. That is going to be so hard, but I have to figure out how to do it. I don't even know what to say."

"Say, 'Robert, I forgive you.' That's it. You don't have to go into detail. As long as you mean it from the depths of your soul, it will free you of him forever. It's not complicated." He hesitated before offering another piece of advice. "And Jazz needs to do it as well. You need to help her do it so she can clear her soul and move on with her life. If her soul is not cleared, she won't be able to communicate with the snakes regardless of your situation. You have to tell her what your mother told you."

Sarah sighed. "You're right. OK, thanks for helping me through this. I feel freer already. I'll take care of this. Let's get home. I need to talk to Jazz tonight."

FIFTY-THREE

he Family was beginning to gather around the fire. Jazz and Mark joined them as usual. Janie arrived a few minutes later.

"Hi, sweetie," Sarah said to her youngest.

"Hi, Mommy, Tommy, Jazzy," she replied as she plopped into her mother's lap.

While the Family was settling in, Sarah turned Janie in her lap and put a hand on Jazz's shoulder, and her oldest faced her mother. "What's up, Mom?" she asked.

"I've been out of sorts because your father is back. I want to apologize for that. I've been selfish. So, Tom took me for a walk to help straighten me up. I meditated while out there and communed with the spirits; my mother gave me a talking-to. So I'm going to share with you her wisdom and Tom's advice, both of which brought me back to reality.

"Jazz and Janie, we have to forgive your father. Janie, I'm proud of you that you've already done that, it seems. Jazz, you and I have to get there."

"But, Mom, I don't think I can."

"Forgiving Dad is for us, not him. Whether he accepts it is irrelevant. We cannot free our souls until we let him go, get him out, forgive him for everything he did to us, and mean it all the way down to our souls. I'm going to do that. I *need* to do that. Jazz, think on it, but I'm not letting you near those snakes until you do and you feel like your soul is free." She stared into the fire then back at Jazz.

"Honey, I know I already feel better. I'm already reconnected to this world. I know in my heart this is the right thing to do. I think so do you, but sleep on it if you want, and we'll talk more in the morning."

Ms. Watson, knowing Sarah's family were having an important discussion, had waited to begin the evening's affairs until they were finished. Ms. Watson stood and commanded the attention of everyone.

She addressed a few minor issues. Gus addressed the horses and cows. Marsha discussed the new barrier extension and asked about when she'd get her bamboo for the new Family home. Then Ms. Watson gazed down at Sarah, who nodded. *Now is the time,* she realized.

Sarah winked at Jazz, who looked uncertain even as she guessed what was about to happen.

"Everyone, I want to apologize for my behavior the last couple of days. As many of you know—well, probably all of you—Robert was my husband in the old world. He's admitted to me that he was brutal during our marriage. He was, and is, an alcoholic. I think he'd admit that now as well."

Robert stood and began to walk around the fire. A sense of trepidation rose inside her. She didn't need him in the middle of this, even though she was forgiving him. Tom stood and put his hand on her shoulder. "He has to be part of this process, honey. You know that. You're way more powerful than he is as long as you keep your soul clear. Don't let him or your past in again."

Jazz stood and moved next to her. Then Sarah felt Janie take her other hand. Robert continued around the fire. He was a few feet in front of her now when he faced the Family.

"Sarah is understating what I did to her. For at least seven years, I beat her, putting her in the hospital twice." (Memories flashed through Sarah's mind: pain, blood, bourbon.) "I'm a horrible drunk. That's the first time I've ever admitted that. It nearly killed me; it nearly killed Sarah."

Sarah could feel sympathy from the Family, sympathy for Robert, as he bared his soul before them.

"I was so trashed most of the time that I don't even remember most of the things I did. The last time I saw Sarah, I was drunk out of my mind and I shot her." As Robert spoke, Sarah reflexively felt the three places where the bullet scars had once been. "Honestly, I wanted to kill myself, but I couldn't bear to die and not take her with me. I needed her in the next world. I have no idea how she survived, but I'm glad she did. Sarah, I still love you." Robert started toward her.

Sarah jumped back. Anger boiled up within her. "Well, I certainly don't love you, or even like you, Robert. Get away from me." Tom grabbed her shoulders in his hands, holding her tight as she recoiled into attack mode. She looked up into his half-smiling, gentle face.

"Calm down," he whispered. "Deep breaths." She complied. She felt her senses return. The Bear wrestled with the anger, dragging it down into her, packing it away, hiding it again in a safe dark space within her. "You stood up for a reason," Tom continued, still whispering.

She wanted to run off with him, to their special place, and fall into his arms for the evening. She knew what she needed to do, gave Tom a half-hearted smile, then tried to exude confidence to her frightened oldest. Jazz was ready to either join in a battle against Robert or sprint away with Mark. Sarah, realizing the importance of this moment, pulled herself together, and Tom released her. She gave Jazz a powerful smile, which calmed her daughter, then turned to Robert.

She took a deep breath, rolled her shoulders back and stood as tall as she could. Robert's 6'4" frame was filling out again, and he towered over her. To her surprise, she felt Jazz beside her. Standing together against Robert gave them both power.

"It's OK, Mom. This is the right thing to do. We both need to forgive him, before the entire Family, and get this behind us." She did not muffle her words or whisper. Everyone nearby heard her, including Robert.

Full of pride, Sarah felt an energy rise within her. It was that wisp of Asha that had entered her after the Storm—pure expansive love. She could actually see the front of Robert light up as she emanated that energy, glowing white. Robert took a step back.

"Robert. First, Jazz and I want to thank you for your confession. It was hard to relive as you spoke, and I'm sorry for the outburst." Sarah was speaking loud enough for the entire Family to hear her. "What you did to me and to Jazz was brutal and inexcusable, whether you were drunk or not. I think you know that."

Robert said nothing, regaining his footing, standing tall and dominant. He was a good two inches taller than Tom, a bit broader and easily the largest man in camp.

"Despite all that, and because you have taken responsibility for your actions, I have decided to forgive you."

Jazz followed immediately, "I do too."

For a fleeting moment, Sarah and Jazz felt freedom, and then Robert's face burst into a huge grin as he came toward them with arms extended.

"STOP!" Sarah growled, and he did. "This does not change the way we feel about you. We have forgiven you, and meant it, to free our souls. It does not mean we want you back in our lives in any way, other than as a resident of this compound. It does mean I'm going to allow you to stay, so long as you pull your own weight and behave."

Robert stood, his face struggling between elation and sadness. There was empathy for him from the Family. Sarah could sense it.

Ms. Watson stepped forward. "Robert, you have been blessed with a new beginning, a new opportunity to live and become part of a wonderful community, free of alcohol, and forgiven for your past sins. There are almost 90 people here. Make new friends. Find a new love. Get to know your children. Rebuild those relationships. Find a new home here."

"Sarah, I love you. I always have and still do. You're my wife. We never got divorced. We're still married to each other. I want you back. You belong to me." Murmurs flowed across the Family.

Sarah struggled to keep her anger controlled and welcomed Tom's hands on her shoulders, "First, as you know, there are no marriages in this community. Our legal relationship in the old world is no longer relevant. Second, I love Tom. I love him more than I ever loved you. As long as he'll be with me, I'm with him. Finally, Robert, that ship has sailed. You brutalized me and tried your best to murder me. You and I are no longer anything—not even friends. And unlike in the old world where you held all the power, in this one, the power is mine." Robert scanned the faces of the Family members around him and saw confusion. "We will coexist.

That is all. Find your way here but steer clear of me, and I will not interfere in your affairs. Do you understand?"

Robert hesitated. Erika rose and stood beside Sarah, followed by Randi, then Ms. Watson and Molly. Marsha, Olivia, Joe and others stood and began to line up behind her in support. Even more of the Family stood. Sarah poured love out into her Family and felt it flow back to her.

Before they could all amass behind her, Robert yelled, "Alright!" Robert's face was hard, anger shining from his eyes. He did not retreat but stood firm, his imposing frame towering over her. "Fine." His voice was menacing. "If you want to play that game, I can play that game with the best of them." Before Sarah could respond, Robert strode off into the darkness.

Someone from inside the Family said, "See, I told you. If we rescued that group, we'd bring another Tony into our Family." Nothing could have alienated Robert faster or more thoroughly. Sarah felt a twinge that she should change this perception, but her anger wouldn't let her do it. After things settled down and they'd lain in their normal places to sleep, a voice in her head said, "You're going to regret that."

FIFTY-FOUR

Sarah struggled through the night again. Nightmare after nightmare woke her in sweats. Robert beating her. Shots. Anger. The ever-present stench of liquor. Tom held her, soothed her, rocked her in his arms until she'd fall asleep, only to wake in terror again a couple hours later. She was not over Robert. The forgiveness had not worked. Something was wrong at a deeper level.

The morning was overcast with occasional drizzle. Sarah worked with the teams preparing for the excursion to secure bamboo the next morning. Robert was nowhere to be found. He'd joined the wood-gathering team, which brought Sarah relief. It took him out of the compound. With her excursions out of camp and his work in the woods, the compound was free of the stress of their relationship for most of the day. Jake had reported that he was a hard worker, though he'd spent a good amount of time exploring to their south against orders. "Still," Jake admitted, "he's huge and can handle large loads and regularly brings in valuable bark, roots and limbs for spears and the like. So, whatever he's doing, it's a benefit to the team and the Family."

Sarah went over the dangers of the bamboo mission, provided instructions and worked with Jazz on communication with animals, though of course, the teenager already knew everything. Sarah did sense that the forgiveness had helped clear Jazz's soul.

A scream came from the eastern woods. Sarah ran to and leaped onto Latifah, as Erika jumped onto Sergio. A guard tossed them spears as they raced out the gates. Joe and several guards sprinted out behind them. Sarah could sense the fear in her Family members in the woods and followed that sensation.

As she and Erika wove between the trees, their spirits connected. The cries for help came from deep within the woods, well to the southeast. Sarah heard shouts from men and women, obviously involved in some sort of battle. As Sarah cleared a small rise, the ground fell off into a dry creek bed. Latifah slowed to navigate down the side and through the uneven rocks at the bottom. The quarter horse did the same. When they climbed the southern bank and cleared the edge, they could see a few members of the wood crew, spears raised, facing down a small pack of wolves. Robert was standing off to the side watching, a sly grin creasing his face as she arrived.

The group backed up to open a path for the two women.

Sarah stopped Latifah and rose up on his neck, facing the eight wolves, who stood their ground but did not advance nor cower before her. "None of these is the pack leader. The pack is much larger. It's farther south. This is a hunting party. What happened?"

"They attacked Joanna," Robert said calmly.

"How do you mean, attacked?"

Joanna was lying on the ground, her right leg bleeding from some sizable tooth marks. She'd been screaming and crying but had pulled herself together. "It was my fault. I strayed from the group. Freddy and I were looking for some bark and leaves that Bethany and Janie need in the infirmary. Robert had been coming down this way, so we thought it was safe."

Sarah never took her eyes off the eight wolves. There was something odd about them.

"Anyway," Joanna, whose pale white skin accentuated the crimson blood, continued, "we crested that hill and stumbled into those guys. I slipped and fell and must have scared them, and one of them bit me. Freddy screamed first. Then I did. Robert stepped in, and the wolves backed away. Then the crew came to protect us."

Freddy, a tall man with dirty-blond hair and beard in his thirties, added, "It's been a standoff ever since. They won't back down, and when we start to retreat, they follow. We didn't want to lead them back to the others."

The rest of the guards, armed with spears, crested the rise behind them. There were now more than 20 humans, all armed, against eight large wolves.

"Let me try to handle this. Everyone, stay back." Sarah slid off Latifah and ordered him back across the gully. He was the sort of animal a pack might like for dinner. Latifah begrudgingly obliged. Erika did the same. Sergio backed off quite willingly.

Sarah focused her attention on the wolves, guiding her Tiger spirit out and through them. She could see four of the wolves in the back begin to back down. She poured fear into them, and within seconds, they broke from the others and raced off south into the woods.

The leader of this group glared at her, engaging directly with her. She sensed anger, an emotion uncharacteristic for animals.

Sarah spoke to her Family without breaking eye contact with the male wolf. "He's angry. That's not right. Animal emotions are utilitarian. Negative emotions in a situation like this should focus on defense of the pack or attack for food, but not anger. That's a human emotion." Sarah paused. "The other three are followers. Part of the pack. No anger. They're simply following their instincts, which is following their leader. But there's something more. Something confusing him."

She focused her spirit on the lead wolf, a big and grey beast that, without her powers, would outmatch her physically. She channeled the Elephant spirit to protect her should he attack, her Bear for strength and, finally, her Tiger spirit, which she aimed at the wolf. Soon after focusing her energy, she could feel her Bengal tiger trotting toward them. The Family members scrambled away as the huge cat passed by. The tiger came up along her right. Erika moved to Sarah's left.

She could sense even greater confusion in the wolf as he glared at the tiger. Anger flared in his eyes. The tiger didn't understand, and neither did Sarah. She could sense the wolf threatening the tiger, and the big

Bengal looked up at Sarah, a bit afraid. Sarah faced the wolf, her courage strengthening the tiger. In the face of such odds, the wolf clearly made a strategic decision to back away. This was not instinctual as it was with the other three. This was a cognitive decision. *That's not how wolves, or any animals, process things.*

Step by step, he retreated, his three cohorts with him. The male looked at Robert, then back at Sarah, then again at Robert, who stood strong and calm with that confident smile. Sarah didn't move. When the leader realized none of Sarah's group were going to follow or attack, he glanced one more time at Robert, turned and sauntered with his team southward into the woods. He moved with attitude, not fear. At the top of the next ridge, the large wolf looked back over his shoulder then howled toward the sky. He returned his eyes to hers, glaring at her. She could feel his anger and determination, an anger aimed at her, and he was promising to return.

As the four crossed a ridge, out of sight, the humans cheered. Robert grinned. Sarah stared after the wolves. *Anger? Where does that come from in a wolf?*

Sarah turned to the tiger, they bowed to each other, and the tiger jogged back north into his part of the eastern woods. Sarah then addressed the Family, "Alright, folks, we may have stumbled into a turf war. Wolves are very territorial. I don't know where they believe their territory reaches, but it's somewhere around here. Be more careful. No wandering off again. Stay armed and in groups. Robert, that includes you." Robert ignored her. "Wolves are smart; they work in teams, and that male, the lead one, was uniquely intelligent. And he's not even the dominant alpha in this pack!"

"What should we do if they come back?"

"They'll be back. That wolf made it clear—they'll be back."

"Did you talk to that wolf?" Freddy asked.

Sarah took a deep breath. "That wolf told me they'd be back. He was pissed off at us—well, at me personally—and the tigers, and his declaration was a clear threat. I don't know how to explain it, but that wolf is different. He nearly spoke to me. He and his team will be back—maybe with reinforcements, maybe for a war." Sarah turned her attention to Robert. His smirk worried her, but she knew he couldn't be behind this. *He can't possibly communicate with these wolves, can he?*

Erika took over. "Joe, put some armed guards on our side of the creek bed when we're working. I'll figure out some defensible positions, but that ditch is a strong divider." She jumped onto Sergio and rode the quarter horse to the east as Sarah continued.

"We need the wood and stuff you all bring back. So, the rest of you, try to be more careful, stay together and work farther north. Try to stay away from the wolves' territory as much as possible." She glared at Robert. Something was up with him. His little "game" perhaps.

Everyone nodded except Robert, who stood defiant and calm while the others scrambled back across the creek bed to perceived safety. Freddy and another man helped the injured Joanna up and back to camp. Erika returned on the quarter horse, riding atop the second ridge above the dry creek. Latifah walked up beside them. Robert hadn't moved or said a word.

Sarah slid down into the creek and leaped in two steps up the northern bank. Standing beside the two horses and her sister, Sarah stared into the dappled forest to their southeast. "I have a strange feeling about those wolves, Erika. Mixed. Confusing. Angry, which is too weird for animals, and desperate, maybe."

FIFTY-FIVE

"Damn!" Sarah exclaimed while Tom worked on a patient in his chiropractic area. A few others were receiving massages from the therapists, including Tanya.

"What?" he asked.

"We may have another huge problem that I have to deal with."

"What now?"

"Really smart wolves who, I think, want to kick our asses."

"Wolves are territorial, right? Maybe we stumbled onto their land?"

"I could feel the lead wolf of the group we ran into. He was angry. Greedy. Mad. Those are not emotions that animals exhibit. Those are human emotions. It's why we fight and wage wars. Only two animals are known to fight wars: humans, of course, and our closest relative, chimpanzees. All other animals avoid confrontation. They may fight for superiority in the herd or pack. That's instinctual. They don't do it because they're mad. They may fight over the edges of territories, but they tend to demonstrate their strength and the weaker side acknowledges defeat and backs off. No anger. Just survival of the fittest."

"So, what's so special about these wolves, exactly?"

"Tom, the lead wolf of this group was pissed off at me. If we didn't have him so outnumbered, I think he'd have attacked. And he would've attacked *just* to attack. We aren't natural food for a wolf. There's a lot of prey out there. Plenty of food. He made a strategic decision to retreat. *Strategic*, not instinctual. He thought it through."

Tom shrugged his shoulders.

Sarah took a deep breath. "And there was something else. I almost felt like he was listening to Robert or something, but that's impossible, right?" Tom shrugged. Another cleansing breath. "It's fine. Not like I have anything else to deal with but a pack of strange, cognitive wolves in league with my crazy, violent ex." Sarah took several steps away then said to Tom, "I have a very weird feeling about those wolves, Tom."

She started to walk away again but stopped and turned back.

"What now?" Tom asked.

"The team is heading out to bring back bamboo tomorrow. What if these crazy wolves attack while I'm gone? Someone always attacks when I leave."

"First of all, and get this through your head, you are not going. Second, they're wolves, not strung-out teens or rebel humans or anything like that. They're just wolves looking for food."

"OK. I know that makes the most sense." She paused. "So why am I not convinced?"

"Then ride down there. Have a conference with this brilliant wolf leader and figure it out. Reach an accord like you did with the other animals. I don't know what else to tell you, sweetheart." Tom held his hands in the air. "We're big boys and girls. We have spears and arrows and knives. This place is impenetrable, certainly for wolves. We can defend this compound against a pack of wolves, for crying out loud."

Sarah stood there, unsure.

"It'll be OK." Tom stood, stepped over his patient and walked up to her. He put one hand on each shoulder and stared into her eyes. "Sarah, my sweet, you're more connected to this place than anyone. Search whatever it is that you search when you meditate. Go to that universe place you took me to. Whatever you need to do, the right answer will come to you. Trust your own instincts on this one."

Sarah took a deep breath. "OK. Thanks."

Tom kissed her on the forehead, gave her a big hug, which she cherished, and released her. "I have a back to fix, so go. You know you can do this." He released her and headed back to his patient. She stood in place and gazed at the barrier inside the edges of the southeastern woods, on the other side of which was the territory of cognitive wolves.

FIFTY-SIX

As they gathered after dinner around the main fire, Sarah was lost in thought, worried about Jazz out alone with the snakes, the new wolf threat from the southeast and whatever Robert's game was. Before Sarah was ready for it, Ms. Watson was asking her to say a few words. Sarah kissed Tom, Jazz and Janie, stalling to collect herself. She scanned the crowd. Robert was not among them. *Where could he be?* Done with expending so much thought and energy on him, Sarah decided to talk about the positives.

"Family, it has been an insane ride. It feels like forever ago that we were spending our days at ordinary jobs, in offices or elsewhere, and returning to our families and our homes that were air conditioned, bug free and safe from rain. When the Storm came through, we were left with nothing and frightened out of our minds." Then she remembered how Tom had put it. "We were frightened beyond our wildest nightmares. All the other nightmares and horror films in the old world ended with a return to a state of normalcy. That won't happen for us.

"We've taken time to mourn those we've lost from the old world, those we've lost from our Family since the Storm, and we've greeted newcomers and welcomed them into our Family.

"We've worked hard. The great thing is that our collective hard work is paying off. We have a secure place to live that is getting more beautiful every day. We have outstanding hunters, fishermen, trappers and gatherers who bring home enough food for us to eat. We have great cooks who turn that raw food into marvelous meals. We've survived the weather, some crazed attackers, a revolution of evil lunatics, rescued 14 new Family members, and we've become one with our surroundings and our neighbors. We have to continue to respect nature, to respect those who share this area with us and to take from the earth only what we need." She could feel connections with the members of the Family grow inside her. Warm and positive kinship.

"We've done this through cooperative hard work. We are diverse peoples. Most of us didn't know anyone else in this Family before the Storm, except perhaps as the parents of another child at the school that was once here. Now we're a Family, working together for the good of everyone. We must keep that up. We have to build this community and grow it. There will be new children born. We'll have more deaths. It's inevitable.

"Life in this new world gets easier but not easy. Summer is coming. There'll be more to eat, and life will get simpler. It's during this time when we must prepare for the winter to come. As most of you who've lived through a St. Louis winter know, it's likely to be harsh, at least for most of the season. Food will be increasingly scarce. We have to prepare ahead, and we must do that together. It will require the entire Family, and it'll be hard work.

"The next major task will be to construct a building for us to all fit in, live in and grow in so that we can get out of the rain and be secured from the frigid cold of winter. Marsha and her team have designed a wonderful structure. They're working on covering the wood so that we save more from the storms. They'll be working on a few other structures to practice and test the designs for our home. They need our help.

"As you all know, Erika and I found a stand of bamboo, and Jazz and I have visited it. Bamboo is a phenomenal building material. We're making our—" Stopping abruptly, she felt her muscles becoming strong and powerful.

The Family's eyes grew big as Sarah's aura suddenly burned bright orange. The situation became clearer to her as the low growl of wolves reached her ears from the woods and the Tiger spirit exploded inside her. *They're in trouble!*

FIFTY-SEVEN

"They need help, NOW!" Sarah exclaimed without explanation. Then with the grace and speed of the big cat, Sarah sprinted toward the front gate, Erica close behind.

Pointing to a guard, she demanded, "You! Open the gate." She grabbed a spear.

Latifah was already in full gallop, coming from the paddock with Sergio close behind. As her big black Arabian raced past, Sarah leaped, grabbed his mane, swung above him and landed gracefully on his back in one swift motion. Erika, channeling Sarah, did the same on Sergio, and they bolted out as the Family stood, mouths agape—all except Ms. Watson. Molly rallied the children to her and led them in a song.

Randi organized several guards, who followed the tiny warrior out of gate well behind the other two women and toward the dark forest, armed with spears. Olivia felt Sarah's spirit beckon, and without questioning, she ran to the infirmary and grabbed a bladder bag filled with the juniper compress and some leather bandages. She sprinted unarmed through the shocked camp and out the front gate.

"Stay," Sarah conveyed to Ms. Watson.

Ms. Watson calmly told the remaining group, "That's all Sarah will need." The rest of the Family settled back to wait.

Sarah, Erika, Latifah and Sergio used the Storm they now shared to become one focused being as she released all awareness of the compound.

Sarah brought forth and felt the ecstasy of the immense power and strength pouring from the four animal spirits into every cell of her being. An aura glowed bright red, connecting Sarah and Erika. They sped into the woods. It was the tiger's cub in danger. She could feel the tigers facing off against the wolves. There were several dozen; the alpha seemed to be there. The angry male certainly was, exuding a desire for vengeance. The tigers were protecting one of their two cubs. The other had been taken.

Sarah's vision, strength and agility peaked as they flew into the phalanx of wolves, startling them. Sarah slashed one with the viciously sharp edge of Jazz's stone tip, ripping a broad gash in his backside. The cry of pain from the wolf echoed through the darkness.

Latifah jumped. A crack joined the echo as Latifah pummeled a wolf's skull with a back hoof. Sarah could feel Erika close behind. Sergio didn't hurdle to avoid the wolves. The big horse's target wolf rolled and whined as Erika ran right over it, crushing it under Sergio's immense weight.

Sarah could feel the cub's panic, sense its location; she directed Latifah, his hooves pounding toward the cub. Erika steered Sergio off to the right to encircle the group of wolves. No words were spoken. All four animals, human and horse, acted in concert as the shared Storm aura flowed through the woods. Sarah focused the powerful Storm's energy forward, and it struck the wolf with the cub, who dropped its catch and whipped its head left and right, preparing to defend itself from whatever was attacking. The other wolves with it bared their fangs, but as the dark, soul-penetrating energy encircled them, they became disoriented, twisting frantically back and forth, trying to determine the source. As Latifah reached the wolf who'd taken the cub, Sarah slid off and drove her spear into its open mouth, through its body, landing on one knee with her hand near the wolf's jaws. Life flickered from his eyes.

Sergio flew in from the woods, landing his huge front hooves forcefully into the side of a wolf as Erika hung from the horse's mane, slashing another with a mighty gash through its side, blood gushing from the wound. A wolf turned on Sarah, its snarl low and guttural. Sarah grabbed the cub in her left arm and yanked her spear out of the dead wolf with her right. Yet another wolf arrived from the darkness. The two males stalked toward Sarah, fangs bared, growling, anger in their souls coming from the big male. They wanted her, but Sarah focused the fear created by the Storm, searing it into them and confusing them.

Latifah returned while one wolf attacked; Sarah advanced on foot, driving her spear into the chest of the wolf as Latifah reared, coming down with force on the other. Latifah leaped past and turned. Sarah jumped astride the pierced canine, tore her spear from his chest and two-handed it into the heart of the one stunned by Latifah.

Erika, on Sergio, raced through the darkness, stabbing her spear into attackers. Sarah focused the Storm at the others. Frightened, they ran farther into the forest. As Latifah rounded back, Sarah vaulted, grabbed his mane and mounted his back with the cub in tow. Erika impaled another wolf on her spear then wrested her spear from the beast, yanking the animal into the air. Another wolf retreated in a run. None of these were the leaders, the intelligent wolves she worried about. *Where are they?*

Sarah raced back to the tigers. She could feel other wolves in the dark woods around them. Sarah could sense their uncertainty, but there were many. Randi was leading the men in defending the tigers as best they could, but the number of wolves had increased. As they reached the standoff, Latifah soared over a wolf and Sarah dropped to the ground, landing next to the male tiger. Latifah retreated, ready to come when Sarah called.

Sarah reached one of the men. "Guard the cubs with your life." Her eyes bore into him like knives, and he knew this was no ordinary order. She held out the cub, but Olivia arrived and took it. Sarah's eyes were wild, glowing red like her aura, consumed by the energy of the Storm. Sarah lost all sense of the men.

Sarah turned to the tigers, who she could feel were frightened. She focused on the wolves around them. A spiritual power much like hers emanated from behind them. There was a faint glow in the woods directly in front of her. *Is it the Storm? The dark side?* She couldn't find the spirit behind the glow, but she sensed the large male inciting the wolves to attack. Anger. Greed. Power. These were not the emotions of wolves. This was a battle of wills, the alpha driving the ordinary wolves forward with anger, and her and Erika's Storm spirit building fear within them.

Sarah looked directly into the eyes of the male and female tigers, whose spirits rallied with the strength of her soul. They reciprocated her courage and ferocity. Now unified, they faced the wolves.

Erika and Sergio galloped in and out of the darkness, attacking the wolves on the far side of the pack, plunging her spear into one and then another. Randi was out among the wolves on the right edge, drawing their attention away from the tigers, spreading them out. Sarah could feel energy coming from her, connecting to something, somewhere.

The wolves, confused and outflanked, started to panic. She felt the male's anger as he tried to organize his troops, rushing back and forth behind them, threatening any who might back down. Two attacked the cubs. A man stepped between the wolves and the cubs and swiped his spear blindly back and forth. One wolf managed to scratch his leg, but Joe drove Trudy, his huge spear, into its side. Erika arrived, thrusting her spear into the other wolf and riding into the woods with it dangling gruesomely.

Sarah and the tigers glared at a group of seven wolves, and Sarah cast fear from the Storm spirit so malevolent that she could feel the animals back down. Her power was met by its counterpart, from the alpha wolf, its glow faint, but it caused the wolves to rebound. Above the growls and yelps, the pounding of hooves and the screams from the men, she thought she heard a voice, quiet and male: "Kill her! She is your enemy." *The alpha can speak?*

The wolves launched their attack. Sarah plunged her spear into the wolf in front of her, lifted it into the air and pounded it into the wolf behind with such force that all around were shaken. The male tiger, her tiger, sliced a huge claw across the faces of two of the approaching wolves, knocking them through the air. The tiger leaped, landing on top of the two sprawling canines before tearing their throats with giant fangs. The female tiger rose high on her hind legs and attacked two wolves at her end, killing one and knocking the other back. She pounced on it, ripping it apart with razor-sharp claws.

Sarah tried to extricate her spear from the wolf, but it was lodged in tight and broke. Two other wolves growled as they approached her, teeth bared. One wolf hesitated. The other jumped high to attack. Sarah rolled back and kicked it under its jaw with one foot and forced the heel of the other hard into its chest, sending it spiraling over her into a tree. The male tiger flew past her left arm, crushing the hesitant wolf's head in his huge jaws. She called to the men, "Spear!" One floated through the air. She snatched it, hurdled over the tiger and embedded the spear directly into the heart of another attacking wolf. Freeing it, she swung the spear with both arms to her left then deep through the shoulders of another wolf.

The men were screaming, struggling, faltering. Sarah removed the spear from the wolf, sprinted to their aid and two-handed it overhead and down through an approaching wolf. She stepped on its side and wrenched the spear free. Erika flew by on her horse and whipped her spear one-handed into the back of a wolf, lifting her spear and the wolf off the ground before the latter fell free with a whine. One of the men stabbed it. More wolves emerged. They were coming from every direction. The male tiger tore a huge gash in one, sending it careening into two others. The female tiger made quick work of another with a swiping claw then another with a crushing bite.

Erika dismounted her horse and joined Sarah. They were one with the tigers. They amassed the power of the Storm, and the two focused a torrent of spiritual power, felt by all present, into the woods at the wolves approaching them. The roar that came from the women, matched by the tigers and heard back in the camp, was all animal—guttural, resonant and ferocious. It was in no way human or female, stunning every creature there.

With concentration deeper than during the encounter with the rats, Sarah and Erika directed the full energy of the Storm toward the wolves. Sarah found the male, the alpha's top commander, and met his spirit. Angry but not evil. Powerful but perhaps not from the Storm. Intelligent but not crazy. There was another spirit, coming from their right, benevolent, connected, but from where? Confused, the big male began to back down. Desperation. Panic. His connection to the other wolves was broken.

Though the tigers, horses and humans were still outnumbered, the wolves that could retreated then ran away. Sarah could feel the male trying to unsuccessfully rally the wolves. Then he seemed to receive an order from the alpha, and he, too, ran off behind them into the darkness. Although the alpha had remained unseen, Sarah could sense that the master wolf was present, but she received nothing from its spirit. Then the faint glow she'd seen disappeared, and the battle was over.

FIFTY-EIGHT

Drawn forward by an invisible force, Sarah took several steps to follow it but was restrained by a strong hand. She jerked herself free, but her spirits, led by the Tiger and mixed with a trace of Asha's spirit, encircled and reined her in. She wanted to follow the alpha, but she knew they would meet again. The alpha and the male commander were the wolves they needed to fear.

In one motion, Erika vaulted back onto the quarter horse and held her bloodied spear above her head, her aura fading as the Storm spirit settled. She screamed into the darkness, "Victory!" On the ground, Joe carefully roamed through the massacre, stabbing the wolves to make sure they were completely dead. There were a few final yelps and then silence.

Erika's celebration brought everyone, including Sarah, to their senses. For the first time, she took in the scene around her. Many dead wolves surrounded them, with a few bodies deeper in the woods. Unlike Erika's jubilation, a deep sense of sadness overtook her. *Why did this need to happen?*

Olivia had treated the injured cub, which was still sitting in her lap as she tended to the guard's scratches. Olivia looked at the approaching tigers with a smile, and Sarah could feel Olivia silently convey to the female, "Just a couple of teeth punctures but nothing deep. The cub should be fine." Then she said aloud to the men, "The cub'll be fine. Roger will be fine as well." Sarah realized that it was their undaunted entertainer,

Roger, whom she'd ordered to protect the cubs. "We'll clean that up back at the infirmary, and I'll get some more antibacterial for it."

"I shall relish this badge of honor," Roger announced.

"That'll leave a scar, so a badge you'll have." Olivia had already applied the salve to the cub and was wrapping a leather bandage around Roger's leg to stop the bleeding. Olivia smiled as the cub licked her hand. She set him on the ground, and the cub trotted over to its mother as though nothing had happened. The mother gathered it in and kissed her baby the way any mother would a child almost lost. Sarah and Olivia could both feel her desire to discipline him for wandering off and to love him at the same time. This whole mess had been his fault.

Sarah turned to the two tigers and stood up tall, spear by her side and a smile on her face. The tigers, too, sat up tall. Then to the amazement of the onlookers, the two huge Bengals bowed their heads to Sarah. She nodded to each of them. She'd lived up to her promise. She'd had their back, just as the Bengal had been there for them. She watched as each adult grabbed a wolf by the scruff of its neck and the tiger family headed into the darkness of the woods. The male tiger glanced back one more time as he disappeared. She felt as close to him as she did to Latifah.

Joe said, "OK, everybody, the party's over. Let's go home."

"Get the wolves in the woods and the rest of these. They're our share. The tigers have all they want," Sarah spoke for the first time. Everyone did as they were told. She felt a hand on her shoulder, warm and kind. She turned. It was Tom. He'd been there. She realized that it was his strong hand that had brought her back from the crazy desire to chase the pack into the darkness of the woods. Tom's love had given her the power over the Storm spirit to return to her senses. Her smile widened, and she jumped into his arms, smearing blood all over his gorgeous body. He caught her and delivered a long, passionate kiss. She didn't want him to put her down, but she relented.

"Erika, lead us in," Sarah said. She nodded to Olivia. Their relationship had strengthened. As Erika gave orders that all the remaining wolf bodies be thrown over Sergio's back, Sarah felt the woods around her.

Robert appeared with three wolf carcasses and lifted them onto Sergio's back. He was unarmed.

"He didn't come out with us. When did he get here?" Tom asked.

As they walked toward camp, Sarah felt a tap on her back. "You wanted to follow her, didn't you?" It was Randi.

"Who?" Sarah asked.

"The alpha," Randi answered. She was about to respond as Erika led the group back into the camp to the cheers of the Family. Randi winked and ran ahead. Sarah walked in last, hand in hand with Tom. The applause grew as Tom pushed her forward and the others on her battle team turned, smiling broadly, to allow her to pass between them, covered head to toe in wolf blood. The Family was beginning to expect this sort of heroics from their leader.

Sarah grabbed Erika's hand and dragged her forward, acknowledging her and addressing the Family, "Thank you. Now, we're going to wash all this wolf blood off, if you don't mind." She blushed then led the band of warriors down to the river.

Gus said, "Bobbi and I'll take care of them wolf hides." The two were already inspecting the stack of dead animals as Michael, Zach and Jack unloaded them from Sergio's back. It'd be a long night for Amy, Gus, Bobbi and the teams that handled their meats.

The hides would be invaluable assets, especially come winter. The meat would be cut up. Sausages would be made from the organs. Both would be smoked that evening in the new larger smokehouse. Tendons would be preserved, largely to spring traps. Connective tissue and sinew would be used by the Seamstresses. Most of the bones would be preserved for tools, though there were more than they could use. Teeth and claws would be extracted for the Seamstresses to use on more necklaces. The rest of the bones, lungs and a few other parts would be taken by Samantha and Claire to the dogs. Tonight, they ate better than they had since the Storm.

FIFTY-NINE

Clean, cold water splashed from the falls onto her back and neck, sending tingles through her body and streaks of red and pink down the racing rapids below. Erika sat to her right, Randi beside her. Olivia had washed quickly and was now tending to Roger's wound. The other men had finished as Tom slipped in beside her and draped an arm around her shoulders. "You, my dear, are amazing. Scary as hell, but amazing. What you did out there today in the pitch black of the woods was off the charts."

She hadn't realized that it'd been that dark until the fight was over. In battle mode, she, Latifah, Erika and Sergio could see just fine. The tigers were cats, so seeing in the dark was one of their special traits. The wolves operated mostly by sense of smell and hearing. Sight was a significantly lesser sense for canines. Apparently, the other humans, including Tom, couldn't see much at all from beneath the thick canopy of the eastern woods. Although not as dense as the forest to their north, they were thick enough to block out what little light came from the crescent moon. She realized that the soft glow of their much smaller fires, or as much of the light that had filtered through the barrier and then managed to sift through the trunks of the trees, had been the only light available.

Sarah gazed deeply into his blue eyes. "Thank you for pulling me back. I was close to running after them." Then she leaned into him as he tightened his hold on her. "Your love brought me back."

"It'll always be there." He kissed her on the forehead as she stared down at the now crystal-clear stream running off through the trees, down to the big lake they'd seen from their secret place.

Her mind relived the battle with the wolves. The power she'd felt when she and Erica released the spirit of the Storm was only the tip of that iceberg. It was violent and nearly overpowering. Now she'd won two battles using the Storm. She'd also gotten her butt kicked releasing it against the crazed teens, though that included the dark side. *Still*, she wondered, *can we truly control it?*

As the battle raged this evening, she'd begun to lose touch with reality, lost within the Storm spirit out there in the dark. Even though she now owned it with Erika, the Storm spirit was elusive, harder to control. *What if Tom hadn't been there?*

On cue, Tom broke in, "We should head up, sweetheart. There's quite the commotion over all this."

Everyone else had already left the falls. She snuggled closer, wrapping her arms around his waist. "Thank you for heading out in the dark woods after me tonight. It took a lot of guts but, most of all, trust in me. Thank you for saving me, and I want you to know how much I love you." They shared a drawn-out kiss, lingering on each other's lips.

The human pain in her body that inevitably emerged from these superhuman battles pushed its way through to her consciousness. "Ugh. Honey, I'm going to need some tending to."

"I bet you are." His lips felt so warm and tender, she almost dragged him up to their secret spot but then decided that would have to wait.

He rose to his feet and reached down to help her up. She reluctantly followed. She felt a few additional pangs as she got up. As they strode up the bank and past the big birch and hickory trees into the fire-lit clearing, the Family rose to their feet, cheering and clapping. Tom released her hand and again nudged her forward to face her people. She felt love from everyone.

Whatever reticence the newcomers had harbored was completely gone. This was her camp, her Family, and she was their undisputed leader. She bowed to them as the applause grew louder. She studied the Family. *Where's Robert?* She scanned the compound for him, but before she could finish, she was engulfed by well-wishers.

SIXTY

The camp was bustling with activity early the next morning. Sarah had had another nightmare, reliving a beating she'd endured at Robert's hands. Throughout the night, Robert invaded her sleep. Now, after several poor nights of sleep, disturbing nightmares and the battle with the wolves, she was sore, tired and on edge.

Today they'd bring home bamboo. Jazz was excited. Forgiving Robert had helped her, at least. Perhaps it was the clear power demonstrated by her mother the previous night. Sarah wasn't sure, but Jazz's connectivity to the world was strong, so that was an improvement. Still, she worried about sending Jazz out to deal with poisonous snakes while she stayed home.

A good-sized contingent was going on the mission. Erika, of course, took charge of the group, giving orders and checking each detail.

Latifah was saddled for Jazz. Sarah stood with him, settling him for the journey without her. Gus would ride Big Gus. Sarah had called in her elephant and communicated with her that they needed help hauling the bamboo back. She connected with her tiger and alerted him to the journey near his territory and asked that he watch over the clan. Claire was taking a large contingent of dogs. Trudy insisted that Joe lead his contingent of armed guards. And, of course, two representatives from Marsha's engineering team would go, while Marsha was staying home with fellow snake-hater Sarah.

Travois had been adjusted from the rescue to allow the elephant, draft and quarter horse to drag bamboo back. Latifah would have none of it, which Sarah told everyone with the exasperated smile of a mother of a willful child. The three other animals possessed enough strength to bring home whatever could be cut down in the balance of the day. Plenty of food had been prepared overnight, largely from the wolf meat, for a hearty breakfast and lunch for the travelers.

By early morning, not long after sunrise, the entourage was ready to head out. Sarah paced back and forth on the hillock at the end of their maze, worried that once they'd reached beyond the limits of her spiritual powers, the entire thing would fall apart. As she paced, a young woman with Down syndrome fell in step behind her.

"Miss Sarah?" The woman tapped Sarah on the hip. Sarah turned and looked down at the dark-haired woman, who was less than 5 feet tall. "Miss Sarah?" she asked, tapping Sarah on her stomach.

"What?" Sarah asked, with too much irritation in her voice.

"I'm sorry." The woman bent her head and seemed to be crying. "I just want to help. I can help."

Sarah pulled herself together and squatted down. The woman looked up, reached out her right hand and touched Sarah on her left shoulder. Sarah had never actually met her, but then, she'd never met Tanya or, she was sure, a few others.

"I'm sorry I snapped at you. I'm nervous about this adventure, for Jazz." Sarah gently placed her right hand on the woman's left shoulder. "How can I help you?"

"I'm Daisy."

"Very nice to meet you, Daisy." Sarah took her hand off Daisy's shoulder and extended it into the small space between them to shake, but Daisy opened her arms for a hug. Sarah obliged. When Daisy's arms encircled Sarah's body, the diminutive woman squeezed her close. As she did, a sensation raced through Sarah from head to toe and then burrowed into her spirit. It was different from any of the amazing connections she'd felt before.

Daisy whispered into her ear, "Now you can see," before releasing her.

Sarah wasn't sure what she meant and, still squatting, stared quizzically at the wondrous woman as Erika and Jazz arrived.

Daisy met Sarah's with bright smiling eyes. "I go on the trip and you can see. You can see all the way." Daisy pointed out of camp.

"Daisy, this is a dangerous mission. You've never been out there. I'd worry about you," Erika said with concern, but there was something . . . something Sarah couldn't put a finger on.

"No. I go. I go on the mission. If I go, Sarah can see." And Daisy put her finger on Sarah's chest. Then she pointed to the animals in the entourage and to all the people who were heading out. "They need you. You can't go. I go, and you can see them. See them through me."

Jazz spoke up, "Mom, Daisy can ride with me. She'll be very helpful. It'll be good for her and all of us."

Sarah asked Daisy, "Can you ride a horse?"

"Yes. I'm a good rider. Good rider. I can ride with Jazz." Daisy's face lit up. Then she reached up and closed Sarah's eyes with her fingers. "Calm, Miss Sarah. Feel me." Then Daisy guided Sarah's hands up to her own shoulders then put her palms flat against Sarah's chest, just above her breasts, which startled Sarah, so she opened her eyes. "Feel me, Miss Sarah. See through me. Close your eyes."

Sarah closed her eyes and guided her spirits into Daisy and found her to be incredibly receptive. She didn't take her spirits in any way but seemed to amplify them. She could feel and then actually see her tiger and bear out in the forests with more clarity than she ever had from the compound. She could sense that they were taken aback as they felt the stronger connection. Sarah opened her eyes and smiled.

"I get it now." She hugged Daisy and then released her. "If you go, I can retain my connection with all the animals and members of our Family, even though they are far away. Daisy, you're wonderful. Thank you."

Sarah stood and addressed the bamboo team. "For everyone who's a nincompoop like me and doesn't know, this is Daisy. She's going on the trip. Through her, I can keep you all connected to my spirits so the trip will be successful. She's riding with Jazz."

SIXTY-ONE

"Alright then." Erika faced the gathering entourage, taking over to lead. "Mount up, everyone. Let's get this show on the road."

"Time's a wastin'," Gus bellowed as he pushed up off a log and onto his saddle on Big Gus's back. He certainly looked like he belonged on top of that huge horse. Gus's smile, which reached his eyes, was broad under his bushy mustache and beard.

He bent his head and closed his eyes. She could feel him trying to connect to the draft horse, and she did her best to encourage the connection. She couldn't feel it. They weren't good friends; in fact, sometimes he rather annoyed her, and with the conflict with Robert, she just couldn't get herself to help him.

"Keep 'em safe, cowboy!" Sarah said with as much enthusiasm as she could muster, but even she realized that it came out stiff.

"Yes, ma'am." Gus's reply seemed mocking. He rode Big Gus to the front of the group onto the ridge at the far end of the valley. It was where Sarah had stood before her momentous stroll back into camp after healing herself for the first time. They'd left for the rescue from this hillock. It had special meaning to the Family, and it was considered good luck to begin a journey from that point. Sarah had learned that this was also where the journey west with the revolutionaries had begun.

Whatever makes them more comfortable, she thought.

The entourage was gathered on the small hills and valleys they all referred to as the maze in front of their gate. Erika would take up the rear on Sergio to watch their flanks. Two male guards walked together on the left nearest their river; Mary and Connie, who'd become rather skilled at sensing the world around them, had their right side, the side nearest the woods. The plan was for Jazz and Daisy to ride Latifah in the middle of everyone for safety. Michael, Zach and Jack, whose job was to cut down and haul the bamboo, and Marsha's two slender engineer volunteers, Patricia and Leonard, who would decide when they had enough bamboo, all walked in the beaten-down wake of the pack animals as the previous crew had learned to do on the rescue. She'd considered sending the two distance runners, but they needed to be with Rhonda's and Samantha's hunting squads, who were already out searching for their evening meal. It was the first adventure for a few on this excursion, and they were visibly excited.

"Head 'em up and move 'em out!" Gus shouted as he steered Big Gus northward. He led the group, and despite the planned arrangement, Latifah moved ahead with Jazz and Daisy to a position next to Big Gus. Erika sat on Sergio atop the largest mound nearest the gate, the one William had stood on before charging at Sarah and into the barrier. The entourage walked out with Erika close behind.

The sun was still rising in the sky. Since it was spring, it would get dark in about 8 hours. She ran to the top of the last hillock and yelled after them, "Erika, be home before dark."

"Yes, Mommy," Erika answered. Everyone chuckled. The Family headed back to their duties, but Sarah stood on that hill as the caravan headed slowly through the grasslands toward the passage east of their river around the northern arc of the eastern woods. She could sense the small animals in the grasses scurrying out of the way. She connected to Mary and Connie and gave them the idea to warn the small critters before them. She felt them begin to do so, moving nearer the front of the pack animals. Erika sensed it as well and looked back at Sarah. Both smiled with pride at the advances their protégés had made.

Sarah built her connection with Daisy. She could feel everyone and everything around the caravan as it moved north across the grasslands and passed between the trees on their right and the river on their left, the area where she'd first run into the zombie teens. This area was still in her range. *What happens when they get out of range?*

The entourage reached the east-west rise and turned right to head east along it behind the wood where the tigers lived. This was the same path they'd taken for the rescue. The connections stayed strong, but she knew she'd lose it soon, unless her connection with Daisy actually worked. She guided her tiger to the edge of the trees to watch them.

Sarah couldn't see what everyone was actually doing, but she could feel the strength of her connections to them, which meant they would retain their connections to their animals, the horses, dogs, elephant and, most important, Jazz's connection with the snakes. She asked her tiger to escort them. She could feel Latifah, with whom her connection had always been strongest, her elephant and then her tiger as he jogged toward Mary and Connie. They greeted him as they'd been instructed, and he settled into pace beside them. Sarah felt better that he was with them.

She stood staring north, feeling, sensing, seeing. It was a long way to the bamboo, especially at the pace they were going, but she was not willing to break from this trance. Not now. She was sure they were nearing the dead zone. *What would happen there? What would happen without me there?*

Tom ambled up behind her, placing his great hands on her shoulders. She didn't flinch. She put her left hand across her chest, laid it on his right hand and tucked her thumb into his palm.

"Tom, if anything happens to them, to Jazz, I'll never be able to live with it."

"Do you sense anything?"

"No. Well, I can feel everything. They've made it to the bamboo. Now for the scary part. Jazz is about to communicate with the snakes." There was a long pause. "I can feel her, but I can't feel the snakes."

"Well, you never could. That's your daughter's connection—one that is personal to her and that has nothing to do with you."

"All these powers come from me."

"Are you sure?"

Sarah paused to focus. "OK. That seems to be working out. Jazz is calm, and I guess she's worked out the accord." Sarah drew in a deep breath and exhaled slowly. "Now, as long as everyone can follow orders. One bite and the victim's dead."

"They'll be alright. You gave them plenty of instructions, and I'm sure everyone is being overly cautious. They all know the dangers out there." Sarah's legs felt like lead, and her shoulders were slumped. She so wanted to sit down but would not let anything break her concentration.

"I know, but Tom, I know those dangers firsthand, and it's taken nearly all my powers to defeat them. I'm way the heck back here, and they're all the way out there. Even though I hate snakes, I should've gone."

"No, you shouldn't have, and you know it. Your abject fear of snakes is precisely what could get someone killed out there. In this instance, you're better off here, and more important, they're actually better off with you here."

Sarah nodded without conviction. Tom squeezed her thumb. Over a long pause, Sarah focused on sensing what was going on in the bamboo party. Latifah and the horses were nibbling on grasses. Everyone was staying away from the dead zone. The tiger was lolling in the sun. Most of the dogs were as well, though a few were chasing small animals in the grasses—a good sign that there was little to fear.

She directed her focus to the dead zone. Her senses there were hazy, at best, and it was way out of range. *What's up with that place?*

Tom stood quietly with her for well over an hour. As she sensed the process moving smoothly, Sarah began to relax. Tom broke the silence. "Glad Daisy stepped forward."

"Yeah. That's crazy, right? It's amazing. I can feel everything, and I know they're out of my normal range. I can sense things almost out to where we rescued those folks. It's all going through that wonderful, brave young woman. I'm very proud of her. I hope she's OK. I hope they're all OK. Hope, hope, hope."

Tom wrapped his strong arms around her chest and held her. He stayed with her for almost an hour as Sarah stared out into the distance, sensing and feeling everything she could, maintaining connections. Finally, she turned to give him a quick kiss. "Honey, I'm fine. This is working. Go back and help people."

He gave her a hug. "It's going to all be fine. Just relax." As he trotted back toward the compound gate in the barrier, she watched his sexy butt and strong back. She sighed and thanked the universe for Tom.

SIXTY-TWO

As Sarah turned back around, she tried to find her connection through Daisy to the group. She couldn't. They were gone. The connection was gone. "Tom! They're gone. I broke my connections to kiss you, and now I've lost them. They're disconnected from all their animals. Jazz can no longer connect to the snakes. Jazz is in danger. They're all in danger!"

Tom started, "I'm sure they're OK—"

Sarah screamed, "Tom, I've lost them! I need to get there. I need to get there now." She swiveled left and right. "The horses are all gone." Of course, they were all with the entourage, except for the extremely pregnant mare. Sarah shot Tom a panicked look then turned and stared through the forest as if she could see through it to the group. She tried to reconnect and then, without warning, began to run. She summoned her Horse spirit and raced faster than her usual amazing speed across the grasslands, up through the passage between the trees and the river. No one could have kept up with her, and no one tried.

She rounded the corner and headed east along the rise. Once she could see them in the distance, her natural connection with the animals and humans kicked in: no panic among them, although perhaps a little confusion. She ran harder, her heart thumping with fear that something may have happened to Jazz, to any of them, to Daisy. Latifah and the tiger turned, expecting her.

254

As she approached, Olivia was tending to someone on the ground. For the first time since the Storm, she was completely out of breath. Sarah discovered that Daisy had tried to dismount from the horse without help and had fallen to the ground. She was fine but a tad woozy.

"I'm sorry," Daisy said to Sarah. "I block your eyes. I had to pee."

Sarah leaned down and hugged Daisy. "It's OK. You're amazing. Not to worry." She helped Daisy up and could feel their connection reestablished.

Sarah watched as Erika and the three young men guided a long piece of bamboo around the trees to the travois attached to the elephant. The draft horse, Big Gus, was already loaded down, and Gus was about to head back on him. Sergio was still waiting, eating grass.

Jazz rounded the corner behind them. "Mom, what are you doing here?"

"Hi, sweetie. Is everyone OK?"

"It was. Now everything's getting tense in there. The snakes know you're here. Get outta here!" and Jazz pointed west.

"Well, I guess Daisy fell and I lost my connection to all of you. I sprinted here as fast as I could, but I was afraid that you'd lose your connection to the snakes and, well, something bad might happen."

"Oh, Mom, my connection to them has nothing to do with you. Thank heavens, 'cause they don't like you *at all*. I came out because they're agitated. You need to leave right now. Daisy's fine, right girlfriend?"

"Yes, Jazz friend. I will help Sarah see again." Olivia was helping Daisy back up onto the horse. "Better eyes from up here."

"Alright, Mom, now get. We have lots to do and times a wastin', right, Gus?" Jazz finished with an imitation of Gus's country accent and a smile at the big man. Then she put her hands out wide and asked, "Why are you still here?" before heading back to the bamboo.

Gus returned Jazz's smile then addressed Sarah. "Train's headed out, Sarah. Wanna ride, or's walkin' more your style?"

Sarah walked up to Latifah, who was standing in the shade nibbling on grass. Latifah nudged her comfortingly, and she patted him on his neck. Exhaustion fell on her shoulders. "I'm coming, Gus. I'll ride." Sarah leaped up and over onto the draft horse behind Gus, a little too close against the hairy, sweaty man and barely on the edge of the saddle. She connected with Big Gus as much as she needed to make the ride home comfortable while maintaining her connection with Daisy.

The trip was slow but steady. Gus rode quietly, which was fine with Sarah. Afraid of losing her connection with Daisy, she was trying to stay focused. As they rounded the bend of the northern reaches of the eastern woods to travel south along the river, Sarah sensed a commotion across the grasslands.

"Damn," she said out loud. "I left the Family. What's going on now? Gus, something's up. Can you stay right here until I figure it out?"

Sarah jumped off the horse, gathered as much strength from her spirits as she could muster and launched into a sprint across the grasslands toward the compound. To the east, in or near those woods, something was happening. She tried to simultaneously run, maintain her connection with Daisy and figure out what was going on near camp.

As she approached, the wolves emerged. The alpha was near, she was sure, but she had no feeling or sense. She could feel the anger of the big male as he led the others out of the eastern woods.

The guards and wood team were backing out of the woods, the guards directing their spears toward whatever was coming out, clearly afraid. The wood team sprinted inside the compound. The guards were collapsing the ranks toward the barrier. One guard broke and sprinted toward the gate. Then another and another until everyone was rushing to the gate.

"Spear!" Sarah yelled as she approached, and the last guard tossed her his. She caught it and faced the emerging wolves.

Sarah was alone along the northern outside wall of the barrier. She tried to stay connected to Daisy and focus on the wolves at the same time, but her signals were getting confused. With too much going on at once, she was feeling drained. The distraction was causing her spirits to be all over the place. She was not ready for a fight, so she took a deliberate step back.

"Sarah, come inside where it's safe. Hurry!" a guard screamed.

OK, focus on the wolves. Jazz and the crew are safe. Figure this situation out, then I'll go back to them. "Close the gate!" Sarah yelled back. "I'll get over it." Sarah strode several yards into the grasslands, faced the eastern woods, took a strong stance and brought her spirits forward and ready for whatever was coming.

She noticed to her left that Gus was entering the grasslands on Big Gus. *Damn. He just cannot follow directions.* Having given up all connection with Daisy, she could only hope they'd return safely. *Damn hope, all the time!*

More wolves started to emerge from the woods into the grasslands. They streamed out, surrounding her, more than she'd expected. A couple dozen. All ages. The male walked over within 5 feet of her, sneering, licking his lips as he approached. Then the wolves parted, heads down, as a huge wolf, a bitch, stepped into the light. She was twice the size of the male, and he was by far the largest in the pack. She was the dominant alpha.

Sarah glanced to her left. Latifah was racing to her aid, passing Big Gus as he galloped across the grasses. Sarah raised a hand and Latifah stopped. Gus stopped Big Gus as well. She could sense her tiger just inside the darkness in the eastern woods. He'd left the crew to be with her. His mate arrived beside him, two sets of green eyes glowing in the rays of the afternoon sun. The bear moved up from the river behind her into the grasslands, and on request, he, too, stopped.

This was not going to be a brute-force battle. If it turned into that, there'd be few survivors, and she likely would not be among them. Sarah took a deep cleansing breath, exuding confidence and love, then lay down her spear.

She needed to try positivity. She poured out love and peace, her spirits guiding it into the surrounding wolves. The male bared his fangs and snarled at Sarah. Sarah nodded calmly, exuding love, which she could sense only served to confuse him.

Sarah reached out spiritually to the female alpha, their leader. The female gave a small growl to her mate, and he backed down.

Sarah gazed into the female's eyes. She was intelligent and wary. Sarah took several centering breaths and settled her spirits, guiding them toward the she-wolf. *Nothing.* No connection. She could barely sense the wolf was even there. It was like with the men in the Family—an awareness that a life form was there but nothing else.

Fear shot up her spine. She'd never been unable to feel, connect with and even intimidate a mammal in this world with her spiritual energy. She looked toward the barrier. The heads of the Family members ran from one end of the barrier to the other, watching the events unfold. She glanced toward the fields. Gus, Big Gus and Latifah were standing well back. She could feel all of them.

Then she regarded the dozens of wolves encircling her. She could feel each one of them. They had the innocent, reactive souls of animals.

Sarah searched her soul for the gentle spirit of Asha, representing peace, love and goodness. She guided that part of her spirit, along with the gentle spirits of nature from all the things around her, toward the alpha. Sarah still felt nothing, but she saw a difference in the alpha's eyes. The male snarled then advanced a step on this lone enemy, unprotected in the middle of the grasslands, but the female had only to look at him for him to back down. The rest of the wolves settled in, sitting or even lying in the grasses, waiting.

The huge she-wolf moved forward toward Sarah, rearing up, towering over her. Sarah heard gasps from the human onlookers. The alpha was massive. She strode with purpose toward Sarah. Sarah could not determine whether she came in peace or wanted to tear her limb from limb. The latter would certainly be justified given the beating Sarah and her comrades had given her wolf family in their last encounter.

Sarah stood strong but emanated only positivity, love and peace. She glowed a pinkish hue, soft and almost misty.

The she-wolf came within a few inches of Sarah and sniffed her. Still no connection. With no idea of the wolf's intentions, Sarah's defenses were down. At this distance, the gigantic wolf could kill her before she could even switch her spirits into battle mode, but she was certain this was the right path. Sarah was trusting her intuition, fighting her mind to do what she knew in her heart of hearts was right.

Sarah conveyed remorse over the earlier event. She tried to convey that she was defending her brother, the tiger, and his cub. She tried to communicate her apologies for those in her pack who had perished. She had no idea what was getting through, if anything, but neither female moved a muscle.

Then Sarah did something that made the Family audibly gasp; she bowed on one knee to the great wolf, exposing the back of her neck in complete submission. Sarah returned to a strong standing position to gaze directly into her big brown eyes, demonstrating respect to the wolf but also her own power. Both stood their ground.

Finally, the she-wolf raised her head to the sky and howled a long and harrowing howl, sending shivers through Sarah's spine. The pack all stood, poised to defend their leader. *Was this the end?* She had no idea how long she and the big wolf had faced off. *Strength against time, and time doesn't matter.*

She felt Daisy and, through her, Jazz. All seemed fine.

As the last of the howl dissipated into still air, her pack encircled Sarah, several wolves deep. Sarah continued to convey love, though now her hands were trembling, and she struggled to continue sending out positive messages.

Then the alpha wolf sniffed right in her face, and Sarah returned her attention to the danger before her. Sarah breathed deeply and refocused her spirits.

SIXTY-THREE

Robert burst from the woods. "Kill her, goddammit! She's your enemy. She's the one keeping your back in that godforsaken forest. Now's your chance. Kill her! Free yourselves. That was our fucking deal!"

The male alpha growled, and the other wolves crouched, ready to attack. Sarah quivered in place but maintained her stance, strong but loving and peaceful. It was her only option at this point. If the alpha wanted to kill her, all her powers combined would be no match for her and her family.

The gate screeched, distracting the wolves and Sarah. Randi came racing through the grasslands toward them, unarmed and yelling, "Wait!" Reaching Sarah's side, the tiny woman stood in front of Sarah with her back to her. The she-wolf lowered her head to Randi's level, nearly lying down to get there. *Randi's connected with the alpha?* Sarah still felt nothing from the pack leader.

Sarah stood still, unaware of what was transpiring between the females in front of her. The eyes of the Family were glued to the image of tiny Randi, barely 5 feet tall and less than 100 pounds soaking wet, standing in front of a wolf many times her size and mass. Few doubted Randi's bravery, but this moment solidified her unwavering courage in their minds. Time again stood still.

Randi turned to face Sarah; the she-wolf returned to an erect, full-height stance, towering above her.

ENTWINED

"Sarah, they need to get past us. There's no food where they live. They're trapped between the cliffs down to the lake on one side and the dead zone on the other. They need to get through, and we and the tigers have been blocking their way out. If we let them pass, they'll move to the far side of the valley, way out where we drove the rebels, and protect the valley from that side. Robert promised them freedom in exchange for killing you. He apparently staged the attack on Joanna and the confrontation in the woods and convinced them to attack the tigers to draw you out. He had no idea how powerful you are."

Sarah was shocked at the last part but quelled her anger, putting forth only love for the wolf and her pack. "Tell her we're terribly sorry, that Robert does not represent us, and that we have an accord. Tell her that we hope to maintain a positive, mutually beneficial relationship among families out here in these grasslands."

Randi spun around and spent several seconds with the alpha, who, it was clear, was attending to her.

"We have an accord, Sarah," Randi said, still facing the dominant female.

"And you have a new job—liaison with the wolves. Excellent. Thank you, Randi." Sarah faced the great wolf leader and bowed again. Randi followed her lead. They genuflected for a few seconds longer than last time. As they stood, the she-wolf lowered her head to Sarah and Randi. The male growled but was rebuked by the leader.

Sarah and Randi backed away toward the barrier, where they stayed to watch the procession.

The alpha seemed to smile. Sarah could finally feel something coming from the large canine, but it came through Randi. The connection to this wolf arose first in her. She was a beneficiary of Randi's connection, not the other way around.

Robert screamed and ran at the wolves, "Noooooo! You have to take her out. She's vicious and dangerous. You saw what they did to your family. They'll kill you. They're human. That's what they do." As Sarah and Randi had moved away, Robert was now the human standing in the way of their path to freedom, oozing negative energy and anger. He was waving his hands and trying to force them back. "Goddammit, you connected with me! You wanted my help. We had a deal. I get you out, and you kill her!"

The alpha turned to the male and nodded. The attack on Robert was swift. He was dead within seconds. There was silence and then, to the surprise of all in the field, someone from the Family behind the barrier began to clap. Others joined in, gaining momentum into full applause. A man yelled, "The next Tony is dead without a war! Thank you to the wolves!" The Family cheered.

The big male, his two front paws atop the corpse, twisted his head away from the noise and growled one more time at Sarah. It almost felt like an apology. *Almost.* The leader howled again, and this time, several additional wolves, mostly young, streamed out of the trees, followed by even younger wolf puppies, running as fast as their little legs would carry them, under, behind and beside the wolves emerging with them. There was an audible "awww" from the Family.

Then the male launched into a run to the west. Other males from the circle began peeling off and guiding the many bitches and their puppies past Sarah and Randi. The Family uttered more "awww"s as the adorable puppies bounded through the grass. As the last of the wolves cleared the trees, the final circle of wolves left to guide them safely west. The wolf family moved across the grasslands then across the river in a winding line, up the far rise and then over it beyond their vision.

Only the she-wolf remained. She trotted over and sat in front of Sarah and gazed into her eyes, finally allowing a connection between them to take place. Sarah thanked the powerful leader. The she-wolf nodded then bent down to lick Sarah's face. Sarah raised her hand and touched the side of the wolf's huge head. They shared a gift. The unusually intelligent alpha wolf could communicate with humans and allow that connection within her pack, just as Sarah could with animals and her Family. The alpha nodded, and Sarah bowed.

The pack's leader headed west at a good trot before breaking into a full run to catch up with her family.

Sarah fell back onto the ground and put her hands to her face. The Family poured out of the gate and began patting Randi and Sarah. Tom carried Janie out, who was confused and crying. Sarah held her tightly. Sarah was breathing hard. Latifah, who'd run back and picked up Jazz and Daisy, galloped toward her.

"Oh my god, Sarah, are you crazy?" Tom said as he gathered Sarah and Janie into his arms. "I thought that thing was going to devour you."

"So did I," Sarah responded. "Thank heavens for Randi. She has the connection to that huge she-wolf. She let me in at the end, but Randi saved the day." Sarah took a breath. "Tom, I should have listened to you. If I'd gone down there to communicate with the wolves, none of this, nor last night's battle, would have happened. I'm sorry." Tom squeezed her reassuringly.

Jazz slid off Latifah and ran to her mother as Tom added her to their little family embrace. Latifah nuzzled the back of Sarah's neck.

The normally quiet warrior, Randi was enjoying being the center of attention and regaled the Family with the story as they followed her back into camp just as the rest of the bamboo team entered the northern end of the grasslands.

Exhaustion flowed through her, and Sarah slipped through the embrace and sat. She let herself feel the warmth of her daughters, her lover, the Family, her animal spirits and her living allies, and the restored harmony of nature as it washed over them all, loving and pure. But something was gnawing at her. Robert was not the threat Daffodil had warned her about. And no matter how intelligent they were, neither were the wolves. Whatever it was, the threat still existed out there, somewhere or, it dawned on her, perhaps not even far away.

Tom reached down, picked her up under her arms, dragging her giggling to her feet, before she jumped into his big safe arms and wrapped her legs around him, warm and happy. She knew something would come around to mess this up, but right now, as he carried her inside, her girls dancing along beside them, she chose to wallow in her happiness.

ACKNOWLEDGMENTS

Entwined is the sequel to *Reset* and follows Sarah as she leads the Family forward into this new world. My passion is writing, and I actually live this story, this world, when I'm in it.

Most of all, I want to thank my wonderfully talented and supremely patient editor, Karen Tucker of Comma Queen Editing, who not only makes me a better writer but also bears with my idiosyncrasies, annoying bad habits and demands on her time. She has been with me throughout this adventure. There is no way this happens without her in my professional world. Thank you so much, Karen.

My wife, Barbara, is so supportive. Getting a writing career off the ground takes time and money. Barbara has supported me, believes in me and is there with encouragement for me on those days when I'm certain I suck at this. She reads my work and tells me it's marvelous. Every writer needs that. Thank you so much, sweetie.

My oldest daughter, Jessica, and my father have become great early readers. While encouraging, they are not afraid to tell me what's wrong with my novels. It's fulfilling to have them push me to do better. Julie Martin, Laurie Zoock, Karen Hoffman and DeeDee Polston have also been reliable and trusted readers, each helping me make my novels better and, as I write from the female perspective, keep my voice for Sarah authentic.

Thank you to all the others who support me in building this business. Jamie Wyatt designs the incredible covers for my books. Laura

Feasline Borders develops and updates my website and has taught me how to do a few things. Scott Crosby and Bill Shoemaker produce my video podcast. Sarah Campbell expertly serves as the voice of the Reset series in the audio books, also produced by Scott Crosby. Finally, I want to thank the St. Louis Writers Meetup, the St. Louis Publishers Association and the St. Louis Writers Guild for their help, introductions and assistance over these last several years.

This is my path. I know it is my path because in my soul it is right, it expresses my passions and allows me to exploit my superpowers, which are getting stronger as I grow to understand them. Most of all, however, it brings me joy. I look forward to each morning when I can return to my keyboard and write or help others to find their passions, superpowers and joy. I hope you, my devoted readers, can find yours!

ABOUT THE AUTHOR

Ned Lips believes that it is never too late or too difficult to Reset Your Life. His mantra is simple: "Do what you know in your heart of hearts is right for YOU, and you will find your path to joy." If you do this, your passions will become evident. You'll develop your own superpowers and find joy that will guide you through the rest of your life.

Ned writes stories inspired by the processes, the hurdles and the steps along one's journey to resetting one's life, discovering personal passions and superpowers to find inner harmony and joy. Ned is the author of *Reset*, *First Steps*, the Reset prequel, and *Entwined*, the first sequel in the Reset series.

Ned, a lifelong writer, is a dedicated husband to Barbara and father to two successful daughters. As his wife introduces him, "He's a recovering attorney, entrepreneur and real estate investor, who is dedicated to becoming the next great author."

CONNECT WITH NED

Please like my Facebook page, Ned Lips – Author, to keep up with my blog posts and writing endeavors: facebook.com/NedLipsAuthor.

Check out my YouTube channel, Resetting Your Life, at bit.ly/NedLipsAuthorYouTubeChannel and my podcast at nedlips.libsyn.com.

Read my Resetting Your Life blog posts at nedlips.com/blog.

Find all my books at my Amazon Author Page and follow me by clicking the button: amazon.com/author/nedlips.

Follow me on Instagram @nedlips, Twitter @LipsIII and LinkedIn at linkedin.com/in/nedlips.

Made in the USA
Lexington, KY
16 November 2019

57149609R00168